DIVIDED STATES

RICK TREON

Black Rose Writing | Texas

The author grants the final approval for this literary material.

First printing

ISBN: 978-1-68433-769-9
PUBLISHED BY BLACK ROSE WRITING
www.blackrosewriting.com

Printed in the United States of America
Suggested Retail Price (SRP) $20.95

Divided States is printed in Book Antiqua

*As a planet-friendly publisher, Black Rose Writing does its best to eliminate unnecessary waste to reduce paper usage and energy costs, while never compromising the reading experience. As a result, the final word count vs. page count may not meet common expectations.

PRAISE FOR THE NOVELS OF RICK TREON

"Rick Treon dispenses well-earned twists and reveals with the stiletto precision of a master."
—Heather Young, *USA Today* bestselling author of *The Lost Girls* and *The Distant Dead*

"Rick Treon does a wonderful job with misdirection and suspense."
—Chera Hammons, PEN Southwest Book Award winner and author of *Monarchs of the Northeast Kingdom*

"Treon knows how to crank up the tension ..."
—Lone Star Literary

"Rick Treon can really, REALLY write."
—Andrew J Brandt, author of *Palo Duro*, shortlisted for 2020 Reading the West Award

"Treon displays prowess as a storyteller ..."
—Scott Semegran, award-winning author of *The Benevolent Lords of Sometimes Island*

ALSO BY RICK TREON

POLITICAL THRILLERS

Deep Background
(Winner of the 2019 PenCraft Award for Literary Excellence in Suspense)

BARTHOLOMEW BECK THRILLERS

Let the Guilty Pay
The Price of Silence

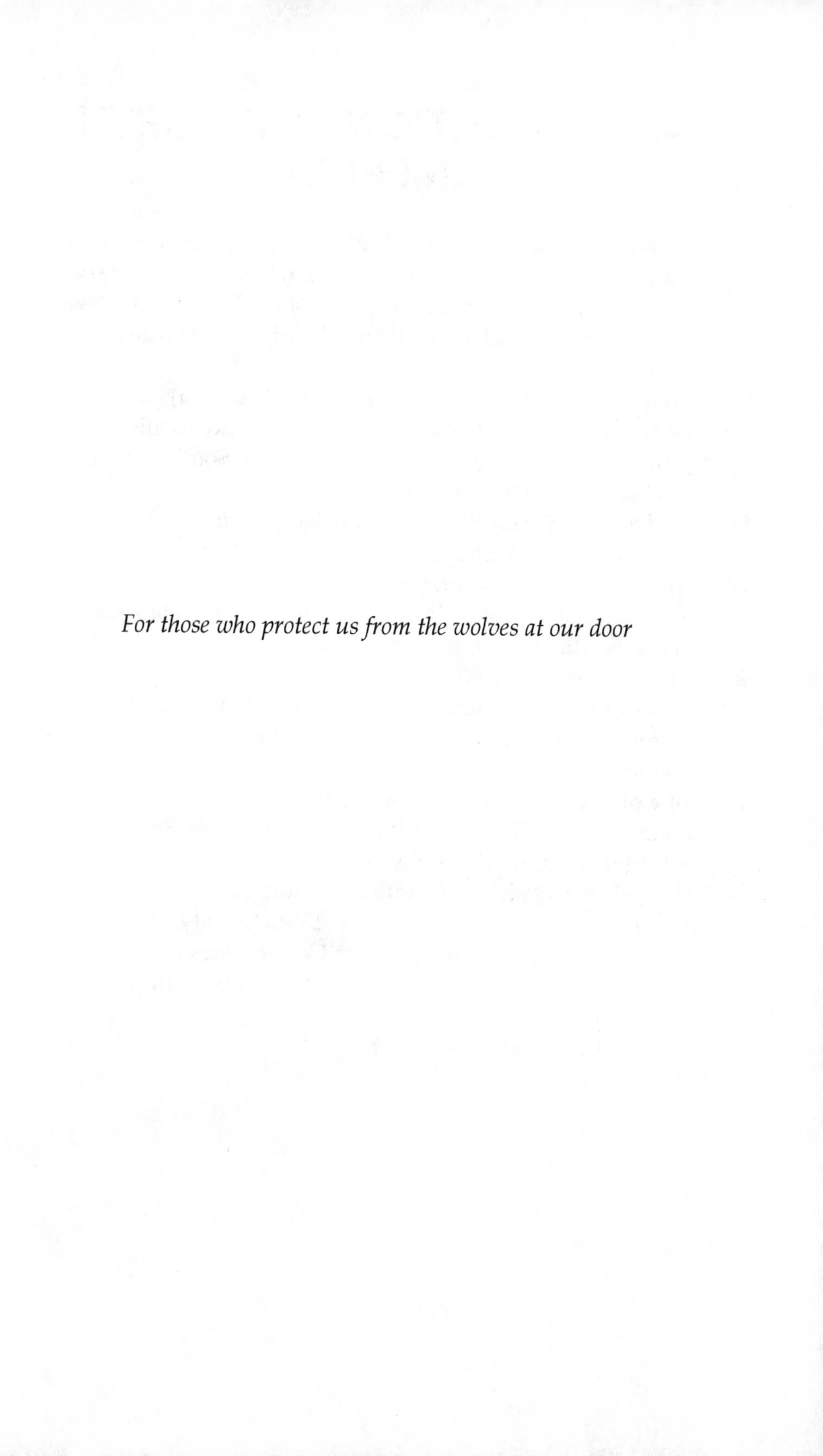

For those who protect us from the wolves at our door

ALLIED NATIONS OF NORTH AMERICA

United States of America (Capital: Philadelphia, Pennsylvania)
Connecticut, Delaware, Illinois, Indiana, Iowa, Maine, Maryland, Massachusetts, Michigan, New Hampshire, New Jersey, New York, North Missouri, Ohio, Pennsylvania, Rhode Island, Vermont, Wisconsin

Federalist States of America (Birmingham, Alabama)
Alabama, Arkansas, Florida, Georgia, Kentucky, Louisiana, North Carolina, Mississippi, South Carolina, South Missouri, Tennessee, Virginia, West Virginia

Liberated States of America (San Francisco, California)
California, Nevada, Oregon, Washington

Western Territories (Denver, Colorado)
Colorado, Idaho, Kansas, Minnesota, Montana, Nebraska, North Dakota, South Dakota, Wyoming

Republic of Texas (Fort Worth)
Capital Province, Central Province, Coastal Province, Eastern Province, Panhandle Province, Western Province, Southern Province

Republic of Oklahoma (Oklahoma City)
Capital Province, Northeast Province, Northwest Province, Southeast Province, Southwest Province

Free State of Southwestern Colorado (Durango)
Archuleta County, Delores County, Delta County, Gunnison County, Hinsdale County, La Plata County, Mesa County, Montezuma County, Montrose County, Ouray County, San Miguel County, San Juan County

Free State of Utah (Salt Lake City)
Single nation-state

DIVIDED STATES

PART I: PINNACLE

1
LORI YOUNG

French Quarter Urban Zone, New Orleans, Louisiana
Federalist States of America

It hits her without warning. Blood rushes to Lori's head and she needs to act fast.

Less-than-ten-seconds fast.

She fumbles with the elegant face thanks to twelve hours of downing vodka on Bourbon Street. But her fingers find the right position and her attention returns to the projection screen, where the ball is dropping in Times Square.

Lori's in New Orleans with hundreds of other vacationers who came to see the concert. She makes sure the watch's hands are set for exactly 11 P.M. And as the timer in the top right corner hits double-zeroes, Lori presses the button.

Perfect execution of a perfect idea. Lori wishes she could turn back time, but she'll settle for resetting it on her new vintage timepiece.

Lori waits for confetti and kissing, but the picture wobbles and cuts away. Music over the speakers is replaced by live gunshots. A bullet pierces her left thigh and sends her tumbling to the beer-soaked turf. Screams fight with gunfire for the loudest noise as panic ripples through the crowd, and drunken partygoers trample each other trying to find two small entrances in the chain-link cage around this block of the French Quarter. Some try climbing the fence, braving the razor wire rather than risk a bullet.

Lori compresses her wound with both hands and scans for the gunfire's source. Bodies lie in a semicircle emanating from a man she recognizes—the security guard who politely wanded her an hour ago.

She couldn't get any closer to the celebrity host, he told her through his handlebar mustache in a lovely Louisiana accent, no matter how pretty she was. Lori loves the Louisiana dialect, so much more interesting than the West Texas drawl she hears every day. Between that and his facial hair, Lori had thought The Cajun would make fantastic hotel room company.

But now he's spraying copper-covered terror thirty feet away. Lori turns to the fence line and sees Urban Zone Police in paramilitary uniforms fighting the crowd. They're at least fifty yards away. She could play dead for a few more minutes and survive, resume what's left of her life, and nobody would know the difference.

But if she's killed fighting The Cajun now, during an event that even the crippled and corrupt media can't ignore, people might remember her as a heroine and forgive the rest.

Lori pushes herself up and, though drunk and favoring her leg, moves quickly as The Cajun marches toward vacationers scrambling across the stage where an actress had fumbled through scripted banter with a Ken doll host.

Desperate screams and gunfire mask Lori's approach, and she summons enough strength to lunge at The Cajun's ankles.

He falls to the ground.

Now it's a fair fight.

* * *

LORI WONDERS who'll pay for the medical care as she sits in the black ambulance. It's only a flesh wound, but it still hurts like hell. She's also pissed about losing the sweater that was tied around her waist, though at least the EMT gave her one of those reflective blankets to put over her tank top.

French Quarter UZ officers dogpiled Lori and The Cajun a few minutes after her tackle. Two officers led him away in cuffs, while two more shoved her toward the bus and told her to wait for a special agent with the Investigative Bureau of the Federalists.

The suit who eventually finds Lori is at least a decade younger. She heard they required a four-year degree, but this guy looks like he came straight from graduation.

"Ma'am, I'm Agent Smalls with the IBF. I know you're probably a little hysterical right now, but I need to ask you some questions."

No way, she thinks. "Your name really Smalls?"

"Yes, ma'am." No sign of a smile or humor in his syrupy Georgia drawl.

He doesn't understand her joke, though she should've expected that when referencing *The Sandlot* with someone so young. Lori was only five or six when her father first streamed it for her.

Lori debriefs Smalls without prompting, assuming the organization was as derivative as its name.

"If I didn't know better," Smalls says, still taking the last of her statement, "I'd think you were one of ours."

"I was a detective in another life."

He looks up, more interested now. "Whereabouts?"

"Texas."

That brings a smile to his face. "Never been to The Republic myself. I want to, but it's hard to get in."

"Speaking of which"—Lori pulls out her Vacation Visa, which looks similar to her driver's license with DEPARTMENT OF INTRACONTINENTAL TRAVEL stamped at the top—"I bet you need to see this."

He swipes the card over a black tablet, which emits the same sharp sound she heard at the Federalist border. This is her first time using a Vacation Visa, something the new nations dreamed up almost immediately after the Second Secessions were finalized. They may not have all the military defense and logistics ironed out yet, but hey, the elite can still spend summer at Martha's Vineyard and winter in Florida.

"Says here you are a saleslady now."

Big Brother's reach still throws her, though it shouldn't. In exchange for relatively easy passage across the continent, Lori gave the department access to everything from bank records to social media.

"Why'd you leave the Amarillo PD?"

Lori clenches her jaw. That's none of his business. This little shit doesn't know a damn thing about her. About what she's been through. But, in the interest of getting this done, Lori relaxes her face and slaps on her well-rehearsed faux smile. "That's a long story, but I'm a saleswoman now because I enjoy it."

"Well, you're certainly pretty enough." He flashes a sheepish smile. "I've always liked brunettes. And that short haircut is so different from the girls where I'm from. That and your tan skin and green eyes. You're so"—he looks to the side, and Lori's frustration grows as he searches for the word because she's heard it a thousand times—"exotic."

You're killing me, Smalls. The joke calms her enough to respond kindly. "Why thank you, Agent Smalls."

Boys and men of all ages have called Lori *exotic* for as long as she can remember, including when it was deeply inappropriate. She watched her mother get the same treatment while she was alive. Misty Young—née Martinez—insisted she was Hispanic. Lori believed she was half until her late twenties.

After her last homicide bust, the perp insisted she had to be part Native American based on the length and hue of her raven hair—which she'd let grow past her shoulder blades—and the shade of her skin. It shouldn't have mattered, but Lori was incensed. The man was human garbage, an always-out-of-work meth-head who'd moved in with a single mother. The little eight-year-old girl in the home *was* half Hispanic, and he'd gotten to study her features through the lens of his video camera while mommy was working. He graduated from taping her to selling the footage for fixes, to realizing he could become part of a kiddie porn chain and make even more.

Then the mother came home early one day. She and her daughter ended up dead, and it took all of Lori's self-control to keep from putting hands on him rather than cuffs—especially after they found the tapes.

So, when that piece of shit said there was no way Lori was the same race as the little girl he'd abused and strangled with a belt, Lori sent off for one of those DNA testing kits and planned to rub the results in his face during a prison visit while provoking him to the point of getting thrown in solitary.

She never got the chance. Lori is about three-eighths American Indian and nearly half Irish with other western European ancestries. Lori knew her white heritage, but she never got much information about her maternal grandparents, except that they'd moved from Oklahoma to Texas as teenagers to escape bad home lives—whatever that meant. They worked the land for a well-to-do farming family, lived in a small brick house in the middle of several fields just west of a small town called Morse, and were never asked to produce papers.

Lori couldn't confirm it with her mother, but Misty was born and raised on the High Plains, so three-quarters Native American made as much sense as being Hispanic.

The lie, however, didn't add up, and Lori was upset she never had the opportunity to reap the small benefits that had existed for American Indians in the USA.

Then the Second Secessions happened, and Lori understood. Her mother, who also kept her hair short, had grown up during a time when being part Comanche or Kiowa or Cherokee could've made small-town life even harder than being a light-skinned Mexican girl.

Now Lori chops off her hair with regularity and keeps expensive highlights, thankful her mother established an alternate racial history at birth.

Lori also leans into the unchecked casual misogyny, like the kind Smalls exhibits unconsciously while trying to be nice in the southern-gentlemanly way he was raised.

Getting upset every time is too exhausting.

* * *

THE EMERGENCY ROOM at New Orleans City Hospital hasn't been updated—maybe not even cleaned—since it was slapped together after the secessions to treat UZ residents and foreign vacationers. Part of Lori thinks she'd have been better off walking to her hotel after getting her wound dressed in the ambulance, but she needs stitches and pain meds.

When a doctor in a dingy coat breezes in, Lori expects him to inspect the wound. Instead, he lifts the gauze from her bare leg, looks her up and down, then replaces it. "You got lucky. The bullet took some meat out of your thigh, but it's nothing a nurse can't handle."

He's out in less than a minute and Lori hears him laugh with a woman outside, calls her sweetie. Ten minutes later, Sweetie pushes past the curtain holding a tray with three needles, one sewing and two hypodermic with syringes.

She picks up the first injection. "This one'll numb the area."

Sweetie doesn't give Lori any warning before pushing a few CCs into her leg. After waiting a minute for the local anesthetic to kick in, she picks up the curved needle and starts stitching the leg with the dexterity of a dry drunk with the shakes.

"Y'all must have your hands full tonight."

Sweetie shrugs. "Not really. We've only had a few people with anything major. You and two other gunshot wounds. Couple of stabbings. Nothing exciting."

Did everyone else die? "Have you heard anything about the shooting in the Quarter?

"Just that we were getting two from there."

Lori sits quietly and prays for the dead. If there is a God, he's showing his angry side tonight. Lori had gone to church every Wednesday and Sunday growing up. By the time she was done working in homicide, she'd lost her faith in God and humanity.

"Okay," Sweetie says, "you're all sewn up. Here's something for the pain before I wrap your leg."

The government-sanctioned heroin is barely out of the syringe when Lori feels the high. She likes her Vicodin and Oxy when she can get it, and this is stronger.

The nurse gestures to Lori's left. "Our payment station is just down that hall."

Sweetie leaves before Lori can ask about crutches. She stands, a bit off balance but feeling no pain, and walks to the kiosk. Standing sentry is a large man who's in no danger of being mistaken for a medical professional. "Card or voucher?"

She pulls out the visa and holds it up for him. After glancing from the ID and back to her, the thick guard points to one of the machines. "That one's for vacationers."

"I don't suppose y'all sell crutches? Or coats?"

He shakes his head and points again.

She slips the visa below a scanner. The screen goes blank, then shows a bill of three hundred dollars for her shitty stitches and shot. That's more than she'd pre-loaded onto the card, so when the machine asks if she accepts the credit terms, Lori taps yes. She'll rack up 20 percent interest each month if she can't pay the balance in ten days.

Then she remembers the ambulance. That bill will be in the mail.

Worst. Vacation. Ever.

***

LORI SPOTS the tail almost immediately. She'd been part of a few drug task forces, and the federal agents taught her some basics.

The two buzzcuts had been on her since she got back to the Quarter. They're young and lean and trying to blend in with their Saints ballcaps and washed-out jeans. Problem is, there's almost nobody on the streets now. And even when there were, the boys were walking too straight and at a pace that kept them exactly a block behind, which is slow given her limp. They must be IBF agents, who can monitor anyone they want inside UZ perimeters.

Lori distracts herself from the tail and the cold by concentrating on the New Orleans Wall, which stays lit twenty-four seven. It was built to keep out monster hurricane storm surges. The Wall is also an outpost for the Federalist Navy. Officers look down on the city from the top. There are rumors of massive cannons up there, too, but she's seen no evidence of them.

Below the lookouts, a steep drop leads to a concave center featuring a hundred-foot-tall screen nestled in the depression. She reads its offerings.

PRESIDENT ANDERSON SAYS SOUTHERN ECONOMY 'STRONGER THAN EVER' HEADING INTO NEW YEAR ...
ALABAMA TO FACE CLEMSON AGAIN IN NATIONAL TITLE, WINNER ADVANCES TO ANNA CFB PLAYOFFS ...
HISTORIC BLIZZARD MOVING THROUGH THE REPUBLIC ...

Business. Sports. Weather. Nothing about the mass shooting. The screen is controlled by the Federalist media, though it was built to mimic the news ticker in Times Square.

"New York," Lori whispers to herself. The live feed went dark just before The Cajun opened fire. Manhattan partiers had no doubt suffered the same fate as those in New Orleans.

If the ball-drop was used as a timer to coordinate the attacks, how many cities were hit? Just the ones hosting New Year's Eve events? Had every city with a large gathering seen dozens—maybe hundreds—die at the hands of some maniac with a machine gun? That would mean UZ celebrations across The South, the republics of Texas and Oklahoma, and the rest of the Divided States.

Fowler might have an accurate count when she gets back. He's got salespeople like her everywhere.

The Buzzcut Twins are still behind her, and foot traffic is getting lighter. She has half a mind to turn around and confront them. Then again, she's technically in a foreign country. She'll shake them and get to her hotel in peace.

Lori turns onto a darkened street with almost no noise and uses her peripheral vision to clock the tail.

But they're not there.

Her heart rate quickens as she flattens herself against a grimy wall between two dumpsters. Lori counts to ninety before she's satisfied the twins are no longer interested in her wanderings. But as she turns back onto whatever rue she'd been navigating, Lori nearly runs into them.

"We need you to come with us, ma'am," says the one on the left. These boys aren't local either. Arkansas.

Lori reminds herself that playing a damsel is her best bet. "May I ask why?"

They stare, stone-faced, and repeat their demand. Playing dumb won't work, so she pulls out her ace of spades.

"You know, I stopped that massacre earlier. Just ask Agent Smalls, he'll tell you."

The slightly taller twin curls his lips. "We know who you are, Ms. Young. And we don't work with Smalls. We're with a"—he pauses, searching for the right phrase—"more important organization."

Lori tries tamping down her escalating panic. *Who in the South is more important than the IBF?*

"Well, I was just in the hospital," she says, trying to sound indignant. "I was told to go straight to my hotel and rest, which is what I intend to do."

Lori tries to split the agents, but she has almost no bounce thanks to the gash in her leg and the opiates in her system. They each take an arm and lift her off the ground. Lori has no chance in a fight, so she stops struggling as a black SUV pulls alongside them.

The slightly shorter one grabs her left wrist, takes off the watch, tosses it to the driver. "GPS."

Lori can't believe he would do this to her. Fowler runs an intracontinental pipeline supply company in Oklahoma. He's also been trying to spark a relationship that will never happen, so the expensive Christmas present didn't raise any red flags. Still, Lori should've told him it was too much and insisted he take it back. But nobody else is giving her expensive gifts, and dammit she earned it.

She also earned this vacation, which thanks to his creepy ass had gone from horrific to whatever's worse than that.

Screw you, Fowler.

Lori tries one more time to jerk free, but Shorty punches her in the gut. As the twins slide her into the backseat, a red flash catches her eye. The Wall's screen blinks red one more time, then comes alive with a new headline.

TERRORISTS ATTACK SOUTH …
IBF SUSPECTS USA, LIBERATED STATES

2
ERIC FOWLER

Fowler Automation Sales and Technology offices,
Cushing, Northeast Province
Republic of Oklahoma

Gunfire and screams blast through the speakers as a herd sprints toward him. Eric replays the fifteen-second video on his computer screen.

Blonde hair tickles Eric's cheek as Rita leans over his shoulder. "Any idea how high the death count'll get?"

"In Oklahoma City?" he asks, eyes still on the largest of his computer's three screens. "Or everywhere?"

His business partner's voice is shaky. "Let's start with the Capital."

Eric can't rip his eyes off the screen as he plays it yet again. "We won't know until tomorrow, and that's if the OBI is feeling generous."

The Oklahoma Bureau of Investigation won't release numbers to what was left of the country's media, but he wants to comfort her. Rita Clarke's sister was on the outskirts of the party in downtown Oklahoma City and escaped with only bruises from the stampede. There'd be at least a dozen dead two blocks away.

He clicks play again. "How long before the shooter was taken down?"

"A minute, maybe ninety seconds" Rita says, her back to the screen. "Thank God they allow open carry."

Eric clicks away from the video and pulls up a browser. "I do know it's not as bad as most of the other shootings."

Reports on the dark web showed at least a dozen more massacres across the former United States of America. Someone built an online map pinpointing the confirmed New Year's Eve mass shootings. Eric clicks on the new USA.

"New York is the third-worst so far, but Boston and Chicago were bad, too," he says. "Dozens dead in each. Nearly that many near the capitol in Philadelphia."

"Which cities were hit worse than New York?"

"Take a wild guess."

Eric moves to the Liberated States. Guns are essentially banned on the West Coast, which would normally put LA as the largest gun-free city on the continent. But never-ending cluster fires made Southern California unlivable last year, so everyone there migrated north or got emergency refugee status in another country.

That leaves two other major metro areas.

"San Francisco was brutal." He clicks on the LSA's capital city. "More than a hundred. The police there only had tasers. They had to wait for the LSA Guard to take down the shooter."

As the cursor hovers over Nevada, Rita sucks in a breath. Rita's mother was killed during the 2017 Las Vegas shooting, one of more than sixty deaths that day. Today's death toll is over eighty.

"Dammit Libs," Rita whispers. "This was bound to happen eventually."

"It just made the death count higher. Someone got into The Republic, too."

"Holy shit. Austin?"

Eric shakes his head. "Houston." He mouses over Texas, which still looks strange on a map. Residents of the El Paso peninsula narrowly voted to join Mexico, and Oklahoma let Texas retake its panhandle. The Republic also has seven provinces now. The state constitution had only allowed for five, but everything was negotiable during the Second Secessions.

Eric zooms in on Houston, capital of the Coastal Province. "Looks like he was taken out pretty quickly, though. So were shooters in The South."

The map shows circles in Atlanta, Miami, and New Orleans.

Eric hadn't heard form Lori, though he tracked her and knows she'd been taken to the city hospital. He'd planned to make sure she made it to her hotel, but when Rita walked in he closed the screen like a teenager watching porn.

Rita puts her hand on his to control the mouse. "I wonder why they bothered with some of these places. The Frontier isn't as wild now, but there were still attacks in Denver and St. Louis."

Good point. "I don't understand attacking the Western Territories, either," Eric says. "Or Salt Lake City. Nobody's messed with the Mormons in months. And Durango? That city's tiny compared to the others."

Rita removes her hand, stands up straight. "But it is the biggest one in ... whatever they call that one."

"The Free State of Southwestern Colorado." Eric studies the map again. "You're right. There was at least one attack in every country."

That's no coincidence. "It was a coordinated attack. Thanks for bringing this to me tonight. It'll really help me get a jump on things."

Rita leans over Eric again. "I couldn't sleep after my sister called. And I wanted to get it off my plate. You'll be busy with this, which means I'll be running the shop." She lowers her lips to his earlobe and slides her hand down his T-shirt. "It also means this is our last chance for a while."

Eric smiles, but it's not real. He's been waiting for the right time to cool things down with Rita. They called off the engagement for a reason. But maybe these attacks—and his upcoming operation—will do it for him. He can also let her misinterpret his recruitment of Lori, which will have to intensify now.

Eric squeezes her forearm with his left hand and minimizes the map with his right, revealing the video again. Rita takes the hint and removes her hand.

"Tall, dark, handsome—and cold as ice." She sighs, every bit the spurned lover she thinks she is. "I better try and get a few hours' sleep before coming in to call our clients."

"Good idea." He stands and puts his hands on her shoulders. "If you keep the business running, I'll shield you from the rest. You've done more than enough."

Eric starts walking her out of the office, slowly, like he's not trying to shoo her out.

"Has anyone else checked in?" she asks at the door.

"Ross called from Billings and said he's fine. Joey's safe in Houston. I'm fixing to start tracking down the rest."

After she leaves, Eric stands in the doorway until he hears the elevator doors close. He waits another ten seconds in case, then rushes back to his desk and pulls up Lori's GPS coordinates again. She's still in New Orleans. He zooms in. She's nowhere near her hotel in the French Quarter or its UZ hospital.

She's near the old Superdome.

What the hell?

The Saints moved inland when the hurricanes became too big and too many to get through a season. The city had turned the stadium into a refuge for displaced residents—until The Wall was completed. As far as Eric knew, the stadium was dormant.

Eric tries Lori's cell again. Voicemail.

He's loath to make the next call, but if Lori called anybody, it would be her ex-husband.

3
JEREMIAH REYNOLDS

19 miles Northeast of Amarillo, Panhandle Province
Republic of Texas

A woman's voice cuts off his favorite Tim McGraw song, so Jeremiah tells his car to turn up the volume.

This is Tommie Thompson here with another update for everyone. Fifteen have been reported dead so far in tonight's deadly attack at Houston's New Year's Eve celebration down in the Coastal Province. We're also getting reports of ten fatalities at a similar event in Oklahoma City. Just a tragic day for these two republics. We'll keep you informed as we learn more. Now, back to more classic country here on KAMA.

He begins mumbling a prayer, so the car asks if he wants the radio tuned to a Christian station. He says no and asks her to turn the volume down again. A second later, she tells him a call's coming in.

The number's unlisted. "Ignore call."

Jeremiah's been driving northeast on Provincial Highway 60 for nearly twenty minutes and praying nobody he knows was hurt. Before that, he was dead asleep. When the call finally woke him up, Jeremiah saw he'd already missed two phone calls from the plant. The night supervisor sounded beyond relieved to finally get a groggy hello out of him. When the guy asked if he was sober enough to come in, he said sure.

As he takes the looping exit onto Farm-to-Market 2373, Jeremiah starts regretting his decision to answer the phone. The plant's always lit, but he's never seen a steady stream of vehicles driving to it outside of shift changes. The last thing the supervisor told him was someone would explain what's happening when he got there.

That someone is his boss's boss, Logan Robb. "Thanks for coming in, Reynolds. Welcome to the shitshow."

The sprawling campus is always busy during the day, but the scrambling near the entrance seems crazy for two in the morning.

"I caught it on the radio driving in. Houston and OKC were attacked."

"Affirmative." Robb rubs his palm over the top of his shaved head. "Plus nine or ten more cities in The South, the West—pretty much everywhere."

Now the level of activity seems appropriate, but the late-night call still made no sense. "Sir, may I ask why I was called in?"

Jeremiah is usually on the road for the Intracontinental Secure Transportation Agency—one of the only institutions that couldn't get dismantled and reshaped. All that changed was the name. And when they added Intracontinental, the higher-ups loved having a usable acronym.

Other than that, his job's the same. When he's home, Jeremiah conducts readiness training and works out in the gym. He puts in seventy hours some weeks, but night overtime is spent in a truck, not here.

Robb looks around. "You're not here strictly as an INSTA employee. We called in everyone with combat experience who's sober enough to pull a trigger."

The plant has its own security personnel. Why call in more resources, especially a guy who hasn't been in for years?

"There's more to this than the shootings, isn't there?"

"We don't know yet. But if there is, I'll be damned if we're caught flatfooted."

***

A FEW OF JEREMIAH'S CREW are waiting, already in their cold-weather gear.

"What took you so long, old man?"

Jeremiah flips off Jesús Ramirez, an ex-Marine and the team's youngest member. "Unlike the mighty Zeus, us old men need sleep. Why aren't you wasted somewhere?"

Zeus puts a finger to his lips. Jeremiah leans in and gets a whiff of tequila and sex despite the fact he's changed. Good thing he's better drunk than most are sober.

"Tell the missus I apologize for interrupting."

Dominic Hansen sidles up to Zeus. "Why are we here?"

Zeus looks up at Dom, a former Special Forces sniper who went into Intelligence Support Activity. Now he drives their blue big-rig. "They're worried about an attack here, dumbass."

Without missing a beat, Dom jabs back. "Then why'd they call in the midget patrol?"

It's always like this with these two. Jeremiah should step in before they end up wrestling on the floor—especially if Zeus is past tipsy—but he doesn't have the bandwidth. He's caught somewhere between herding those two and trying to get real information from the higher-ups. And Jeremiah's only heard from Robb, not his direct supervisor, Greg Daniels.

The group turns when they hear footsteps.

"I'll never understand why they always call boys to do a woman's job."

That woman looks like the coach's wife from *Friday Night Lights* but younger and built like Wonder Woman, a five-eleven redhead who takes no shit. The kids wave her off, but Jeremiah's happy to see Shaye MacLaughlin. She handles communications for the team—and whatever else Jeremiah needs.

Dom and Jeremiah laugh at her dig, but Zeus takes umbrage. "Whatever, Mac."

Jeremiah tells the guys he'll be back and walks alongside Mac to the lockers, causing a chorus of catcalls and kissing noises. Mac gives them the bird over her shoulder.

"Glad you made it," Jeremiah says. "I was *not* looking forward to a night keeping those two in line by myself. Especially with nothing to keep them occupied."

It's never easy keeping stride with Mac—they're the same height, but Jeremiah gives up at least an inch in the legs—but when she's this amped, it's nearly impossible.

"You sure nothing's going to happen?"

He pauses before answering. There's no proof. The story is they're here to reinforce the plant's safety after what appears to be a coordinated attack, and Republic honchos are trying to piece it together.

Something's not sitting right with him, but that doesn't mean Mac should worry, too. "Nah. We're just a precaution."

Mac stops at the door to her locker room and stares into his eyes. "Those baby blues of yours are distracting, but I can still see when you're lying."

She ducks into the women's locker room without giving Jeremiah a chance to respond. He's about to enter the men's when his cellphone rings. A second call from an unknown number.

"Whoever this is, you better hope we don't ever meet in person."

"It's Eric Fowler. I'm trying to find out if Lori's okay."

His ex's asshole boss. Lori still vents once in a while about the sales calls he gives her. She tells him Fowler is demanding and is constantly trying to win her affection. Jeremiah has no right to be jealous—they've been divorced for years—but it still pisses him off.

More upsetting right now is the fact Fowler has never called Jeremiah's number, not even when he and Lori were still married.

Something is wrong.

"Why wouldn't she be?" Jeremiah asks.

"So you haven't heard from her tonight?"

Jeremiah's about to ask why she'd call so late, but then it clicks. "New Orleans was one of the cities, wasn't it?"

Fowler says yes, and panic rises from Jeremiah's gut to his face. He tries to remember if he knows anyone in the city. The state? Nobody comes to mind.

"Are any of your other salesmen nearby?"

When Fowler pauses, Jeremiah gets pissed and nearly ends the call before he finally speaks.

"Yes. But I'm not calling him unless …"

"Unless what?"

Another pause.

"Unless what you cryptic mother—"

"I'll call you back."

The call ends before Jeremiah can respond.

4
LORI

Unknown location, New Orleans, Louisiana
The South

Lori's in the dark but trying to remember the turns and approximate distances. Problem is, she didn't study a map of the city, so it probably won't do any good even if she does find a way to contact someone. Fowler's watch won't help anyone find her either. She heard one of them open a window for a few seconds, which means they tossed it.

The point of coming here was to leave everything behind for a few days. But being moved to God-knows-where with a sack over her head, which the buzzcut twins added shortly after grabbing her, was not what she had in mind.

"The bag's a little cliché, don't you think? I'm not struggling. And I had no idea that watch was a tracking device, so you're wasting your time with me."

Fear is giving way to anger. If she's about to die, she's going out having told these two what pieces of shit they are.

The SUV stops in the middle of her tirade. Doors open. Bodies move.

The sack doesn't come off.

"Hey, Tweedledee and Tweedledumbass, you forgot something."

As if in response, one of them grabs her arm and jerks her sideways, so she bucks her hips and twists.

Lori's butt barely leaves the seat.

"I can't take off the handcuffs if you keep doing that."

Lori turns and throws a haymaker as soon as her right hand is free and nearly falls over when she doesn't connect. *That's why they didn't take the sack off first, stupid.* She rips it off and sees an office building. A six-story gray square with pane windows in neat little rows and no lettering on the side.

"Guys, I hate to be the one to tell you this, but that's the shittiest evil lair ever."

The boys pull her out, one on each arm. One asks the other if he knows who *Tweedle-whatever* is. She's docile for a few more steps as they discuss the dated *Alice in Wonderland* reference, then stomps on a foot with her right bootheel and jerks her arm free. As she drops to one knee, Lori balls her fist and connects with the other's crotch like a boxer on the speed bag. The goon doubles over, angry words caught in his throat.

With both arms free, Lori bolts forward. But she only gets two steps before one of them dives and trips her up, the pavement digging into her palms and burning her cheek.

She turns over just in time to see the butt of a pistol.

* * *

LORI WAKES on a couch, hands bandaged and head pounding.

"You made that a lot harder than it had to be."

His voice is new. Calm. A distinct East Texas accent.

Lori eases herself up until she's sitting and facing the man, who's dressed in a suit and standing beside a large executive desk, complete with a large calendar, desk pads, gold letter opener, and one of those things with the ball bearings that smack each other rhythmically.

"I'll remember that the next time I get kidnapped."

"They say sarcasm is the lowest form of wit."

Lori waits, wondering if she should say it. Her mouth's gotten her in trouble before. Then again, she's in some executive's office with a head wound.

Before she makes up her mind, the man rolls a chair toward her and sits so close she can smell his sweat. "I understand you're upset. But if you give me a minute to explain—"

Lori spits in his face.

She braces for a slap or worse. When the man reaches into his black suit jacket, she wonders if she overplayed her hand and he's fixing to shoot her.

Instead, he pulls out a red handkerchief and wipes his face, which takes a few passes over his thick stubble. "We didn't kidnap you, Ms. Young. We're recruiting you."

This is bad. Real bad. "What the hell are you talking about?"

He smiles and replaces the soiled cloth. "My name is Robert Moore. I lead a group of covert intelligence officers, and we need your help. And if you can stop your self-destructive behavior and start caring about people again, you'll save the world."

He laid that cheese on way too thick. But she'll bite. If she keeps him talking, maybe he won't start beating her. Or worse.

"Oh yeah? How's that?"

"First, you need to know that Eric Fowler's business isn't just a pipeline sales company. It's a front for another group of intelligence officers. For simplicity's sake, he's the bad guy, and I'm the good guy."

Though her molars feel like they might crack, Lori works them in lieu of speaking. Because of that goddamn watch, this clown thinks Lori is part of some underground spy organization. Fowler is dead if she gets out of this alive.

"Look Mr. Secret Agent Man, I have no idea what'n the hell you're talking about."

Moore narrows his eyes but leans back, relaxed. "I believe you. I believe you have no idea how Eric Fowler has been manipulating you. It's his specialty."

5
ERIC

FAST offices, Cushing, Northeast Province
Republic of Oklahoma

Eric felt lucky earlier when he saw Lori was wearing the watch. It had been a safe bet, though. She'd told him about missing a similar one, lost after a one-night-stand on the road where no numbers were exchanged.

Now he wishes she'd left it at the hotel. At least then she'd have been Schrödinger's Traveler, both safe and in danger until he located her. But Lori hasn't moved in thirty minutes, and the tracker shows her on the edge of a public park, nowhere near any benches or swings or anything else to sit on.

She's not wearing the watch anymore.

Or she's lying there dead.

Lori left the Superdome parking lot and was riding in a vehicle, and he assumed she called a cab or—though he hated the thought—let someone she met there take her home.

Reynolds has called three times, but Eric won't answer. Not before he calls Boudreaux. And that can be dangerous. But when you need someone found and extricated in Louisiana, Boudreaux is the man you contact and hope the body count isn't high when it's over.

Eric pulls a satellite phone from his desk and punches in the numbers.

"Speak." Boudreaux's voice sounds like someone poured gravel down his throat. That's not new, but he sounds nothing like the young soldier Eric met decades ago. It's still jarring after long communication blackouts.

"It's Fowler. I need an extraction in New Orleans."

"One of yours?"

"Yeah. ETA?"

"Two hours."

Eric fills him in on the details. It's not much to go on, but Boudreaux's never failed Eric.

After replacing the satphone, Eric rubs his eyes and leans back. That was his last call of the night. His twenty-two officers are safe. He doesn't count Lori, who's not yet an officer but a high-value target. Posing as salesmen, Eric has two officers each in The Liberated States, Western Territories, Free State of Utah, Free State of Southwestern Colorado, The Republic of Oklahoma, and The Republic of Texas. There are four each in the Federalist States and United States, and one each in Alaska and Hawaii.

Alaska is technically a Western Territory, but it's worth making sure the land's not annexed by Russia. Or—and he laughs every time he thinks it—Canada. Hawaii stayed with the USA to maintain its economy and military defense, assuming correctly that Asia would become more volatile after the split.

The Oahu post isn't under the cover of working for Eric. Phoebe's a former colleague there to hit the panic button if anything happens at Pearl Harbor.

All of Eric's officers used to work under him in the Directorate of Operations. None of them left by choice.

The Second Secessions left the intelligence community with the impossible task of divvying up resources, and many were forced out of the Agency. Eric had left early and was ready to scoop up officers unsatisfied with civilian life.

Deputy Director for Operations Randall Gates had known the secessions were coming and told Eric to retire just before Alexia Ramirez was re-elected POTUS. Gates retired a few months later when Ramirez—as he'd predicted—selected a new Director of the CIA with the mandate to clean up his shop.

That's why Eric started his own company. He and Gates would run the show carte blanche.

When the time came, leaving operations to start the business went smoothly, especially when an old friend with a Stanford MBA moved back to Oklahoma because she couldn't stand to live in ultra-liberal Palo Alto or San Francisco. He and Rita bought a struggling sales firm, recruited a couple of officers, taught them about pipelines and valves and actuators, and made it profitable again. For a while, their covert activities seemed to take a backseat to bringing in cash by the wheelbarrow.

Then the secessions came, and Gates dropped the bomb.

He had a new adversary on the other side.

Time to scale up.

* * *

ERIC'S NEARLY ASLEEP when his cell rings. He expects Boudreaux, but it's only been ten minutes.

Reynolds. Again.

"I have someone on it," Eric says.

"What does that mean?"

Reynolds is whispering and Eric hears other voices in the background. One of them yells. He's at the plant, which is unusual. Eric listens for another moment before answering Reynolds.

"It means I've called the hospitals and she's not there. The police are too busy to take my call, but I have another salesman in the area who's on his way into the city to check her hotel room and physically ask someone at the police stations around the city. I should know more in two hours."

Reynolds ends the call without comment, but Eric gets the message. He'll provide Reynolds with regular status updates. Lori would want that.

What Eric wants is sleep, even if it's just for the next two hours. But it won't come now. There's more going on than a series of coordinated mass shootings.

How else can he explain the increased activity at Reynolds' plant—the only facility in the Western Hemisphere that still assembles and disassembles nuclear warheads.

And somebody yelled *load up*.

6
JEREMIAH

The Plant, Panhandle Province
The Republic

The night is dragging. Jeremiah and Mac are outside running drills with Dom and Zeus, but it's pointless with only four of them.

And where the hell is Daniels? Jeremiah has his number for emergencies, but so far this hasn't qualified.

The plant is always considered a target. Old-timers say everyone in Amarillo was worried on 9/11 after the Twin Towers fell. Security was heightened after the secessions were finalized, too. The continent hadn't been that vulnerable since the Second World War.

But nothing happened then.

And nothing will happen tonight.

Speaking with Robb would settle his nerves, though. If nothing else, Jeremiah should find out how long they're staying. If it's all night, the four of them will catch sleep in shifts. He also needs to know if more of the team is coming.

Jeremiah puts Mac in charge and starts walking toward the massive but aging administration building. It's three miles away, so he flags down a kid hauling ass in a utility terrain vehicle—what his father used to call a souped-up go-kart. "Can I hitch a ride to admin?"

The kid nods.

Jeremiah doesn't know the guy's name. More than three thousand workers stream in and out of the twenty-five-square-mile compound every day, and he doesn't interact with most of them or understand what they do. That hasn't bothered him until now.

The ride is short, so neither of them engage in small talk. Jeremiah checks his watch. He's still got a while before Lori's boss is supposed to call, but that doesn't keep Jeremiah from worrying. She was the last woman he'd loved. And they connected frequently enough that she almost felt like his girlfriend again.

When the ride stops, Jeremiah doesn't notice until the driver starts talking. "Crazy night. You know what's going on?"

Jeremiah shakes his head. *Not yet, anyway.*

Getting to the building is just the first step. Jeremiah's annoyed by the heightened security. Then there's getting to Robb's office, one of a thousand in the three-story structure occupied by whichever government contractor was earning billions in guaranteed profits to run the plant. And, of course, Robb's office is on the far end.

The door is open, but Jeremiah knocks on it anyway before entering.

"Reynolds, how are your two guys and a girl?"

Robb laughs at his own joke. Jeremiah doesn't get it, but he feigns amusement. "Good one, sir. They're fine."

Robb's not a forward-thinking man, but for someone in his mid-fifties raised in Arkansas, he could be worse. He did greenlight Mac's hiring, though the fact Jeremiah knew her while they served and personally vouched for her abilities probably helped.

Robb motions for him to take a seat. "What's on your mind, son?"

Why does everything about tonight feel off? "Just wanted to see if you had a timetable for us yet. Are more resources coming in later to relieve us, or should we plan on sleeping in shifts?"

He purses his lips, and Jeremiah hopes he hasn't been too relaxed with Robb. He's a folksy guy, but perhaps that's just a show. When he leans back in his chair and opens the desk drawer, Jeremiah nearly blurts out an apology in hopes of not getting written up.

Then Robb pulls out a bottle of bourbon. "You still dry?"

Jeremiah tries not to let his body react to the shock. "Yessir, going on five years."

Is he allowed to drink in here?

"Good man. Do me a favor and shut the door."

Nope.

When Jeremiah returns to his chair, Robb is pouring into a rocks glass.

"I don't drink much either, but this is good enough to make a preacher sneak a taste." He lifts the tumbler to his nose then takes a sip. "I don't usually let people know I have this, but I feel like I can trust you. Can I trust you, Reynolds?"

Jeremiah improves his posture. "I was a SEAL, sir."

Robb nods and downs his drink. "I used to care so much about shit that doesn't matter. Like having one or two at work." He pours another, toasts an imaginary drinking partner, and shoots the bourbon again. "I always thought chain of command and security clearance were sacred, too."

They are. But Jeremiah stays frozen. Interrupting now might keep him from getting answers. Jeremiah's had higher clearance than him, so whatever Robb's struggling with can't be heavier than what Jeremiah's had to carry.

Robb is looking down at the glass in his right hand when he opens his mouth. "I was given intel last week. Intel I had no business getting, but I guess that doesn't matter now."

When he looks up, Robb is sweating, and Jeremiah can't tell if it's from the alcohol or what he's about to say. "We've always had nukes pointed at us, but the threat never felt real." He turns to look out of his corner office at the night. "Now it is. And we need to be ready."

Both men flinch when someone knocks on Robb's door. He turns around, opens his drawer, replaces the contraband and pulls out a pack of gum. Jeremiah stands, and they walk to the door.

Robb throws it open. Jeremiah doesn't know the intense face staring him down, but Robb calls him *Novak* and chomps his spearmint like nothing's wrong.

"Reynolds, thank you for stopping by." He slaps Jeremiah on the shoulder. "I appreciate your insight."

As he's walking down the hall, Jeremiah replays the conversation. If he understood Robb correctly, there's an imminent threat of nuclear war. Robb didn't get a chance to say it, but the New Year's attacks and his presence here are no coincidence.

The enemy's plan is already in motion.

7
LORI

Covert field office, New Orleans, Louisiana
The South

Lori's still trying to wrap her head around it. Fowler told her on a drunken night that he was a spy in the old CIA, and she guessed he was high up the food chain before it was broken up.

But Moore is lying about the rest. Has to be.

After giving her a tour of the unimpressive *field office,* Moore opens the door to his office. She takes the captain's chair and lifts her feet onto the desk.

"Here's what I don't get. If Eric Fowler is such a bad guy, why are you hiding out here instead of bringing him in. You and your guys are official, right?"

They're not officially associated with the Federalist government. That's the obvious part. What she's trying to suss out is whether he's gullible enough to believe her when she agrees to become a part of his team. Or group. Or whatever the hell he calls it.

Moore eases himself into the chair across from her. "It's a little more nuanced than that."

"No, it's not." She swings her legs down and scoots toward the desk. "You're either working for one of the governments or you're doing the same illegal shit you're accusing Fowler of. No better. Probably worse."

When Moore looks at his chest and flattens his tie, Lori smiles. She's getting to him.

"What do you think intelligence officers do? We don't arrest people. We gather information and pass it on."

He had Lori there. Her experience with government work—even if it was just the Amarillo PD—had been about getting the information *and* making the arrest. More efficient that way, in her opinion.

"Who do you give your information to?"

Moore leans back in his chair. He's getting comfortable again and Lori knows her advantage is slipping.

"We'll get there. But first I need you to understand how dangerous Fowler is."

"First, I don't believe he sold government secrets just before the country split. That's the setup for a bad spy movie. Second, there's no way in hell he helped orchestrate any assassinations. The guy has plenty of faults, but psychopathy isn't one of them."

"You don't have to be a psychopath to order a hit."

The way Moore frowns and softens his voice, Lori knows she's picking at an old wound. It's not exposed, but the scar's worse than the one she'll have on her thigh. That's something she can work with.

"Okay," she says, trying to match his change in tone. "Let's say you're being straight with me. What would motivate a career patriot to do those things?"

He sighs. "Money, usually. Or power."

"Now I know you're lying." Lori smiles. "Fowler has neither."

"I disagree."

Whatever game Moore is playing, he's grossly misinformed. She doesn't even try to suppress the *bless your heart* look from spreading across her face. "He makes good money from the business, but not the kind you're talking about. And if his salespeople were spies—which we're not—I'm betting the little information they've gathered so far hasn't been earth-shattering." She means to stop there, then realizes something even more insane about Moore's theory. "Plus, if he were some power-hungry genius like you say, you really think his seat of power would be a small town in Oklahoma? Hell, they had to trade their panhandle for funding and The Republic's protection."

That last part is only partially true, but it's how most describe the events that led to the new map.

Moore shakes his head, obviously uninterested in Lori's low opinion of Oklahoma. "I know it's hard to see past your small life right now."

I'm going to kill you before this is over. Lori's jaw hurts, but she keeps her mouth shut and lets him continue.

"You make a living working for Fowler's company, but you're far from his top earner. You can't carry on a relationship, so you sleep with your ex-husband when you get drunk and horny. Then you go to Oklahoma for his monthly meeting and drink some more with Fowler, and you probably think about sleeping with him, too. But you don't because there's something off about the way he interacts with you. Then you go home and do it all again. Sound about right?"

Lori fights her heart and lungs, hoping she isn't showing panic. Moore's people have been following her.

"But think about what you and Fowler talk about when you get hammered together. What does he ask you about, and what do you say?"

Not that it's any of Moore's business, but Lori and Fowler mostly talk about their messy relationships and bitch about exes they can't stay away from. If she wanted to, she could recall every one of their conversations verbatim. But even without doing that, she knows what Moore's getting at. She's told Fowler about Jeremiah's job, his schedule, his routes.

"Lori, you have to believe me when I say Eric Fowler is a conniving sonofabitch, and the man he works for is worse." Moore looks at the inside of his left wrist, revealing the face an oversized black watch. "I have to jump on a conference call, but someone's coming who can confirm everything I'm saying. It'll be a while before either of us are available, so I'm going to leave you in here. If you need food, coffee, anything, Tommy and John are right outside."

"Who?"

One corner of Moore's face ticks up. "Tweedledee and Tweedledumbass."

Lori lets him leave without protest and waits a minute before poking around. She doesn't expect to find anything—what self-respecting kidnapper would leave her in a room with something she could use against them—but it'll help pass the time.

First she checks the desk. Nothing in the shallow drawer just underneath the top. Same with the top drawer on the right and left. Both bottom drawers are also empty. She checks them for false bottoms and strikes out.

Next she crawls beneath to make sure nothing's secured to the underside.

No way. A letter-sized envelope is duct-taped just above where her knees had been while Moore was giving her shit. Her heart races as she peels away the tape and she has to take a deep breath before returning to her seat at the desk.

The gold letter opener seems to appear from nowhere beside her right hand. She carefully slips it in, slices open the envelope, finds a sheet of copy paper folded into thirds. The back is blank.

When she flips it over, a fire burns so hot she stands and hurts her knuckles punching the desk.

Nice try. – R. Moore

Lori pictures the laugh he's having at her expense and curses spew from her mouth like lava. Between her voice and the punch, she expects the guards to rush in. When they don't, she falls into the chair, spent and—for the first time that night—feeling helpless.

Then, through burning eyes, Lori sees it again, lying beside the letter. The cherry on top of this elaborate joke at the expense of a woman and her *small life*. But they obviously didn't study that life hard enough.

They left her with a letter opener.

Big fucking mistake.

8
ERIC

FAST offices, Cushing, Northeast Province
Republic of Oklahoma

Eric is missing something. If Lori got treatment at the hospital, even a city hospital in The South, and was somewhere else an hour or so later, she's probably alive. Then again, there's a chance someone slipped the watch off her wrist while taking her to the morgue.

He pulls up the log to see how the tracker got from A to B. She wasn't in the hospital long, probably a good sign. From there, she walked back to the French Quarter. An even better sign, though the path doesn't take a straight line to her hotel. There are a few unexplained turns, and one long pause in an alley.

"Idiot," he whispers. *Why didn't I see it earlier?* She was either tailing someone or trying to lose one. Though she rarely acted like it anymore, Lori had been a smart detective once. He's glad she still had some of those instincts. She'll need them.

Just after her stop, Lori returns to the street before moving the opposite direction in a vehicle that drives straight to the Superdome parking lot.

Whoever was tailing Lori kidnapped her.

Eric opens a browser and logs onto a secure messaging site. While ISPs and revenue were chopped up according to geography after the secessions, the web's infrastructure didn't change. Much of the Rural Bloc tried to filter out USA and Lib news sites, but the internet remained porous and accessible to hackers.

After glancing at his alerts, Eric finds the handle for Randall Gates and types a new message.

DDO: Do you have current location for RM?

The last time Eric asked for Robert Moore's status, Gates said the traitorous bastard was working as the top intelligence officer for Federalist President Ace Anderson in Birmingham, Alabama.

Eric tries to track Moore, but Gates has more time and resources. He left the Agency with a sizable retirement and pension. He also has family money. Then there's the cash *lost* overseas after 9/11 that ended up as digital currency in Switzerland and Grand Cayman. It added up to a Wyoming ranch, a private jet, and an office in the valley where one-percenters congregate.

Waiting on Gates to respond had become a pastime, but Eric knows his old boss will be awake in Jackson Hole, either at his computer or waiting for his encrypted phone to ding.

The response comes in less than a minute.

DCI: No. RM not in Birmingham. Operational again.

DDO: I may know where.

He has no proof, but when Eric steps into Moore's shoes, there's no target better than Lori. She has access to some of the most critical intelligence on the planet. Lori doesn't know she's being worked, but she's given Eric more intel about the continent's nuclear program than any of its new leaders possess.

DDO: Asset missing in NOLA. BX en route. Will advise.

Eric wants to be wrong. If Moore gets out of Lori even a fraction of what she knows, it could ruin everything Eric and Gates have been planning—which has been his former best friend's goal since the states broke up.

But Eric's sure he's right, so he calls Boudreaux.

"It's Fowler. She may have been detained by Robert Moore."

"Do you have his location?"

"No."

So much for that. But at least Boudreaux knows what he's getting into now. Moore travels with a pair of armed guards in addition to whatever personnel he feels necessary for the assignment. And though he's in his mid-forties, Moore can still take almost anyone one-on-one.

Boudreaux falls into the almost category.

With nothing more he can do for Lori, Eric drags the virtual conversation with Gates to the monitor on his left. On the center screen, Eric opens a map of the Allied Nations of North America—the official designation for what most called the Divided States or DS, a much more palatable acronym for most military types than ANNA. Each nation is a different shade, including Canada and a slightly larger Mexico, which absorbed the former New Mexico and Arizona.

Billed as a solution to the porous southern border, all Mexican nationals were given a year to move to one of those states if they wished, and American citizens could move or apply for dual citizenship, subject to approval by the Mexican government. Mexico was happy to collect tax dollars from the cities and assumed the power to help the American Indians in the new region, dubbed Los Estados Méxicanos de Norteamérica. Indigenous Peoples residing in the Republic of Oklahoma were also urged to relocate to the EMN, but few did.

American Indian relations in Oklahoma had maintained a pre-secession status quo for a while, though the tribes received even less financial aid. Then Oklahoma became more comfortable with its autonomy, and rumors of higher-than-usual disappearances on tribal land started surfacing. Eric believes some of it's true and feels guilty, but he knows a successful reunification with the USA and its humanitarian rights laws is the only first step that will yield positive results.

He isn't sure there's any hope left for the EMN. The reality in Los Estados Méxicanos de Norteamérica had been bad from the start, and protests by residents of the former Arizona and New Mexico—particularly those in the cities—turned into bloody riots that sprang up for months until The Republic's military stepped in. Republican tanks, Humvees and helicopters flooded into the cities and lifted or escorted American expats to safety. Refugees were told they could live and work in The Republic for two years while applying for citizenship there or in an Allied Nation.

But the Republican Guard took more than people from the former state of New Mexico.

One of the new force's first operations—during the chaotic months just after the secessions were finalized and things were falling through the cracks—was to work with select members of INSTA and travel to Albuquerque. Officials at the nuclear transportation control center and Air Force base there were getting orders through a firehose each day, trying to keep straight which resources were being diverted to which new nation.

During the chaos, and with what appeared to be official authority, the Guard and a set of INSTA's top agents took thousands of nuclear warheads from the base's underground storage complex and transported them to the Amarillo site.

They'd done it with nobody watching, but Jeremiah Reynolds was one of the people duped into carrying out the heist.

That's how Eric knows his map of available nuclear weaponry and transport routes is the most up-to-date on the continent.

9
JEREMIAH

The Plant, Panhandle Province
The Republic

Mac grabs Jeremiah by the arm as soon as the door shuts behind Dom and Zeus.

"You tell me what the hell's going on, and I mean right now."

Jeremiah tries to look confused, purposely knitting his brow together and even cocking his head. "What?"

Turns out, he's a terrible actor. She glares at him as workers hustle past them in the breezeway between the galley and another building, most wearing blue coveralls beneath hoodies or long johns.

"We need to trust each other," she says. "Isn't that what you said my first day on the job? I was hired as a federal agent, just like you, so I can handle whatever Robb said."

Jeremiah looks down. Mac was one of four women to complete Air Force Special Warfare training, then decided that wasn't enough and joined the 24th Special Tactics Squadron as a combat controller. Members of 24 STS are Tier One just like he was. She puts almost everyone else on their team to shame, and there's nobody he'd rather have at his side if a transport jackknifes.

He also wants to protect her. Mac doesn't need it and would tell him so, but it's still his natural instinct. And why should he bring her into this—whatever the hell this is—just because Robb got loaded at work and said, without evidence, the sky's about to fall? She could lose a career. Or worse.

But in situations like this, you have to trust someone.

Jeremiah motions for her to follow. They move to the back of the building and find a spot that's not lit up. Their heavy black coats, pants, and combat boots blend into the dark, and her head seems to float behind the condensation from her breath.

"We got cut off, but Robb said he received classified intel last week that there's an imminent threat of a nuclear attack on the United … on the Allied Nations."

Mac's a pro and doesn't react, but he knows her tells. She chews on the inside of her bottom lip for a few seconds and the cloud around her disembodied face thickens.

"That's an awful joke to make after what happened tonight."

Jeremiah looks around, then grabs her by the shoulders and yanks her close. "Look at me," he says over her protests. "Do I look like I'm fucking around?"

She studies him for a moment. Mac knows his tells, too, but she doesn't find any.

"What does he want us to do about it?"

He releases her shoulders and shrugs his. "Like I said, someone interrupted us."

Mac turns her head as Zeus starts singing *Mac and Master Chief, sittin' in a tree.*

"Go screw yourself," she says, then grins and walks toward him like she hadn't just heard the worst news in their lifetimes.

Jeremiah smiles, too.

He picked well.

* * *

ZEUS WALKS UP to Jeremiah with two silver Yetis full of awful break room coffee and hands one to him without conversation. The kid's high is wearing off, and Jeremiah can tell he's pissed that Dom and Mac are sleeping and he's not.

It was an easy decision. Dom needs to be rested if he has to drive a load out of the plant, and the person in charge of comms can't be dozing off in the middle of a transport.

But Jeremiah empathizes with him. "I appreciate you coming in tonight. I've had a hangover hit in the middle of a shift. More times than I'd like to admit." He takes a sip of the coffee, which is only drinkable when it's half milk and sugar. "It's better to stay awake and work through it. Trust me."

Zeus takes an impossibly long draw of the sludge. "Yeah, right. You coming here drunk. Like I'm going to believe that."

If you only knew. The divorce—and the events that led to it—gave Jeremiah the excuse he always wanted, and he dove into a bottle of whiskey with no plans to come up for air. He'd been at the edge for as long as he could remember. That first taste of hard lemonade sitting around his uncle's campfire, then graduating from bitch beer to the real thing at fifteen. Bud heavy at first, but switching to light when he realized he could drink more and still be lean for football. From there, life gave him plenty of reasons to stay drunk during his downtime.

Now, with Lori missing, Jeremiah wishes he'd been more sober. Perhaps they could've worked through it.

"Ask Daniels," Jeremiah says. "First time he caught me with liquor on my breath, he gave me a choice. Come with him to a meeting that night or pack my shit."

That gets a grin from Zeus. "I'd totally call your bluff if he was here." His expression changes, as if he just realized it. "Where is he, anyway?"

Though that's the question of the night, Jeremiah plays it cool. "He took the family on a trip out of town. Down near the border."

Zeus accepts the answer without pause.

It's not in Jeremiah's nature to lie, especially to someone he might fight alongside if shit does hit the fan, but he also can't put people more on edge. The faces he sees hustling around the campus are already agitated, some bordering on frantic.

In fact, the more he studies them, the more Jeremiah realizes his people are the only ones not scurrying around.

He turns to Zeus. "I'm going for a walk. Turn to the secure frequency."

Jeremiah's not familiar with most of the structures at the plant. He knows where to eat, where to work out, and where to run drills and train on new weapons and tech. There was never much of a reason to concern himself with the rest. The cargo is precious, and his team takes the parts wherever they need to go.

He starts walking toward the center of the compound. He's familiar with the facilities near the entrance, but Jeremiah knows the weapons are handled near the middle. Past that, the research happens in another cluster of buildings about twenty miles due east.

As he nears the edge of familiar territory, many of the workers look like they could be at any industrial workplace. But as he gets farther away from his territory, the dress code changes in subtle ways. The coveralls are not blue, but shades of green and white. Some of the men and women wear rubber gloves.

Two green UTVs sit facing the open space that leads to rows of white domes, which are usually nonthreatening but now look more like intercontinental ballistic missile silos at the ready. Nobody's guarding the vehicles, so Jeremiah slips into one and takes off, first on a designated path, then cutting across the prairie.

He parks fifty yards away. Jeremiah doesn't know if he's allowed to use the UTVs or spy on the goings-on, but his strategy is to get there inconspicuously then act like his presence is routine. As he gets within twenty yards, Jeremiah hears a murmur. Voices. Doors opening and shutting and opening again.

Jeremiah rounds a bend and finds the source, a swarm of plant employees taking off or putting on purple and red hazmat suits as they rush from structure to structure. He's out of place in his dark uniform but nobody seems to notice until an older guy passes without his hood.

"Help you with something?" he says, sweat streaming down his cheek from silver sideburns despite the January air.

"No, just making my rounds. I was brought in for extra security tonight."

The man nods. "Glad they at least have the brains to do that."

It sounds like he's in the mood to vent, so Jeremiah gives him a reason. "They sure do have y'all scrambling tonight. You usually work night shifts on holidays?"

"Brother, I've been here thirty years and we've never had an assembly bay this full of overtime workers."

Someone yells in their direction and the guy hustles away. Jeremiah wanted to ask more questions, but he got the most important piece of information.

Assembly bay.

He and the others aren't here for added security. They're here for a transport. But that doesn't make much sense with only four of them. They're missing a dozen others.

As he starts mentally tallying who's not there, Jeremiah realizes who is. Dom to drive the rig, Zeus to shoot anyone who tries to breach it, Mac to call it in, and him to coordinate.

Everyone needed to get a package on the road.

But nobody to escort the truck.

10
LORI

Covert field office, New Orleans, Louisiana
The South

Lori raps on the door, trying to strike a balance between sad and angry. She smooths out her hair and puts on a Mona Lisa smile because starting innocent is key.

When one of them opens the door, she takes a step toward him. He looks defensive until she lowers her gaze slightly, tucking a bit of hair behind her ear. "Are you Tommy, or John?"

She looks back up and his eyes have softened.

"Actually, it's Thomas." He nods toward the other one. "He's Jonathan. But Moore likes to say it the other way because he's a baseball fan. You know, the surgery."

Lori grins. "Or the underwear." Getting them to picture her without clothes is an important step. "He sounds fun to work for. I've had bosses like that."

As Thomas returns the camaraderie, Lori's mouth goes full Cheshire. She has him.

"I wanted to apologize to you both for earlier. If I'd known you were the good guys, I wouldn't have fought so hard."

Thomas reflexively folds his hands together and holds them between his legs. "He told us you'd be squirrely, but you are one tough lady."

Jonathan jumps in. "I'm sorry I had to hit you like that."

Lori reaches out and cups his elbow, rubs her thumb on his skin. "I keep in shape. But all that struggling and sweating has worn me out a little. Do you think you could bring me a cup of coffee?"

They look at each other, pigs silently deciding which of them deserves her more. Thomas tells her he'll be back in a minute. Makes sense. She did punch him in the junk earlier. Lori steps back into the room and Jonathan shuts the door.

The plan's working so far, but it's about to get harder. She kneels in front of the couch and reaches underneath, making sure the letter opener is still in the right spot. Satisfied with the placement, she slips off her boots and socks and sits on the end farthest from the entrance.

When Thomas opens the door a minute later, her left arm is draped over the side, a grin inviting him to come sit down beside her. He turns to Jonathan and gives him the gimme-some-privacy head bob, and she hears his bootsteps as Thomas shuts the door.

Good, you arrogant prick.

Before he can offer the drink, she pats the other cushion with her right hand. "Take a load off. You deserve it."

Thomas obliges and hands her the foam cup, which she places on the floor below her, bending in a way that invites him to look down her shirt.

"So, Thomas, how old are you?"

He adjusts his seat and moves his right arm to the back of the couch. "Twenty-seven, ma'am."

Lori acts offended and puts a hand to her chest, drawing his eyes there again. "*Ma'am,*" she says, mimicking his accent. "Just how old do you think I am?"

He looks her up and down, smiling, considering. "Well, my mamma always said it was impolite to talk about a woman's age."

The time has come to be more forward, so she leans in. "Well, your mamma raised a very polite young man. And so handsome."

She hates herself for what's coming next. But it'll be worth it.

Lori places her hand on his inner thigh and pulls, opening his legs and scooting herself closer to him. He licks his lips and leans down to kiss her. She lets him get 90 percent of the way, then stops him with an index finger. Thomas looks confused until she bites her lower lip and begins sliding off the couch.

He leans back and interlaces his fingers behind his head. The cocky little shit is going to make her unbutton his jeans and lower them.

Just like she knew he would.

She does it—even manages to maintain a pleasant demeanor in case he sneaks a peek—and gets the jeans just above his ankles. That's when she reaches under the couch and grips the blade.

Lori wants to do it then. And, if it were one of her knives, she could. But a letter opener isn't as sharp, and he's wearing tighty-whities that aren't so white anymore, so she takes a deep breath and reaches up with her left hand to grab the elastic. Thomas obliges by lifting his butt, allowing her to slide them down to the jeans. He spreads his knees as far apart as he can and slides his butt to the edge of the cushion.

She works the hand back up his leg and Thomas grunts in anticipation. After making sure she has just the right spot on his inner thigh, Lori raises her right hand and plunges it as hard as she can into his femoral artery, twisting and churning the gold-plated steel for a second to ensure maximum damage.

Now comes the hard work.

Thomas pulls both hands down to his bleeding leg and cries out. Lori hopes the walls muffle the sound and his friend's far enough away, though it only lasts a moment. By the time his hands grab the letter opener-cum-dagger, Lori has already wrapped her legs around his torso and covered his mouth, pinning his arms to his side and muffling his screams as a crimson river of life flows out of him.

Lori squeezes her thighs tight, fighting the pain of her stitches pulling at taut skin. She keeps one hand over his mouth, the other palming the back of his head. He stands and tries to take a step, forgetting about his pants and pathetic undies.

When Thomas falls on top of her, Lori hopes the other twin mistakes it for rough sex. Also problematic is her own leg wound, which has torn open, blood beginning to soak through her jeans. But his movements are getting weaker, his breathing shallower, his blood colder on her exposed lower back. Lori bears the pain for his last moments and, when there is no more fight left in her victim, she rolls over and straddles him.

Lori pushes herself up despite the shaking. She doesn't have long until the other one comes back, and she needs to be ready. The letter opener is no longer in Thomas's leg, and Lori turns frantic when she can't find it.

Calm down. Focus. She scans the floor and sees a sliver of gold in the pool of blood. It's slick and so is her hand, but his shirt is mostly clean and makes a suitable towel.

If she can get one clean opening, Lori might get out of this hellhole.

She settles into her new post near the door's hinges. The wait feels excruciating, but when there's finally a knock on the door, Lori slows her breath, steadies her hand. When Jonathan gets no response, he opens the door and rushes to his comrade's side with a flurry of murmured curses.

As he hunches over the lifeless body, Lori jumps and lands a clean shot into Jonathan's neck. Though stunned, the bigger of the boys turns and grabs her arm. She struggles but can't shake free. Another quiet death was her goal, but that's not going to happen now, so Lori quits pulling and bull rushes him. They move backward as one, an awkward dance that ends when his legs hit the desk.

Jonathan's momentum stops on a dime and she times her jump perfectly, sliding across the polished wood on her hip like cops on a cheesy TV show. She's weak, though, and doesn't stick the landing, her shoulder crashing into the wall.

She scrambles to her feet and bolts for the door, expecting to get intercepted.

But Lori makes it.

Lori pulls up Moore's guided tour as she stumbles into the hall and sprints to the closest exit. Lori is nearly at a door marked STAIRS when it flies open and she nearly barrels into a large man with a thick beard.

She changes direction, but Blackbeard moves fast for a big man and swallows her in a tight bear hug. She struggles, but it's useless. His arms are as large and strong as her legs, but with a few more tattoos. Despite her screams, she hears a man yelling in the stairwell. Blackbeard spins her so they're facing the entrance.

Though she's physically and emotionally exhausted, Lori has enough for one more round of kicking and screaming as Robert Fucking Moore walks toward them.

"Looks like you've been up to no good," Moore says, his smooth tone now replaced with a sharp edge.

She sets her jaw but stops struggling. Lori knows she can't escape Blackbeard's grip, and if they were going to kill her, they'd have done it by now. After she's been still for a moment, Blackbeard releases Lori and steps aside.

Moore points to Blackbeard.

"Lori, meet Boudreaux."

11
ERIC

FAST offices, Cushing, Northeast Province
Republic of Oklahoma

He hates the taste of energy drinks, but nothing else has ever allowed him to stay awake and think clearly. So, like he has since his first overseas post, Eric pours the skinny can's contents into a tall glass and mixes it with carbonated mineral water and a twist of lemon. He learned the trick from Boudreaux, though he drinks black coffee—with a touch of pharmaceutical enhancement.

Boudreaux should be close to New Orleans, but Eric still has time to scratch an itch.

Who ordered the massacres?

Eric can think of only one person more connected to the kinds of animals capable of carrying out that attack.

Randall Gates.

DDO: Expecting confirmation on RM location soon. Meantime, what intel do you have on NYE attack?

He doesn't expect Gates to know yet. But if he has a lead, Eric wants to provide support. Their goal from the beginning has been to ensure the relative peace that's been found on the continent. The mission evolved some over time, but few people know that. This new adversary believes they struck the first blow in a campaign against Eric and Gates.

DCI: Obviously organized by RM.

Gates never liked Moore. He didn't recommend Moore to replace Eric, and when Gates's own retirement left another void in the command structure, he again blocked Moore's career advancement.

Moore joined Anderson's cabinet before the ink on the FSA's secession documents were dry.

Gates has an axe to grind with Moore, so Eric will need more evidence than Gates's gut feeling.

Especially since it conflicts with his own.

Moore is an expert tactician and infinitely dangerous when in the wrong hands, but executing civilians is not in his repertoire. The officer he worked beside and trusted to run myriad operations simply wouldn't give that order. No end could justify those means. Eric is sure Moore would rather leave President Anderson's administration.

DDO: Proof?

DCI: Will have to discuss later. Shootings have accelerated timetable for MANIFEST. Contact from Firestarter is imminent.

Eric chugs his drink and stands to make another. He and Gates had spent so much time planning the operation that it had become more fantasy than reality, a thought experiment designed to inspire a cure that could never be achieved.

Then war was declared at midnight Eastern.

As soon as he was told about the massacres, Eric had known someone would trigger MANIFEST. The flagword Pinnacle is being used right now in the new USA capital among defense and intelligence chiefs, classifying the coordinated attacks as an incident that could lead to nuclear war.

Eric and Gates were supposed to keep that from happening. They were the continent's peacekeepers, and they'd been caught sleeping. The union's dissolution had caused enough global instability. But now the Divided States appear to be at war, and one of the superpowers in Asia or Eastern Europe will take advantage unless they act fast.

He and Gates conceived MANIFEST as an answer to a Pinnacle incident, which had become an unfortunate eventuality the moment Texas declared its independence again.

Eric returns the map of nuclear weapons and transportation routes to his center monitor. Then, on the screen to his left, he pulls up the same map, only the dots and lines represent major oil and natural gas pipelines and transfer stations.

All that remains is the call from Logan Robb.

12
JEREMIAH

The Plant, Panhandle Province
The Republic

Jeremiah elbows Zeus. "Thirty more mikes, then you can sleep."

"You're a hardass," Zeus says, eyes still closed. "I ever tell you that?"

"Every day."

Zeus can sleep standing up—doesn't even need something to lean on—and Jeremiah let him do it for the better part of an hour. He had a feeling Zeus wouldn't make it to the cots inside.

As if on cue, one of the loud UTVs whips by, then turns and skids to a stop in front of them. The guy who hops out isn't one of the plant workers. Not in a leather jacket, slacks, and no ballcap. Must be with administration, somewhere in middle management.

"Master Chief Jeremiah Reynolds?"

"Once upon a time." Jeremiah takes a step forward. "Who's asking?"

He closes the gap between them until he recognizes him. It's the man who interrupted Robb. Novak.

"He needs to see you."

Jeremiah turns to Zeus, who looks ready to throttle this Novak guy if given the word. He's not much for the higher-ups sticking their fingers in the team's business.

"Get the others," Jeremiah says. "And start another pot of coffee."

***

NOVAK IS NOT middle management. He was shooed in at every checkpoint and security called to let Robb know we were coming, all done without uttering a syllable and despite the fact he has a pistol on his hip.

The intensity of the situation is on full display when we step off the elevator to the third floor and Robb is waiting. Jeremiah should wait for Robb to initiate the discussion, but as far as he can tell, protocol has been tossed out of the boss's corner window.

"We're here for a transport." It's not a question for Jeremiah at this point, but a statement that'll hopefully get Robb to cut through the bull.

Robb turns toward his office. "Not out here."

As he walks, Novak pulls beside him. Jeremiah studies the new player's posture and gait. Ex-military. By the way he's standing shoulder-to-shoulder with the top brass, Jeremiah isn't sure if he works for Robb or the other way around. He may not even work at the plant. Is he with the government? The Guard?

Novak shuts the office door, and everyone remains standing, Novak blocking the exit.

Robb sighs. "Yes, we're preparing a load for you. But not for the reasons you think."

"It has nothing to do with the New Year's attacks?"

"No." He bobs his head. "And yes."

Just like a goddamn bureaucrat to use doublespeak and avoid the answer. If Daniels were giving the order, Jeremiah wouldn't question it. But he doesn't trust Robb. In fact, this guy is pissing him off.

"If you don't start being straight with me, you'll have to find someone else. I'm not—"

The next noise Jeremiah makes is the bastard child of a scream and a war cry. Novak has him on his knees, one of them on fire after receiving a boot from behind. One of Novak's hands is gripping his shoulder. He can't see it, but Jeremiah knows the other is pointing a muzzle at his skull.

"You said this one would cooperate." Novak's voice is as calculated as his takedown. "If he won't, there are people we can bring in who will."

The look on Robb's face confuses Jeremiah. The man in charge of this plant—one of the most protected, classified dots on the globe—is now a kid in the principal's office. Jeremiah also catches Novak's phrasing. *This one*.

"No," Robb says. "We need him and his team. Just give me a chance to explain."

Before he can continue, Jeremiah asks the question, though at this point it's rhetorical.

"Where's Daniels?"

Though Jeremiah's eyes sting, his jaw is set in rage as Robb starts offering his pathetic excuses.

"Daniels started fighting and it got out of hand. He didn't understand. Didn't see. But you will. You told me earlier tonight that you were a SEAL before the secessions. You swore your allegiance to the United States Constitution."

"So did Daniels."

He didn't just serve under Fifty Stars. He was in Delta. Jeremiah can't picture these two clowns getting the better of Daniels, though he'd been in his fifties. Robb's roughly the same age, but Novak can't be older than thirty-five.

"Daniels was stubborn," Robb says. "He didn't understand the operation. He thought the ends didn't justify the means. But they do, Reynolds. I swear to Christ they do."

Before Jeremiah can protest, Novak presses the muzzle of a pistol into the back of his head. "You're either in or out, Master Chief. Right now. Your answer doesn't matter to me, really. I just need to get things moving."

The honorable thing would be to let Novak shoot him. He wants no part of a military coup. Jeremiah doesn't know all the players or the overall objective, but nobody massacres innocent people and moves a nuke in the middle of the night with good intentions. He can't be a part of it. He needs to stop it.

Then again, dead men can't stop anything.

"Fine," Jeremiah says. "But I'm not doing anything until you read me in. And I mean all the way."

When Novak holsters his 9mm, Robb looks like a test just came back negative.

"Okay." Robb pours another drink, slams it back. "You remember when we picked up that package in New Mexico?"

13
LORI

Covert field office, New Orleans, Louisiana
The South

Lori can't scrape the dried blood from under her fingernails. She's been trying for half an hour, sitting in another office chair with nothing to use but a business card she found lying in the bottom of a desk drawer.

This Boudreaux guy tossed her a towel, a pair of oversized gray sweatpants, a matching T-shirt stamped with CIA, and a pair of thong sandals. Boudreaux, who's six-three if he's a foot, is her new guard. Lori won't test him.

She's still working on a nail when one of them knocks—as if she could refuse them entry—and cracks open the door. When Lori doesn't attack, Moore pokes his head in and smiles. She'll wipe it off his face if they're ever alone.

"Thank you for your patience," he says as the pair walks in. "We're running behind, but I'm optimistic." Moore takes the chair across the desk while Boudreaux—still in clothes stained by her blood—remains standing. "First, let me say that I'm extremely disappointed you killed my guys. That said, if you took them out with a letter opener, they obviously weren't right for this job."

Lori goes back to work on her nails. "They were pretty stupid."

"Seems that way. You also showed us just how valuable you can be. You obviously have talents we didn't know about."

He doesn't know the half of it. In addition to her combat skills, Lori can recall every conversation she's ever had. Every song she's ever heard. The score and dialogue to every movie she's ever seen. The secrets of everyone who's ever trusted her. She's a walking voice recorder incapable of shutting off. It seemed like a blessing in school and when she was working murders.

Now it's a curse that won't let her sleep without booze or drugs.

"I know you don't understand why yet, but your continued relationship with your ex-husband makes you one of the most important people on the planet."

Making her seem important is a nice move. Lori looks up, takes a moment to consider her options. She can't fight her way out. She'll have to engage with Moore and hope she can talk her way out—even if it means acting like she believes his batshit crazy nonsense.

"Actually, I do understand why. He thinks I still worry about him when he's on the road, so he tells me about his schedule and routes, even though he's not supposed to. And when I get drunk with Fowler, he asks me where Jeremiah is going next, and I tell him."

Moore flashes *that* look, the one every man makes when a woman understands a concept that should be beyond her understanding. It's infuriating. But, in this case, useful. The smarter she seems, the more valuable she'll become, which means he'll keep her alive.

"Very good. I take it you also know how damaging it can be to reveal that information?"

"Don't know. Don't care."

"Forgive me if I don't believe you, detective Young."

Lori settles into her chair. Depending on how far back he goes, this could be a long interrogation. "Those days are long gone."

Moore leans forward, elbows on the table, fingers laced. He's trying to establish dominance. Trying to rattle her.

"You can act like you've changed, and you've done a good job hurting yourself, but you're neither uncaring nor unintelligent. If you were, you'd still be on the force."

This asshole thinks he knows her. Moore's obviously read Lori's jacket and decided she was in the right that night. Or he only wants her to think so. Either way, he's playing good cop.

Lori doesn't want to know what Boudreaux's bad cop looks like.

"Let's say you're right," she says, mimicking Moore's dominating lean. "Maybe I do care about drunkenly discussing information that could make our nuclear arsenal vulnerable to terrorists. But if I'm so smart, I've realized the risk isn't as bad as you seem to think it is. Maybe Jeremiah's told me that there are so many safeguards in those big rigs that hijacking one while it's on the road is impossible. Literally can't be done."

The nod she gets in return is telling. Moore already knows everything she just said, yet he's continuing down this road.

"You're right. If a team tried to take a truck by force, some of them would die in the firefight trying to take out the escorts. If they brought enough people, a few might make it to the trailer. The first may not survive the electric shock—unless they've accounted for that and used some fairly advanced tech to disable it. But could they neutralize the expert marksman inside the truck? Or get past the foam that floods the trailer? And even if they did all of that before police or military arrived, the exploding axels would keep them from moving the trailer."

"That's what I'm saying. So, if Fowler really is this evil spy like you say, what good is the information on Jeremiah's schedule and routes?" That question isn't part of her act. Lori honestly can't see where he's going.

"Wrong question. If acquiring a nuclear device by force during transport is impossible, then what good are *you* to Fowler?"

She waits for him to spin another lie, but he doesn't. With his silence, Moore is giving her time to think about the question, to consider the possibility he's telling the truth. But she's done playing.

"Near as I can tell, I make him money. And I'm sure he hopes one day I'll break down and sleep with him."

Another infuriating nod. "You can't see the answer because you're looking through the wrong lens. You assume I'm the bad guy behind today's shootings and Fowler's not."

No shit.

"But," Moore continues, "what if Fowler is the bad guy? And what if he's not using the information you've unknowingly given him to hijack a truck, but to know where and when governments are expecting the nuclear weapon to be, where they'll look first if the tracking is disabled and communications are broken? And let's say he comes to you one day and tells you about his group, says if you work with him, you can help save the world."

"Didn't you tell me the same thing a few minutes ago?"

A laugh. "I did. But consider one last thing. We know from surveillance that your ex still cares about you and that you can persuade him with relative ease."

He's not wrong. He also hasn't made a point yet.

"So, what if Fowler wanted you to persuade Jeremiah to do something? Something he'd never consider under normal circumstances. What could you convince Jeremiah Reynolds to do for Fowler, who wants to steal a nuclear weapon but knows he can't take it by force?"

She tries not to answer the question, but Moore was right earlier. She is smart.

Less-than-ten-seconds smart.

"Jeremiah's going to deliver the nuke to Eric."

14
ERIC

FAST offices, Cushing, Northeast Province
Republic of Oklahoma

As Boudreaux's deadline to check in approaches, Eric rehearses the operation one last time.

It starts with the perfect location. Gates and Eric couldn't secure a better place to execute Phase One of MANIFEST if they'd built a town from scratch.

Though the Liberated States are developing technology that will phase out fossil fuels, every industrialized country on the planet still runs on oil. And on the map Eric's been staring at, nearly every major pipeline runs through Cushing.

The town has been known as the pipeline crossroads of the world for decades. It has also been a global economic hub since the New York Mercantile Exchange began using Cushing's West Texas Intermediate crude as the benchmark by which all oil futures are priced. That was in the mid-eighties, and Cushing's infrastructure and financial importance have remained through all the booms and busts.

But most of the world's population has no idea how important Cushing is to their lives.

That's why Gates chose it.

Eric nearly jumps when his phone buzzes. Boudreaux's two minutes early.

"Status?"

"Target secure."

Thank God. "How is she?"

"Injury to her left leg, but fine otherwise. We're on the road now."

On the road? That news wakes him up faster than one of Boudreaux's modafinil pills. "You're driving? She needs to be in Amarillo by morn ... by sun-up. At the latest."

"Negative. Unscheduled flight over Republic airspace is a no-go. We'll just get escorted to Lackland or Sheppard."

Eric had been so preoccupied with making sure Lori was still in play that he forgot about the logistics of getting her in position. The Republic had the most sophisticated air defense on the continent, a stark contrast to Oklahoma.

Oklahoma! "Can you bring her to me instead?"

"Affirmative. Three hours."

Eric can make this work. It's a change in plan, but the result will be the same.

Lori was supposed to get home from New Orleans, work on Reynolds a bit longer, then bring him in. Make sure he was ready when Robb gave the order. On paper, he'd be transporting components from Amarillo to Oak Ridge, Tennessee. But his rig would have assembled warheads, and instead of staying on Intracontinental Highway 40 the whole trip, he'd exit early and drive north to Cushing.

But with those shootings moving up the timetable, getting Lori to Cushing is the best he can do. Eric can still get Reynolds to comply. Lori didn't convince him to go willingly, but he'll do it to save her.

That's what Eric will tell Robb, anyway.

He wants at least a few minutes to rehearse, but the phone is still in his hand when it vibrates.

15
JEREMIAH

The Plant, Panhandle Province
The Republic

Jeremiah strains to hear the other half of Robb's conversation, but it's useless. Before making the call, Robb had walked toward his window into darkness and kept his phone tight against his ear.

"MANIFEST is a go," he says. After a beat, he inhales deeply. "That's not what we discussed."

Novak, who had only listened but not contributed to Robb's explanation for the night's events, creeps away from his post at the door.

"You can't just change plans like this," Robb continues.

That sends Novak into a sprint across the office, and he jerks the phone out of Robb's hand.

"This is Novak. What the hell's going on?"

Jeremiah tries not to look relieved that their so-called plan is unraveling. Though he understands the logic behind what Robb told him, it's also dangerous and won't work.

"How could you let ... I don't care if you were tracking her."

Lori. It's no coincidence she went missing on the same night these two idiots are trying to pin down the location of a woman while coercing him into something out of an old Brad Taylor novel.

"Well, you left us no choice." Novak says. "But if this doesn't work, it's your ass, not mine."

Jeremiah and Robb stare at Novak as he ends the call and looks out the window. When he turns around, Novak is more collected than Jeremiah expects.

Robb isn't. "So, it worked?"

"Perfectly," Novak says as he hands back Robb's phone. "In fact, Fowler thinks it was his idea."

Jeremiah stands, trying to appear calm. It was a performance, the loud steps and jerking the phone away, all meant to fool someone who thinks he's on the same side. Lori's boss, who was tracking her before she went missing, runs something a hell of a lot more dangerous than a sales company.

And now she's neck deep in whatever it is.

"What've you done with Lori?"

Novak puts up a palm. "Relax. She's safe for now."

Jeremiah walks to Novak until they're nose-to-nose. "What does that mean?"

"It means as long as you do what you're told, she'll be fine."

"Who the fuck do you think you are?"

Novak laughs and turns to Robb. "You take this one." Novak's eyes are wild when he turns back. "I hate bragging on myself."

***

NOVAK SLAMS the brakes in front of Jeremiah's team.

"We understand each other, Master Chief?"

As an answer, Jeremiah stares at Novak until the asshole's pupils dilate and nostrils flare. He now knows Novak's rarely challenged, which'll make him impulsive and easy to manipulate later. The staring contests lasts a few more seconds. Then, just as the prick's about to lose it, Jeremiah grins.

He barely makes it out of the Polaris before Novak speeds away.

Zeus follows Novak with his eyes, but he addresses Jeremiah. "Who was that?"

"He's from INSTA's HQ. We have a transport tonight."

That gets everyone's attention. Zeus looks excited to finally feed his ADHD. Dom, who's about to get behind the wheel of a Safeguards Transport rig, rubs his eyes and starts chugging his coffee.

Mac doesn't tip her hand unless you look at her bottom lip. "When do we leave?"

"Soon. And the protocol has changed."

Jeremiah reaches into his jacket and pulls out a large plastic bag. Inside are four Transcontinental Travel Licenses and related paperwork. "Tonight we have to be more covert than ever. Take these, learn your new names, DOBs, and addresses."

Dom starts to protest, but Jeremiah puts up an index finger. "Save your questions. We're taking material to Oak Ridge. We'll take Alpha route with some modifications. And, since we're not announcing our presence, we can't have any escort. It's just us."

After a beat, Dom nods. "But what's with all the cloak and dagger? If there's a threat, shouldn't we have more security, not less?"

Before the secessions, Dom would've been right. It was easy to stay incognito, just another semi on open highways flanked by passenger vehicles with USA government license plates. But now there's at least one border crossing no matter which facility they drive to, so INSTA's presence is always announced, and they were likely monitored while in-country.

"Since we don't know who's behind the attacks, we can't risk anyone knowing our location."

Now Zeus has a question. "Then why are we moving anything? We shouldn't be operating without sufficient intel."

"Under normal circumstances, you're absolutely correct. But our neighbors in The South want to be fully stocked until they know what's what."

Zeus shakes his head, disgusted. "Whatever. This is some bullshit."

While Jeremiah agrees, he can't let his team know it. Not if his plan is going to work.

"Look, this is the job. If you don't like it, I can accept your resignation right now and you can get back to your wife."

Questioning Zeus's loyalty and manhood is usually a bad decision. But, despite the bravado, Zeus knows he's lucky to have the job, so he nods and holds out his hand to accept the fake passport.

Jeremiah distributes the materials. "Since we're going covert, I want everyone but Dom to leave behind your cellphones. I'll procure other communications on the way, but I also want you to write down names and phone numbers to call in case this doesn't go right. Keep them on you."

That gets their attention. After a transport or two, INSTA transporters forget their packages are nuclear, and the job becomes cake. He's glad they won't feel that way tonight.

Jeremiah tells Zeus and Dom to go get Big Blue ready. Mac stays behind.

"We're not taking parts to Tennessee. Not if we're under imminent threat of nuclear war. We're fixing to move live warheads, off the books, to someone who isn't supposed to have them, aren't we?"

He doesn't answer, but Mac's gears are still turning. He appreciates how smart she is, but tonight it might be a liability.

"And Daniels isn't on vacation."

"No."

She hangs her head. When she looks back up, Jeremiah expects to see tears, but is met instead with rage.

"And you're just going along with this? I know we have a chain of command, but if you go along with this, you're not the man I thought you were."

It's subtle. Nobody else would've noticed, but Jeremiah sees a shift in her expression when she mentions Jeremiah's integrity, from anger to disappointment.

"No," Jeremiah says, "I'm not going along with this. But we have to pretend for now. They have leverage."

"Nothing's worth doing this."

Almost nothing. Jeremiah had checked his voicemail on the drive from the admin building. Fowler said his *guy* in Louisiana had found Lori. The story is that she went back to the scene to help the UZ Police after being released from the hospital with minor injuries.

But Fowler doesn't know his guy is really Novak's guy, and anyone taking orders from Novak is out of his mind.

Jeremiah thought about why both sides want him to deliver an armed hydrogen bomb to Cushing, or why they think he's stupid enough not to realize Lori dies in that scenario, too.

His conclusion? It doesn't matter.

"They have my ex, Mac. They have Lori."

Mac didn't like Lori when they were married, and much of what she knows about the divorce is bad. But Jeremiah still cares about Lori, and Mac knows it.

"Okay," Mac says. "What do we do?"

"We go get her."

16
LORI

Lakefront Airport, New Orleans, Louisiana
The South

The jet is fit for a Fortune 500 CEO, not the grizzly bear escorting Tiny Tim toward a graying pilot.

"I was picturing a stealth fighter or helicopter," Lori says. "I mean, aren't you a military badass?"

"If we were coming out hot, maybe," he says in a maddeningly unplaceable accent. "But when you have an old friend who flies private jets, it's much more comfortable to have him change a passenger log."

A lot of people trust Boudreaux. Still, Lori isn't on board with the plan he and Moore have cooked up to *save the world* from Fowler.

After exchanging pleasantries with the pilot, Boudreaux takes her crutches and helps her into the luxurious cabin. He points to a white leather seat that stretches along half the fuselage. "Keep your leg elevated. I patched you up, but the more you let it rest, the faster you can ditch the crutches."

"I don't need the crutches. I'm a lot tougher—"

"Look, you've got nothing to prove to me. I got your background from Moore. But I just stitched you up for the second time, and you're going to want your leg to work later."

He has a point, and the couch looks comfortable. As she settles in, Lori feels the inevitable crash following a night of adrenaline. Sleeping isn't an option, though. Boudreaux may have the loyalty of everyone else, but he hasn't earned hers. He's strong enough to snap her in two, so she should at least be awake to fight back.

"They serve coffee on this flight?"

"You read my mind." Boudreaux stands and walks to the back. He returns a minute later holding two paper cups with cardboard sleeves, though he nearly spills them as the jet starts down the runway.

"He had coffee waiting for you. That's some friend."

Boudreaux hands her a cup and sips from the another. "Combat brings people together like that."

"I know," she says between drinks. "My ex was a SEAL."

"And a damn fine one at that."

"So everyone says. He didn't talk much about it."

He did every time he had two too many, but Lori knows better than to tell anyone Jeremiah had spoken about SEAL Team Six—even to his wife.

Lori also isn't interested in telling a stranger about the cold days and the drunken nights or the suppressed anger that led to the destruction of their marriage and her career, so she changes the subject. "You should know that I am not convinced that Moore runs a spy agency. I just went along with him to get on this plane. And now that we're in the air, and we have time to kill, I have a few questions about this ridiculous plan."

"I thought you might."

"For starters, whose side are you on? Fowler thinks he sent you to save me, and Moore thinks he's sending us to spoil some doomsday plot."

The silence didn't last long, but it was enough for Lori. He's as conflicted as she is. Rather than call him out, she waits, lets him convince himself. "I'm on the side of preventing nuclear war and taking down the sonofabitch who ordered the slaughter of innocent people tonight."

The answer catches her off guard. Moore made Boudreaux sound like a mercenary. Boudreaux could be lying—she doubts anyone's been straight with her all night—but there's something in his deep voice that rings true. A familiar hurt that's impossible to fake.

"How does delivering me to someone who, according to you, wants to start a nuclear holocaust, accomplish that?"

He takes an impossibly long drink—a stalling tactic Jeremiah uses when she asks about his job. Boudreaux has no reason to trust her. But dammit, he's asking Lori to risk her life.

"Look," she says, "if I don't know the endgame, why should I play? What's keeping me from outing you to Fowler? Especially since I still think this is all bullshit."

He leans back and smiles, white teeth peeking out below his impressive beard. "Moore said you're not big on chain of command."

That kind of comment used to piss her off. She'd rage and curse and threaten. But she'd learned not to let other people determine how she feels about herself. "How would you feel if I judged you by the worst moment of your life?"

People usually shut up quick when she pulls that card. But not Boudreaux.

"That's not the worst moment of your life." Boudreaux stands and moves next to her. Not uncomfortably close, but near enough that she notices the faded scar on the left edge of his face, a line of stitches that runs from his hairline to his beard. Boudreaux's now in tactical gear like Jeremiah wears on the road, but her ex never wore it like that.

"I don't know what that moment was," Boudreaux continues. "But I can tell it was bad, and you haven't forgiven yourself yet."

If you only knew. It feels like he does know, though she knows he can't. Still, she finds herself looking into his hazel eyes, transfixed, uncomfortable but in the best way.

"I can also tell you're a survivor by the way you took out those kids today," he says. "Stopping the shooter may have been your police training kicking in, but not what you did to them. I know Special Forces guys who couldn't pull that off."

He inches closer and Lori hides behind her coffee cup, hopes he thinks the blush in her cheeks is from the coffee's heat.

"Don't worry. I don't need to know your life's story. In fact, your ability to keep secrets will be a useful asset for what we're about to do."

For a moment she thinks he might lean in the rest of the way. When he doesn't, Lori brings herself back to the task at hand.

"And what are we about to do, exactly?"

Lori asks the question with no snark. She hasn't wanted to take any of this seriously, but Lori can't ignore Boudreaux's earnestness. And if he's all in, maybe she really has been sucked into some bizzarro world where conspiracies are real.

"I deliver you to Fowler, acting like I rescued you from Moore. When Fowler thinks his plan's coming together, I'll neutralize him. Then you'll let your husband know what's happening."

She doesn't mean to do it, but Lori feels the corners of her lips curl, an unconscious reaction, a true smile—the one she never shows anymore.

"*Ex*-husband. And I'm going to need just a few more details."

"We'll get into the specifics, but first"—Boudreaux brushes Lori's hand as he takes her paper coffee cup—"we need more of this."

Lori watches him walk to the back again. She still can't place him. Not his accent. His allegiance. His true nature. Boudreaux is as mysterious as this new reality.

She'll just have to enjoy both while she can.

17
ERIC

FAST offices, Cushing, Northeast Province
Republic of Oklahoma

He's nodding off when the computer chimes. Gates has responded to the status update, and it could go either way.

The plan has been ripped apart and Frankensteined back together. But Eric had no way to anticipate a multination terrorist attack during Lori's vacation, or that the attack would move up MANIFEST's timeline so drastically.

DCI: Good work.

Eric sighs in relief and feels safe asking the questions that've plagued him since their last communication.

DDO: Current time?

DCI: 5 seconds.

It's worse than he thought. Much worse.

Though the Bulleting of Atomic Scientists haven't announced a change in their Doomsday Clock since the secessions, it's still the best metaphor for the threat of global nuclear war. Last January, Gates said they were thirty seconds away.

Eric is sure of the next answer, but he asks the question anyway.

ECOO: Current threat?

Russia always had its intercontinental and submarine-launched nuclear missiles on hair-trigger status, and several other overseas nations likely had their arsenal at the ready.

But, as he'd feared, Eric gets the worst possible answer.

DCI: China.

Russia has twenty times the number of warheads and had used the size of its arsenal to bully former Soviet republics into rejoining the band, but nothing more.

China, on the other hand, has used nuclear force.

Twice.

Japan was the first target. Despite its history with atomic bombs, Japan came to the aid of Taiwan, which was fighting hard to stave off realization of the mainland's One China policy. Japan's superior technology and strategy nearly crippled the Chinese Communist Party, so in the same desperation the Allies felt in the Second World War, China became the second country to use nuclear force.

Much of the world signaled its disgust with the People's Republic of China.

Then did nothing in response.

In the Western Hemisphere, Texas and the Liberated States had just seceded, and Washington was still negotiating terms with them while trying to keep the rest of the states united. Like the capital's namesake once did with France, the USA felt it was on ground too shaky to intervene on Taiwan's behalf.

China declared victory, but Japan had other plans. It continued to support Taiwan, and the air and sea assault continued to deplete the mainland's resources. With China's economy in freefall and no other nations coming to Taiwan's aid, the CCP felt it could nuke the island into oblivion. Given China's dire economic straits, reunification had become primarily about preventing another superpower from setting up shop in Taiwan—a goal that could also be achieved by turning it into a radioactive wasteland.

Overseas, the USA was trying to tamp down its own border skirmishes after losing The South to secession.

The rest of the world's nuclear powers also declined to respond. Those in Europe were in a cold war with Russia, and the Middle East was preoccupied with Israel and a newly nuclear Iran.

China and Japan focused on rebuilding, as did the Allied Nations of North America.

But reconstituting the western hemisphere's nuclear arsenal had yet to become a priority.

All former USA submarines had been recalled to the mainland while the secessions were negotiated and remained dormant as governments, economies, and infrastructures were rebuilt. Though much of that was now complete, none of the Divided States could justify redeployment of the subs under new flags, so their SLBMs remained indefinitely useless.

As for ICBMs, though United States President Alexia Ramirez retained possession of the Football, nearly all the personnel needed to physically execute an authorized nuclear strike reside either in the South or on the Frontier. It only takes four people turning their keys to launch the missiles, but should those troops now act on the orders of a foreign president?

For those two legs of the nuclear triad, the United States would likely need a string of concessions like ones made by Ukraine, Kazakhstan, and Belarus after the Soviet Union fell. Russia ended up with the nuclear arsenal, but it took five years and nearly two million American dollars.

The few bases with bombers and caches of nuclear weapons could deploy independently, but the time and visibility involved rendered the point moot if China let loose any of its missiles.

Gates had foreseen this scenario and several others, all of which require the same preventive solution.

MANIFEST.

But the New Year's attacks have truncated the op's timetable. And if the clock is this close to midnight, China must be recalibrating their missiles and putting ANNA cities in its crosshairs.

The plan may be perfect, but can they execute it in time?

Before asking Gates, Eric calls Robb to make sure the payload left on time.

"This better be important." It's Novak, not Robb.

You better hope I never see your crazy ass in person. "Gates wants me to confirm everything is operating according to schedule."

"Yes, it is. And Fowler ..."

Novak remains silent, waiting for Eric to acknowledge him. Eric's first instinct is to end the call. He got the info he wanted. But, for reasons Eric can't fathom, Gates brought Novak into MANIFEST and put him in charge of logistics, and this situation is too explosive for internal bickering.

"Yeah."

"Gates has my number. Lie to me again, and you'n me'll have a big problem."

The line goes dead before Eric can tell him to take a flying leap.

The anger subsides quickly, though, and Eric knows Gates wants reassurance from his Number Two, not the guy in charge of shipping. Knowing now that Reynolds left the plant on time, he and the payload should be approaching the border.

DDO: Phase Two currently on schedule for 0730. Acceptable?

DCI: Yes.

Good. The world's safety now hinges on Jeremiah Reynolds's love for his ex-wife.

PART II: EMPTY QUIVER

18
JEREMIAH

Intracontinental Highway 40,
2 miles west of Texola Border Crossing
The Republic

Jeremiah's eyes snap into focus as they approach the border. It's only been ninety minutes since leaving the dock, but watching the flat, endless blacktop through the windshield had him hypnotized.

How does Mac do this all day?

Jeremiah's riding shotgun—a position usually reserved for Mac, where she mans Big Blue's comms. They're much more sophisticated than a CB radio and give her a direct link to the new INSTA operations center inside the Plant. The change is fresh enough that Mac occasionally says ABQ when she means AMA. She's also the second driver, which allows the team to finish transports without stopping overnight.

Jeremiah usually drives his own vehicle, a modified SUV that trails the rig with a few other INSTA agents. A second escort vehicle would ordinarily travel alongside, loaded down with a collection of the fiercest badasses they can find. Except for Zeus. He's the best of them and rides in the trailer with the payload—the warrior of last resort.

But, since this transport is off the books and unguarded, Jeremiah decided two men in the cab would attract less attention when they were inevitably pulled over for Dom's lead foot, so she's in the overhead compartment with Zeus. Mac's presence in the cab always makes Guardsmen, Rangers, and sheriff's deputies stick around and chat—even after Jeremiah smooths out the speeding ticket.

The only thing less conspicuous than two men in the cab is one, so Jeremiah stands as Dom slows down for the crossing, which would be nothing more than a toll booth were it not for the guards with modified M4 rifles capable of fully automatic fire—the same models provided to INSTA transport teams.

"You got this," Jeremiah says. "Remember, you can't use the express lane and there's no sign-countersign." He puts in a Bluetooth earpiece and dials Dom's personal cell. "And I'll be on this if you need me."

Dom nods, but Jeremiah can tell he's uncomfortable. Though he drives what looks on the outside like a standard tractor-trailer, the big man has never had to pass for a trucker. No matter which country they're entering, INSTA passes through the lane designated for military and law enforcement. To pass through, Dom and the border guard exchange a verbal code: the guard says a letter of the phonetic alphabet and Dom responds with a corresponding letter. Both sign and countersign change each month.

But as Jeremiah climbs into the cab's overhead compartment, Dom steers instead toward the far-right civilian truck lane, where he'll provide his fake passport and falsified paperwork. Novak said the guard there is in on it, but they'll still be subject to an inspection by the rifle-wielding guards.

Best-case scenario if it goes wrong? An international incident. But the ingredients for a deadly firefight are present.

Either way, Lori dies.

Zeus is sprawled out on one of the overhead beds sounding like a hog rooting for truffles. The compartment was designed to hold two at most, so Jeremiah squeezes inside and sits thigh-to-thigh with Mac.

"Think this'll work?" she whispers.

"Seventy-thirty yes."

Mac gives him the *yeah, right* look, an oft-used expression in their nonverbal repartee.

"Fine. Sixty-forty."

Mac opens her mouth, but the truck stops and Jeremiah puts an index finger to his lips. He pushes the Bluetooth farther into his ear.

"Alpha Charlie," Dom says before stumbling. "I mean, morning sir."

Mistakes like that are rare for Dom, though Jeremiah's never asked him to lie. And the flub doesn't disrupt their ID and paperwork exchange, so Jeremiah keeps his face neutral. Mac seems to buy it.

"A little early to be on the road, isn't it?" the guard asks. "I know the laws are more relaxed now, but I'm required to see your log between midnight and five."

A doctored electronic log is in the truck, but Dom's never had to worry about it. He struggles to turn on the device, which he signals by talking to himself using colorful language.

A full minute later, one of the guards finally speaks. "Mr. Torretto, I need you to pull into to our inspection area.

"May I ask why, sir?"

"Pull into the inspection area please."

Shit.

The truck lurches forward. Zeus yawns and sits up. Mac gives Jeremiah a questioning thumbs up. When Jeremiah shakes his head, her communication goes verbal.

"Dammit Dom. And you," she says, eyes cutting through him. "You should've listened and let me drive."

She's right, which happens more often than Jeremiah will ever admit. Mac's recounting the various reasons why she should've been in the cab when Dom starts talking in his ear.

"I'm looking at three guards. Two armed with rifles, one with a pistol on his hip. It's cold as balls outside, so they don't look happy."

Jeremiah turns away from Mac. "Stay relaxed. We've got this covered, too. And do not, under any circumstances, pull your weapon."

"If they try to detain me, I'm sure as hell not going to just let it happen."

"I'll come down and straighten things out if I have to. But I won't let you get shot over this. Understood?"

"Yeah, I copy."

Zeus nods down to the rifle next to his feet. Jeremiah shakes his head as the truck stops.

"Step out of truck, please," a guard tells Dom. "Leave your earpiece and bring your bill of lading."

Jeremiah rips out his Bluetooth. "They made him leave the earpiece. Dom's on his own."

Mac and Zeus curse under their breath. Jeremiah stays silent so he doesn't confirm their fear, but he shares it.

Several things must go right from here for the mission to stay on track. First, these guys will have to buy the fake BOL. That's not a high hurdle, though. Novak had Dom fill it out, so the handwriting will match and he can pass a quiz on the contents.

The next part is out of Dom's control. Out of everyone's control.

The trailer's double doors are programmed to stay locked unless the truck's inside one of INSTA's facilities. And even then, the perimeter is small. Jeremiah doesn't know exactly how the tech works, just that it does.

When Jeremiah brought this up, Novak said he'd taken care of it. Asked to explain, Novak told Jeremiah he didn't have a high enough clearance. Jeremiah's is Secret, which means Novak has Top Secret. Or—and Jeremiah finds this far more likely—Novak is lying about his TS clearance, he has no idea how to disable the door security, which may or may not be possible, and they're all screwed.

But even if Novak's not full of it and the doors open, the border guards will have to stay on the ground and not see past the wall of palleted boxes concealing the rig's real cargo. The BOL says Dom's hauling nonperishable food as part of a trade agreement between the Republic and Oklahoma. Texas provides free canned goods and other foodstuffs to impoverished Oklahomans and Indigenous Peoples in exchange for oil exports.

There was just enough room in the trailer to stack a few columns of boxes to the top after loading the real cargo. But if the guards step up and look hard enough, they'll see it's all for show.

Jeremiah's head is down when he hears the creak of metal hinges. All three nervous faces turn the direction of the trailer even though they can't see what's happening.

As they hold their breath, Zeus reaches for his rifle. Jeremiah doesn't stop him. When he turns to Mac, she does the same and nods. *Got your six.*

The doors shut less than a minute later. Jeremiah stands, ready to get out and try talking their way out. Mac and Zeus raise their weapons.

The next sound is Dom shutting the cab door. "We're good," he says into Jeremiah's ear before the MX-13 engine roars to life. "Apparently they're required to inspect all trucks with this trade cargo, but all they really do is make sure the truck's not empty. Hell, one's an Okie and thanked me for doing God's work."

Jeremiah pulls out the earpiece. "All good guys. Mac, I'll have Dom pull over at the Love's up ahead so you can take over."

She raises one corner of her mouth.

Damn right you will.

19
LORI

Somewhere over Arkansas
Federalist airspace

Lori's frustrated. She thought there was chemistry between them, but Boudreaux has been clinical and sitting at an appropriate distance while explaining their plan. And military jargon she's known since early childhood. In depth. Several times. He doesn't know about her memory, and she knows it's not his fault, but she can't take much more.

When he takes a drink, and pauses for a moment, she thinks he's finally done—until he clears his throat. "So, to summarize—"

"Will you shut up already." Lori sounds more frustrated than she should, but she can't help it. "I understand exactly what we're going to do from the second we land. I have every detail memorized. I promise."

Boudreaux shakes his head. "I know you think you do. But when we get into it, you'll be glad I went over all this a few times."

She considers a few things before responding. If she tells him, Boudreaux may think she's damaged, say she has a mental disorder like her mother. Or he might be like every other man and use her.

But Lori told herself she'd trust Boudreaux, and he's given her no reason to change her mind.

"I remember everything I've ever heard." She pauses, ready to absorb his laughter or confusion or refusal to believe. When she gets a single nod, Lori takes it as a gesture to continue. "Well, since I was about one. We never figured out what started it, but a doctor said it was probably trauma, either psychological or a TBI. Of course my parents never copped to anything like that."

Boudreaux leans forward, focuses on her face. "I've heard of hyperthymesia but never met anyone with it."

The fact he knows about the condition is surprising, though not quite relevant. "It's not that. At least, not fully. I don't remember the other senses with nearly as much detail. Only sound." She laughs. "I didn't even know it was weird until my dad started testing me all the time. When I was young, I was scared he'd take me to a doctor or shrink or something. Instead, he told me to keep it a secret. His secret weapon."

The soft look in Boudreaux's eyes tells Lori she made the right call in letting him in. "I'm sorry I treated you like you're stupid."

"Don't be. You couldn't have known that about me."

"There's a lot I don't know about you."

Lori contemplates whether to keep up the subtext or just ask.

She doesn't arrive at an answer before the pilot's voice crashes into her thoughts.

"Just wanted to let you know we're approaching Oklahoma airspace. All the paperwork's in order, so assuming there are no issues, we should arrive in about twenty."

You interrupted me for that? By the time he's done talking, Boudreaux is standing.

"Time for you to change back into your bloody clothes."

He hands Lori the clothing as she walks to the bathroom. She starts to close the door but doesn't. He can't see her from where he's standing, but maybe he'll take her up on the invitation.

"What about you, Mr. No-First-Name Boudreaux?" she asks while lowering the borrowed sweatpants. "You a mercenary? Assassin? Bearded James Bond?"

"None of the above. I'm just a guy who helps when he can."

Now naked and frustrated by that answer—among other things—Lori pokes her head out from behind the door. He's facing away from her. *Dammit.*

She returns to her clothing change but keeps talking. "I'm fixing to put my life in your hands, and that's all I get?"

"How about this? You answer a question, I answer a question. Tit for tat."

At least he still wants to flirt, even if he's not trying to sneak a peek.

"Sounds fair. I'll even let you start."

Dried blood has made her skinny jeans stiff and painful to pull up, and her socks are sweaty and gross. She'll be thankful for the distraction of answering his question.

"How'd you get those hand-to-hand combat skills?"

Or not. But she can be vague and still not give anything away.

"My dad was an Army officer and knew that nailing the boss's daughter would eventually become a game for his men, so he decided to make sure I could defend myself when things got out of hand. As you can imagine, I'm exceptionally easy to coach, so it wasn't hard to get the best in the world to instruct me."

Lori surprised herself by mostly telling the truth.

She slips into her boots and is about to take her turn when Boudreaux speaks.

"Wait, your father was Wyatt Young? The Colonel at Fort Bragg?"

Shit. He put that together fast. But she doesn't have to answer just yet. "I believe it's my turn to ask a question, soldier."

She hears an exasperated sigh. "I suppose it is."

Satisfied with her dodge, Lori pulls down her tight tank. She knows looking tattered and bloody is necessary to fool Fowler, but that knowledge doesn't dampen the gross factor as she thinks of a question that'll keep Boudreaux talking. She needs time to formulate an answer about her dad.

She needs him to tell her a story.

Lori steps out of the bathroom and points to the left side of her face. "How'd you get that scar?"

Not all veterans like talking about their tours, and by the way Boudreaux pauses and looks at the floor between them, Lori can tell he's one of them. "I can't talk about that. It's classified."

"First, that's a bullshit excuse at this point. Second, I know your next question." She steps closer. "If you want the answer, you better start talking."

For some, like her father, divulging classified information is like gossiping to a drinking buddy. For those with integrity, it's more like deciding whether cutting off a limb is worth saving the rest. While Lori knows he might clamp shut after his prolonged silence, she's pleased to know Boudreaux is, at his core, a good man.

When he looks up, she can tell he's also haunted.

"It happened during an exfil," he says. "I was part of a small Army group working at the United States embassy in Brazil."

"Ranger or Green Beret?"

"Special Forces."

Don't do it, Lori. Don't you do it. "So, a Ranger."

She did it.

Lori knows civilians call Army Special Forces the Green Berets, while the 75th Ranger Regiment gets shortened to Rangers. She also knows that frustrating Boudreaux can only hurt her chances of living through the day. But Lori can't help it. She loves poking fun at all types of Special Operations Forces guys. When she was growing up, Lori told herself it was okay because she was a military brat. Later, she said it was fine because she married a SEAL.

"Look," Boudreaux says, less annoyed than she anticipated. "I was in the seventy-fifth's Special Troops Battalion, then Special Forces, so I don't care what you call me. You want to hear this story or not?"

"Sorry," she says. "Old habit."

Boudreaux clears his throat. "Like I was saying, I was working in Brasília as part of a Military Liaison Element."

He pauses to let her search for the term. Yes, she's heard it. During one of his post-transport rants, Jeremiah said an MLE gathered intelligence on terrorists in foreign countries but didn't take them out, then called them pussies compared to his precious SEAL Team Six. In fairness, Jeremiah was drunk, which is why he proceeded to mansplain how they're technically a group and are a tier above the teams. Lori thought Jeremiah had forgotten who her father was. Then Jeremiah said she would've made a hell of a stand-in wife with him and his DEVGRU Black team—if her father would've been alive to let her join the Navy. Yes, Jeremiah really said her father would've had to *let her* join the branch of her choice.

Lori fast-forwards through the rest of his terrible, scattered monologue to more relevant info: MLE operators reported to United States Special Operations Command rather than local CIA officers or American ambassadors.

Lori nods for Boudreaux to continue.

"I hadn't been SF for that long but was told I had an aptitude for intel, so they sent me and another guy to help the CIA. The Agency officers didn't like us operating in their territory. Until they needed us, which happened when their Chief of Station was named by the Brazilian government in a public document."

"Oh shit."

"Exactly. He had to leave in a hurry. Since we were down there anyway, SOCOM had us escort him from the embassy. We were nearly done when it happened. I'll spare you the details, but I ended up one-on-one and the enemy was good with a knife. I was better."

"So you got the CIA guy out?"

Boudreaux grins. "I believe it's my turn to ask a question."

As the laugh escapes, Lori realizes it's too loud and too giddy for the situation. Though he could make fun—or a move—Boudreaux asks the question.

"So. Your father?"

While he was telling the extraction story, Lori failed to come up with an answer that wouldn't reveal at least part of her damage. So, she sticks with simplicity and hopes he doesn't ask follow-up questions.

"Yes."

That one word says many, many more. It says she's the daughter of the infamous Col. Wyatt Young, the subject of rumors for decades after his administrative discharge from the Army. Those uninvolved in the proceedings were told he resigned, but he didn't leave voluntarily, and his discharge was under other than honorable conditions.

Most of the rumors had those details right. But an OTH can be handed down for many reasons. A few savvy soldiers may have looked at the timing and connected the colonel's discharge with civilian press clippings, but the newspapers didn't dig deep and only got half the surface facts right. After the years and her father had passed, Lori assumed those in the know kept their mouths shut and the documents watertight.

Amarillo Slim's poker face wasn't as good as Boudreaux's is now, so Lori can't judge exactly how much of the story he knows. Even the bare bones are too much for her comfort, though.

The silence and tension are about to make her scream when the pilot gets back on the intercom.

"We're about to start descending into Cushing Municipal. We'll miss the blizzard blowing in from the southwest, but the wind is picking up so you'll want to sit down and buckle up."

Boudreaux moves toward her and smiles. "You heard the man." He sits on what'd been Lori's seat and leaves just enough room for her. "Looks like you have time for one more."

As she sits, Lori considers what to ask. The game's flirty nature is gone, and the thought of landing in Oklahoma—where if she's outed as part Native American could be problematic—is making her uneasy, so she decides it's time to skip the foreplay get information that'll be useful later.

"How do you know Fowler?"

Boudreaux laughs. "Man, that really sucks."

"I don't follow."

He shakes his head. "You just wasted your last question."

20
ERIC

Cushing Municipal Airport, Northeast Province
Republic of Oklahoma

Eric blows into his hand before replacing his glove. Though the hangar breaks the wind, cold is creeping through the black leather. He should've waited longer at his office, but the key to being on time is allowing for plans to go awry.

The three-mile drive to the airport before seven in the morning went quickly, and with the nearly empty roads he could appreciate the rows—and rows, and rows—of massive oil tanks that store about 13 percent of the oil pumped and transported by the nations of the former United States.

Eric still has at least ten more minutes for them to land, but he was anxious to get confirmation of Lori's safety and MANIFEST's viability.

It'll also be nice to have Boudreaux here for this. Eric wanted him onboard from the beginning, but Gates said the op required a scalpel, not a Ka-Bar. Boudreaux carries a different knife, but Eric understood the metaphor and, after a bit of convincing, agreed. And when Eric said he'd enlisted Boudreaux in locating and delivering Lori, Gates made it clear he was not to read Boudreaux in.

Eric was not big on disobeying orders. But he also knew Gates chose him for his instinct. Gates once called Eric the best targeting officer he'd ever seen, which meant there was no better judge of character. When MANIFEST was complete, Gates would thank Eric for his operational agility.

Having Boudreaux shave wouldn't hurt. Eric smiles. He's had the beard since they met, though back then it was shorter and might've seen the bristle-end of a brush once or twice.

Eric had just secured his first foreign posting as a targeting officer. He was probably too inexperienced, but Eric used the same charm and expertise in the office that he so deftly employed on assets. And he was qualified for the job, having traveled extensively through Latin America after getting his undergrad degree. He spoke fluent Portuguese—in addition to Spanish—and knew the customs. He even remembered Brasília well enough to avoid looking lost when he touched down.

His COS, however, wasn't happy having such a green officer, and Seamus Garrett let Eric know every chance he got.

After six months, Eric was wondering if he'd made a mistake. The locale wasn't exotic to him and, while targeting was fun, he was getting nauseated every time he thought about dealing with Garrett.

Then his boss found another outlet for his anger.

The military.

More specifically, the pair of Special Forces soldiers who were sent, according to Garrett, to muck around in their backyard. Worse, Garrett couldn't boss them around despite the fact they were there to gather intelligence. MLE service members also didn't worry about operating covertly.

But they're spies, all right, Garrett would say. The DOD sends these shitheels here to report on our operation, not al-Qaeda or Hezbollah. Liaisons my ass.

Eric was never convinced SOCOM cared much about what he and Garrett were doing, but it was nice to have someone else drawing his ire.

It was another few weeks before Eric met Boudreaux. He'd seen photos of the SF guys and studied their files—Boudreaux wasn't a bad-looking guy underneath his face weasel—but they didn't shake hands until the embassy Christmas party.

They had a lot in common. Both from small towns, both fans of single-malt, both far too young and wild for marriage or families. They got friendly over the next month, though to call them friends would've been an overstatement.

Then the Brazilian government screwed Garrett.

They said it was unintentional, that they were following their country's laws. While the Brazilian freedom of information laws required names and positions for all high-level meetings, the CIA operated there for decades without using the name of the Agency's COS in a publicly available agenda. The timing was also suspicious, given the meeting between Garrett and his Brazilian counterpart was essentially a going-away party. Garrett's posting was nearly over, so outing him in a public way gave enemies of the CIA one last chance at a ceremonial victory over America's all-powerful intelligence community.

The Agency and SOCOM put aside their pissing contest and had the pair of SF men escort Eric and Garrett to a plane bound for the states. Boudreaux drove Eric in the lead SUV and Garrett rode with another soldier in the follow.

The initial route took them along the north shore of Lago Paranoá. Eric and Boudreaux were cutting up when traffic slowed and scanner traffic indicated a crash ahead, just after the Ponte das Garças—the oldest of the three bridges across the lake in Brasília's federal district.

Boudreaux radioed the other vehicle to change the route. They were going to cross the bridge, but the soldiers were on high alert. The next five minutes were tense, but all four made it to the airport, through security, and onto the apron.

Then came the second piece of evidence that all but proves the memo leak was no accident.

A man later identified as al-Qaeda flanked the four of them, firing an AK. Boudreaux and his buddy returned fire, forcing the terrorist to scramble behind a larger plane's landing gear. Garrett had made it onto the plane bound for D.C. and the other soldier was hit in the gut.

Eric picked up the Beret's M4, and Boudreaux signaled for him to provide cover while he made a wide approach to flank the shooter. When he was in position, Eric ran toward the terrorist, drawing his attention and fire as Boudreaux rushed him from the side.

His view was obstructed, but when Eric got to the men, Boudreaux's face was flayed open. The other guy's throat was slit with both men's knives sticking out of his stomach. That he opted for a gun rather than a suicide vest felt like divine intervention.

Afterward, Eric was awarded a Hostile Action Service Medal and promoted. Boudreaux was similarly cited and ended his service as a member of the Army's 1st Special Forces Operational Detachment-Delta, where he occasionally crossed paths with and outperformed Eric's officers on covert ops.

Boudreaux would've made a hell of an asset, and Eric tried to recruit him. But his friend—like many in his position—had a profound distrust for the Agency, so Boudreaux declined the offers, instead finding a way to put his intelligence skills to work within the Army.

* * *

ERIC IS WAITING at the bottom of the jet's fold-out staircase and greets Boudreaux first. Lori's bound to be mad as a bull in the chute, so he's putting that off as long as he can.

"Didn't think that thing could get any gnarlier," Eric says, referring to Boudreaux's comically out-of-control beard.

"And I didn't think you could get any uglier."

Decades go by and the greeting doesn't change. Boudreaux, on the other hand, has.

"You look like the old Boudreaux," Eric says, "the one with twenty-five-inch biceps and a hilarious name."

Boudreaux's smile is big enough to see despite the beard. "Being freelance has its advantages. More lifting, less goddamn running."

Delta always did prioritize agility, speed, and blending in over looking like a pro wrestler—Boudreaux's natural default when left to his own training regimen. He reaches the bottom of the steps and Eric hugs him.

Then looks up at Lori, arms crossed over a bloody shirt, one leg of her jeans torn, her scowl a jagged scar stretching across her face. Eric slides off his Carhartt and ascends the stairs.

Lori doesn't accept it immediately.

"Is your name even Eric Fowler?" she asks through clenched teeth. "Or is that a lie, too?"

When Boudreaux brings it up, Eric will blame his wet eyes on the freezing wind. "Ninety percent of what you know about me is true, I swear."

Lori rolls her eyes and yanks away his coat. "Whatever."

He's about to start what will surely be a string of apologies when the pilot pokes his head into the doorway.

"Hey, we have another jet landing. Better get a move on if you don't want anyone knowing about this lovely reunion."

As he thanks the pilot, Lori brushes past Eric, muttering something about him being a lying sack of shit. He checks his watch before descending into the dark.

Eric has until 0730 to get her on board.

He may need every second.

21
JEREMIAH

I-40, 23 miles west of El Reno, Capital Province
Republic of Oklahoma

Snow? No, it's sleet getting swept away from the windshield as Mac speeds down the dark highway listening to some new-wave pop tune. She's not much younger than Jeremiah, but sometimes her taste in music makes him feel ancient.

She reaches for the dash, but her hand doesn't land on the radio. Her fingers are nearly to the communications controls when Jeremiah grabs them.

"We can't use the comms."

"I'm just checking the roads. If they're bad, I'll need to find another way there."

Mac keeps her arm extended, so Jeremiah keeps his hand wrapped around her fingers. "Novak said he took out the LoJack, but we can't turn on the comms. They don't just alert the plant. Every INSTA post from California to Pennsylvania would know they have an empty quiver."

Mac's hand shivers at the mention of the INSTA communications parlance for a stolen or lost nuclear weapon—a term that's been around since the fifties but never used by the USA or any of its new offspring. "Well, we still need road conditions."

Travelling along I-40 is almost second nature for the team, but Mac's never done it without relying on INSTA's technology. She's a Florida transplant by way of Illinois who hasn't visited either parent since Daniels hired her.

Jeremiah, on the other hand, has been driving on this stretch of Route 66 since before he was of legal age. He switches the radio from satellite to FM and tunes it to 89.1, the local public radio station out of Clinton.

Neither of them cares for jazz, so Jeremiah turns the volume down while they wait for the next weather update.

"Thanks," she says. "Sometimes I forget you grew up around here."

"Half the time, anyway."

"How is your old man?" she asks.

"Hanging in there. Worse since Mom passed, though. Dad never stopped loving her. They just couldn't stand living together."

The saxophone gives way to a voice, and Jeremiah's thankful for the distraction as Mac turns it up.

The Oklahoma Bureau of Investigation still hasn't released the number of victims in last night's mass shooting in downtown Oklahoma City. The OBI also hasn't released the identity of the shooter or a possible motive for the massacre. We have received reports of similar events in The Republic's Coastal Province and across The South, and we're trying to confirm rumors of other cities on the continent, though Canada and Mexico have said they are not aware of any New Year's Eve attacks.

The other major event this morning is a massive blizzard moving into central Oklahoma at more than twenty miles-per-hour from the southwest. The Oklahoma Department of Transportation is monitoring the situation and says it expects to shut down Intracontinental Highway 40 within the hour. The storm is causing whiteout conditions along I-44 southwest of Oklahoma City and has already dumped more than twenty inches in its wake.

In entertainment news …

Jeremiah turns the radio down and looks at Mac.

"Your call," she says. "We're doing this for your ex. And you know the roads."

The sleet has intensified in just a few minutes. If the whiteout conditions don't make the roads impassable, the ice and snow will. He can't see the lights yet, but he knows there's a small rest area a few miles ahead. Yesterday's Jeremiah would've told Mac to pull over there and wait it out.

But Yesterday's Jeremiah wouldn't be on the road. That guy would've left a day earlier or two days later.

And Today's Jeremiah has no idea what will happen to Lori if he doesn't get to her, or what will happen to his payload if he's stranded in two feet of snow with no escort.

Cushing is to the northeast. If they speed up and take smaller highways, they can skirt the storm.

"Step on it."

Mac obliges with a smile. "What's the plan?"

"When we get close to El Reno, take the business loop, then turn north on Oklahoma Highway 81."

***

TURNING NORTH and pushing the truck to its limits was working. The trailer caught the crosswind occasionally, but Mac seems fine as they approach an oasis of illuminated parking lots and red neon lights.

"It could be Armageddon outside and there'd be suckers in there playing penny slots," Jeremiah says. "And I'm not just saying that because of the old man."

Jeremiah's father chose a casino—and a few of its cocktail waitresses—over his mother, so she moved back to the Texas Panhandle with her folks when he was in eighth grade. He stayed in Tulsa.

He was a good dad, though, and once-a-month visits weren't enough. Jeremiah technically stole his mom's rusted-out Bronco at fourteen. His backside hurt for a week, but his parents went fifty-fifty after that.

"I never liked gambling," Mac says. "If it weren't for bad luck, I wouldn't—"

A gust turns the truck into a sail. Mac jerks the steering wheel to correct, sending the boys crashing to the edge and floor overhead.

"Sure you don't want me back down there?" Dom yells, clearly unhappy to be shoehorned up there with Zeus. "I mean, I can drive this bad if it's what you want."

"Screw you," Mac says under her breath.

Jeremiah snorts. "Everyone okay up there?"

After they answer in the affirmative, Jeremiah leans over. "Seriously Shaye, you good over there?"

Mac flips him off.

Jeremiah tries not to use her first name. He doesn't use anyone else's, so it's patronizing to single her out, as her gesture reminds him.

But that's not the only reason.

Mac was stood up at a bar about a year ago. The appropriate response was to drink until she didn't care. Knowing he was divorced and dry, Jeremiah was the logical person to call for a sober ride home. He obliged, and even walked her to the apartment door and said *goodnight, Shaye*. That's where she kissed him. Sloppy. Hungry. Mac told him not to call her Shaye unless he wanted to come inside.

He left.

The next day, Mac was hungover but thankful for the ride. No mention of the kiss. The next time he used her first name, he got the usual annoyance. No residual feelings from that night. She'd been blackout drunk. Or wanted him to think so.

Now, needing to break the cab's silence just in case he was wrong, Jeremiah turns to the subject he and Mac can discuss for hours—the weather.

"Winter storms like this used to happen once a decade around here. Now it's twice a winter."

"No joke," she says. "Remember when we had to go to Oak Ridge via Birmingham?"

They laugh because there's nothing else to do. The Earth is two generations away from an unlivable climate, and there's nothing they can do.

"I'll tell you what, though, these storms beat the hell out of the constant tornadoes when I was a kid. This used to be Tornado Alley."

"I'm sure the South would give the twisters back. And the hurricanes."

They fly by the casino, and Jeremiah's glad any chance for tension has passed. He's about to launch into a rant about INSTA needing to up their hazard pay during winter when Mac explodes into a fit of cursing and slamming the steering wheel.

Jeremiah looks past Mac to her side mirror. Blue and red lights are speeding alongside the truck. Mac slows and the car pulls in front of them. It's a Canadian County Sheriff cruiser, driven by a deputy who was looking for drunks leaving the casino.

"Stay calm, everyone. We'll just take the ticket and deal with it later."

Mac mutters something under her breath as her window lowers.

"What?" Jeremiah asks.

"You really think Novak and Robb had time to alter information in the TTD? They had someone at the Texola crossing to grease us through, but there's no way our licenses will get through this guy."

Shit. She's right. The Transcontinental Traffic Database is as secure as any in the Allied Nations, and though the team's TT licenses look right, the barcode probably won't have the right information—if they're not blank.

Jeremiah doesn't have much time to formulate a plan. The deputy, tall and young, is already halfway to Mac.

He needlessly sweeps the beam of his flashlight across the windshield and settles on Mac, holds the position until she blocks it with her hand. The guy's either sexist or a bully. Probably both. If he flirts with her, maybe she can work him. If not, Jeremiah will ask if they can talk, man-to-man.

The flashlight stays trained on Mac until he's under her door. "TTL and BOL." His voice is even, but he snatches the items out of Mac's hand. "I clocked you at eighty-eight. Surprised she can handle that much speed."

Mac looks ready to lay into him, but Jeremiah leans forward and puts a hand on her knee. *I got this.*

"It's a modified engine," he says. "Built just for us."

It's the truth. It also gets the deputy's mind off Mac.

"And who's us?"

"It's a bit of an explanation, sir. Mind if I come down and explain it, one-on-one"—he tips his head toward Mac—"It'll be quicker that way."

The kid mulls it over by flashing his light over the documents. "All right," he says, not looking up. "I'm going to hang onto these while we talk."

Jeremiah squeezes Mac's knee before opening his door. *Thanks.*

As he crosses in front of the truck, Jeremiah tips his head again, away from the cab, toward his car. The deputy translates correctly, assuming Jeremiah wants to have this conversation out of a woman's earshot. They meet between the vehicles, just at the edge of the glow of headlights.

"Thank you, sir," Jeremiah says before blowing into his hands. "I'm training her and don't want her to get any more hysterical than she already is."

"What kind of training means driving ninety in the middle of the night?"

Jeremiah leans in, close enough the vapor from his breath mixes with his. "We're part of a team of intracontinental agents who transport hazardous material across the Divided States."

This time, Jeremiah's hoping the truth will impress a man who wants to feel important.

The deputy doesn't say anything, but glances back at the rig.

"There's nothing in it now, so no need to worry, deputy ..."

"Jones." He turns back with a neutral expression Jeremiah can't read. "So then what are you doing out here?"

Jeremiah turns toward the cab and exhales through his nose, dual streams drifting toward Mac. "She's related to one of my bosses and he said I needed to hire her to do something. She sure as hell can't provide any security, but I think I can get her to at least drive without killing us."

When Jones doesn't smile, Jeremiah questions his initial read, which is rarely wrong.

"Let's say I believe you. I still don't see why you'd have her drive down my highway that fast."

As if he divined it, the smallest pieces of sleet begin hitting Jeremiah and Jones in the face. "I'm using this storm to train her in outrunning and driving through bad weather."

Jones purses his lips, then shakes his head.

Dammit.

"People tell crazy stories to get out of speeding tickets, but that's the dumbest one I've heard yet."

Jeremiah doesn't fluster easily, but the cloud between them gets thicker as his mind races. He needs Jones to understand the situation. The weather's caught up with them. Lori's been taken hostage. There's a nuclear bomb twenty feet away from them and only four people protecting it.

He takes a step toward Jones.

Jones yells for Jeremiah to step back as he reaches for his hip. When Jeremiah doesn't comply immediately, he takes a step back and draws.

His view of the truck is blocked, but Jeremiah has faith.

"Now'd be a great time, Mac."

Jones pivots toward the cab, allowing Jeremiah to see his number two leaning out of her window, the pistol from the dash's hidden compartment now fixed on her target.

"Drop it, asshole."

Jeremiah allows the stalemate to go on for nearly thirty seconds before speaking again.

"Okay Zeus, time to wrap this up."

The best marksman Jeremiah's ever worked with steps out from behind the truck and takes three strides toward Jones, his automatic rifle ready.

Jones's pistol bounces between the two, with occasional glances to a smiling Jeremiah.

"I wouldn't," Jeremiah says. "There's another one of us out here. And you have no idea where he is or what he's packing."

There's no way to know if Dom's out of the truck and hiding somewhere, but the bluff works. Jones lowers his pistol. Zeus rushes him with instructions to get on his knees and interlock his fingers behind his head.

"What are we going to do with him?" Zeus asks.

Jeremiah hadn't thought that far ahead. They can't kill Jones, though it's the cleanest option. Kidnap him? No.

"Mac, go kill his radio."

Though her look says she's unsatisfied with the plan, Mac trots to the car.

"You out there, Dom?"

"Back here." His hulking figure steps out from behind the ass-end of the trailer, rifle at his shoulder.

"Go flatten two of his tires."

Jeremiah looks down at Jones through the thickening sleet. "Give me your phone."

The Canadian County deputy's scowl is defiant, but after a ten-second staring contest, Zeus presses his rifle's muzzle into the base of his skull.

Jones digs out the cell and hands it to Jeremiah.

"Now, when you're found, you're going to say you let us off with a warning. Then, just as we pulled away, you were ambushed by a group of rednecks from the casino and couldn't make out the license plate through this weather. Sound fair?"

He nods.

"Load up," he says before offering a hand to Jones. "You, too."

Anger gives way to confusion as he stands.

"Is what you said true?"

"All but two things. She's more of a man than you or me"—Jeremiah points to the trailer—"and that's not empty."

Jeremiah wonders if he should've told him. But he didn't say what was in the trailer. And it was worth it to see the worry on Jones's face.

Back in the cab, Mac's face is harder to read.

"You really saved my ass out there."

Nothing.

"I know you disagree with what I did, but that guy was a dick. The only way I was going to—"

He stops when she grins. *You're welcome.*

Present crisis averted, Jeremiah allows himself one of Mac's awful songs to relax.

Then it's back to figuring out how to save Lori without giving her kidnappers a nuke.

22
LORI

FAST offices, Cushing, Northeast Province
Republic of Oklahoma

Lori doesn't need to use the restroom. She needs to get away from Fowler's East Texas whining.

He's sorry. The guiltiest man in history. Lori let him apologize five times for lying about the nature of their conversations, nine for having to tell her about his *operation* like this, and thirteen—a damn baker's dozen—for tracking her on vacation. When he started talking again, Lori stood and walked out of the office and down the hall to the small but clean bathroom that always smells of the sink's small soaps.

Five minutes is pushing it, though, so she stands and reaches for the knob.

Then, footsteps. Boots. Cowgirl boots because they're connected to a woman's voice, whispering but angry. The steps move closer, then drift away, pacing the hall outside Eric's office.

Lori puts her ear to the door. The hushed tone and door distort the voice enough to avoid a match. That's twice Lori's brain has betrayed her—and on the one day she might need it most.

"I can't believe you would think that," Puss 'n Boots says, trailing away from the bathroom. "How many years have I been here for you?"

There's noting inherently sinister about the words. The delivery doesn't give much away, either. For all Lori knows, Fowler hired a new secretary, had her come in because of the shootings, causing an argument with her boyfriend.

Puss 'n Boots starts back toward the door. "So, we're good?"

She stops pacing. "Right. See you then."

The steps quicken and she's nearly outside the bathroom. Lori reaches over and flushes the toilet just as the door opens.

Rita Clarke yelps and jumps back. "You scared the crap out of me," she says in a phony drawl, trying to add back in what California's homogenization took away. "I didn't know you were here."

You've got to be kidding. On top of everything else, Lori's going to have to deal with the bottle blonde, too?

Clarke keeps the books, which means she's constantly on Lori for expense reports and mileage—when she's not questioning her timesheets. They only interact in person at company-wide functions or if she interrupts Lori's monthly meeting with Fowler. Clarke's more concept than woman, an email address that somehow manages to sound passive-aggressive every time they trade messages.

"I just got in from New Orleans."

Hearing the location seems to trigger something, and Clarke finally notices Lori's clothes. "Oh my Lord, were you? I mean, is that ..."

"Blood. Yeah. I took one in the leg, but it's not bad."

Clarke gasps. Literally, like she's on stage auditioning for an off-off-off-Broadway show. "I think I have something in my office you can wear. Pants may be a little tight in the thighs, though."

Tossing aside the dig at her legs—which are all muscle and proved useful in New Orleans—Lori detects something else. After the yelp, Clarke's reactions were forced and her speech unnatural.

She's being disingenuous. But about what?

Lori follows Clarke to her office. It's the most boring room she's ever seen, decorated on one wall by a map with pins in each salesperson's home city and a mosaic of color-coded spreadsheets on another. The rest are bare, save for one landscape oil painting that looks like it came with the place.

Clarke crosses the hardwood to her psychopathically neat wooden desk and reaches into the side drawer. *What woman keeps nice clothes in her desk?*

She pulls out neatly folded dark jeans and a black silk blouse. "I keep these in case a big-wig client comes in. It's saved me a time or two on casual Friday."

Lori buys that and accepts the clothing. "Do you mind if I change in here?"

"Oh, sure, go ahead. I've still got to use the bathroom and let Eric know I'm here."

As she leaves, Lori notices one other detail. It's well before dawn and she lives in a different country, but Clarke never asked Lori why the hell she's here.

Lori waits fifteen seconds after the door closes, then starts looking around the office. Moore and Boudreaux want her to play double-agent, conveniently ignoring the fact she was never an agent in the first place. Nevertheless, Lori's come to trust Boudreaux, and Eric's given her no reason to believe anything he's ever said.

And then there's Clarke's behavior, strange even for a woman who admitted to a string of out-of-town rendezvous with other men, then lobbied to stay and help run the business rather than letting Fowler buy her out.

Lori's snooping starts with the cartoonishly large map. Cartography's importance exploded after the first meeting between Texas Governor Levi Cole and U.S President *Alex* Ramirez, who must've dropped the vowels at the end of her name to scoop up votes from uninformed misogynists. Though most GPS navigation apps were updated quickly and seamlessly, physical maps had become the most popular item sold in any office supply store. Lori had small ones at home and in her truck, but she rarely looked at them. For Texas citizens with transcontinental licenses, getting into Oklahoma was simple, and this disaster of a vacation was her first travel outside of either of the republics.

But, as promised, the travel was relatively painless.

At first, Lori didn't pay much attention to the Texit talk. Political rancor, outsized state pride, and a history of national independence was nothing new. Then Cole was accused of corruption and murder by the *New York media*—Texan for liberal East Coast elitists—and most of the state dug in around its beloved governor.

The scandal became all anyone could talk about, including Lori. The secessionists, once considered part of the tin foil hat crowd, were taken seriously when asking for proof of the accusations. The national media, led by cable news anchor Regina Watkins, obliged.

Half the country believed Watkins, including the United States Department of Justice and President Ramirez, a native Texan. The President's apparent disloyalty made an already toxic situation worse.

When a federal grand jury didn't indict Cole, his sympathizers exploded in joyous rage. Texas retailers began selling flags with TRAITOR written above Ramirez's mugshot and full first name, the last two letters painted in menstruation red.

A week later, thousands of men and women in Western garb marched in Washington calling themselves *White Hats* for their western headwear ranging from convenience-store straw to custom-shaped Stetsons. They protested. Then after an inflammatory social media post from Governor Cole, they rioted. Only ten minutes passed before a dozen White Hats were gunned down by Secret Service after sprinting across the North Lawn, a mass casualty event carried live by all the networks and cable news channels. The Amarillo newspaper headline read 12 EXECUTED BY SS ASSASSINS above photos of sinister-looking agents behind scopes and muzzles.

Television stations refused to re-air the massacre. Websites declined self-censorship, however, and soon the footage was on every social media feed worldwide. A massive public outcry led to the Big Three pulling video clips, but that traffic just went to sites who quickly branded themselves as the First Amendment alternatives.

Hate boiled over on both sides. Everyone felt aggrieved. Nobody was in the mood for talking or healing or bipartisanship.

Governor Cole, claiming the White Hats acted on his behalf, declared their execution at the hands of the United States an act of war. Like the rest of the world, Lori was glued to the television when Cole and select legislators gathered on a dais during a live news conference at the old statehouse in Austin. Cole told residents they were drafting secession documents. They said a template existed for post-separation relations—the European Union. Texas could still use the dollar. Traveling from The Republic of Texas to the United States of America would be as easy as EU residents crossing into member nations. Texas already had a state legislature and executive power structure. Hell, its capitol building was taller than the one in Washington.

Texas leaders even had a plan for the military. The state's National Guard becomes its military, and all personnel stationed in Texas can choose to join or move, with a one-year period to get your affairs in order. Possession of material and assets within its borders falls under the nine-tenths rule.

Why did Ramirez take any of it seriously? Texas owned the mineral rights to nearly half of America's unrefined oil and natural gas. It was also home to the largest companies that extract it, transport it, and refine it.

Then there's the infrastructure. Much of what Lori sells is manufactured in Houston, so even if America wanted to stop the flow in and out of Texas, they may run out of valves, actuators, and myriad other components needed to physically divert the hydrocarbons. The proposed Republic of Texas would also annex Oklahoma, adding to its stranglehold on the world's most popular fuel.

Cole used this leverage and secured a secession discussion with Ramirez. The historic summit wasn't public, but the outcome didn't matter. Its very existence was the first domino.

California requested a secession meeting the next day, a liberal response. Having the world's fifth-largest economy was enough to secure the meeting. Then Oklahoma rejected Texas's terms and secured a trilateral summit with Ramirez and Cole. That opened the door for California to come back with a plan to add Nevada, Oregon, and Washington to its new nation.

In six months, the Divided States had agreed in principle to the new map—except for the Free State of Southwestern Colorado and the doomed Cimarron Territory.

The latter was an irritating strip of Oklahoma once called No Man's Land—stolen soil Cole wanted to reacquire.

After being taken from American Indians, the Oklahoma Panhandle—a patch of prairie 166 miles long and 34 miles wide—belonged to New Spain, then Mexico, then the original Republic of Texas.

As a state, Texas amputated its tip to stay southern enough for slavery, but the strip went unassigned. Left to its own devices, the area operated independently as the Cimarron Territory until 1890, when America pinned it to the ass-end of Oklahoma.

Nearly 150 years later, during the free-for-all that was the Second Secessions, counties in the panhandle added a ballot proposition re-establishing the Cimarron Territory.

The measure passed in a landslide, but wasn't taken seriously by Texas, Oklahoma, or the United States. President Grover Cleveland never formalized the Cimarron Territory, so how could residents now *re-establish* it as a sovereign nation?

But other negotiations allowed Mexico to annex the El Paso peninsula, and Cimarron Territory Rebels were outraged that their lawful vote had been disregarded.

The Republic attributed El Paso's exit to cultural differences and geopolitics, which was much more reasonable than the weird wishes of less than thirty thousand Okies. Incensed, the Rebels took up arms and stood guard at Cimarron Territory's southern border.

Oklahoma City tried to step in, but Beaver County residents worked twenty-four-seven and erected 34 miles of fencing along the eastern border. It was mostly symbolic, but tensions soared.

That was when The Republic decided it was done and sent a military occupation to the southern border fit for Grenada. Rebels and Oklahoma City saw no need for physical fighting over No Man's Land. Instead, they used the USA's distain for Texas and jointly negotiated minimal financial and defense support from The Republic in exchange for annexation of panhandle counties.

Amarillo media reported the events with the headline REPUBLIC REGAINS LAND LOST IN 1820 and Oklahoma media reported OKC NEGOTIATES AID, MILITARY SUPPORT FROM TEXAS with neither mentioning the tanks and Humvees.

Then came the Free State of Southwestern Colorado.

That coalition of rural Colorado counties, galvanized by a local marijuana farmer and dispensateur, added a measure to their secession ballots similar to Oklahoma's. And like that effort, Colorado

Territory didn't recognize the creation of the Free State of Southwestern Colorado.

The difference became clear when Southwestern Colorado began what became the bloodiest siege of the Second Secessions, one of many that some call the Second Civil War.

When word made it three hundred miles east, Cimarron Rebels re-erected their fences. When the Republican Guard came rolling back in, emboldened Rebels emptied their AR mags, only to quickly realize that—unlike the mountainous region of Southwestern Colorado—there is no high ground on the High Plains of Oklahoma and Texas. Without such fortification, it only took a few rounds of tank fire for the Rebels to again accept their status as Texans.

The action was far less one-sided in the San Juan foothills, where a coalition of preppers and sympathetic defectors from several Western Territories brought in military armaments. The Colorado Guard could've won, but Denver decided the death toll wasn't worth control of such a small, politically insignificant area. The Colorado Territory capital told its Guard to stand down, calling an end to the battle and allowing for the rest of the Allied Nations to formally recognize the Free State of Southwestern Colorado.

The tiny nation-state now looks like a mistake on Clarke's map, but its only alterations are large, bulbous push-pins securing the name of Fowler's other salespeople. Or should she call them his *officers*?

Nothing looks out of place until she sees a pin in Hawaii. She's never heard Eric talk about doing business there. The pin is next to Pearl Harbor and secures a slip of paper with the name *Phoebe*. It's probably nothing. A new hire she isn't aware of.

But in case she's wrong, Lori wants to remember it.

"The map on Clarke's wall has a pin in Pearl Harbor indicating a FAST employee named Phoebe lives there."

Lori's voice gets recorded, same as everything else. She used to sound like a crazy person at crime scenes, muttering to herself. Same for APD's homicide bullpen, reading case files aloud.

She hustles to the desk and starts opening drawers. They're nearly bare. Nothing extra. In the side drawer that didn't hold the spare clothing are folders, all of which are neatly filed, labeled in smooth handwriting, and full of documents that appear to be on the up-and-up. There may be secrets in them, but it only takes so long to change into clothes.

The rest of the drawers are similarly free of odd or superfluous items. Lori pulls the painting from the wall and finds no safe behind it or documents fastened to the underside. Clarke must not be a part of Eric's covert operation, just a business partner.

Satisfied with her effort, Lori peels off her clothes once again. She'll have to wear the socks and bloody boots again, but she'll enjoy the hell out of fresh pants and a nice top. Lori sits in Clarke's ergonomic chair and pulls off the footwear. She stands to take off the rest, then takes a moment to stretch, exhausted. Her shirt and pants are piled on the floor, and she'll leave them there. Let Clarke deal with it.

She lifts the jeans off the desk and puts in one leg. Clarke was right. Pulling them over her thighs and ass isn't easy, but she'll live. Lori sits to slip on her socks and boots but feels something press into her ass, so she lifts her right cheek and reaches into the back pocket to pull out the object, a wad of crumpled paper.

It's a receipt. She smooths it out on the desk. The charge is for coffee from a shop on the Frontier, and not a city marked on Clarke's map. She must've used her Thanksgiving vacation to visit a boyfriend. A sugar daddy, based on the location and price of the drinks.

Apparently the outfit was for more than unannounced visits from whales.

She starts to crumple up the receipt for depositing into Clarke's deskside garbage can.

Then she hesitates.

Just in case.

"I found a crumpled receipt in the back right pocket of a pair of Clarke's pants. It's from Northtable Café. The address is thirty-seven twenty-five Village Lane, Teton Village, Wyoming, eight three zero two five. The date is November twenty seventh, just over a month ago. The charge was for two cups of coffee, one pumpkin spice, one black with half-and-half, two pumps of vanilla and C-N-M-N, which if I'm reading it right is cinnamon."

Pumpkin spice doesn't tell her much, other than Clarke might be a little more basic than Lori thought.

The other order is much more specific.

23
ERIC

Eric's thankful Lori made up an excuse to leave. She wasn't reacting well to his apologies, and he wasn't sure how to move the discussion along.

Plus it gave him time to catch up with Boudreaux, who's sitting on Eric's couch and in the middle of a story when the door to Eric's office opens behind him.

"I was beginning to wonder if you'd fallen in," he says without turning around.

When Lori doesn't respond, he turns around to find that it's not Lori. He checks his watch.

"A little early to start calling clients, isn't it?"

Rita doesn't respond. Her eyes are wide and looking past him at Boudreaux, who stands.

"Oh, right." Eric stands, too, remembering how much pride Boudreaux takes in his manners. "Rita, meet Boudreaux."

Her eyes widen further. "*The* Boudreaux. The one you met in Brazil?"

"Sounds like me." He steps toward her, right hand extended. "It's a pleasure to meet you, ma'am."

Boudreaux's hand hangs for an awkward moment before she lifts hers. "Please, call me Rita. I'm Eric's business partner."

Eric can't tell if Rita's smitten with Boudreaux, reacting to putting a face to the stories—and she's only heard the mild ones—or just too tired to function properly.

"Did you get any sleep?" he asks.

Rita takes her eyes off Boudreaux for the first time since walking in. "Not really. Kind of hard given the circumstances, so I thought I'd start compiling the list of our most important clients so I can start rolling calls at eight."

"Smart."

"Sometimes. By the way, I ran into Lori and gave her some clothes to wear. Poor thing looked awful." She turns to Boudreaux. "Did you two fly in together?"

Boudreaux nods. Before he can explain, Lori's in the doorway. "Ears burning?" he says. "You clean up nice."

He's not kidding. Eric's never seen her in denim that tight, which would be inappropriate to wear for business—even one where looking good is her ticket into the offices of blue-collar buyers. He's seen the shirt, but it fits differently on Lori, hangs more loosely. She's also washed her face and arms and smoothed out her hair.

Lori walks past him toward Rita and Boudreaux. Eric smells soap. He owns this floor of the building and knows there's only one restroom, but for a second Eric wonders if she found a secret shower.

Boudreaux's captivated.

Rita's less impressed.

"My shirt looks good on you," she says, setting up an insult. "A little loose in the chest, though."

They've never been friendly, but Rita usually keeps her claws retracted until Lori leaves. Eric's the reason she dislikes Lori more than any of the other salesmen. He lets Rita believe a romance is brewing with Lori. Necessary to keep her from knowing too much about MANIFEST, but unfair—perhaps cruel—to the woman who remains in love with Eric.

But he also knows Rita can love him and want to sleep with other men. Men like Boudreaux, whose presence is the new variable tonight.

"I think you look just fine," Boudreaux tells Lori. "Especially given how I found you."

"And how was that?" Rita asks.

"Like a mouse drowning in her own blood."

A succinct and colorful way to put it. Lori coldly described the massacre and being kidnapped by Moore's men after leaving the hospital. Boudreaux took over from there, equally clinical in recalling a conversation with a military contractor who pointed him to the office building, his neutralization of Moore's bodyguards, and a car chase to the airport where his pilot buddy was waiting to sneak them into the country.

"Sounds like we're lucky you came."

The overt flirting is making Eric uncomfortable. He's not in love with Rita anymore, but it's still not fun to see.

Even Boudreaux's not sure what's happening, and Eric's seen women fall over themselves trying to get his attention.

"Who else needs some coffee?" Boudreaux says. "Break room?"

Eric points. "End of the hall."

Boudreaux starts toward the door, but as he passes, Rita puts a hand on his chest, now free of the flak jacket and covered with a black T-shirt.

"I'll go get you some. How do you take it?"

"Thanks. Black." He motions to Lori. "A splash of milk and two packets of sweetener for her."

Rita frowns but leaves without objection.

"What about you?" Boudreaux asks Eric. "Still not man enough to drink coffee?"

Lori's snort might ordinarily bother Eric, but he's preoccupied with Rita. He needs to get ahold of this situation. He doesn't know exactly how her behavior could jeopardize MANIFEST, but if Eric, his operators, or his assets are emotionally compromised, chances for error increase exponentially.

"Nope, still drinking your caffeine cocktail." He picks up the empty aluminum can and glass on his desk. "In fact, I should go make myself another one."

Eric leaves Boudreaux to describe the drink's origin. On the way to the break room, he rehearses the lecture. This is an extraordinary night, but she's at the office. Boudreaux is a guest of their company. Lori's her employee.

He enters the office, sees Rita leaning against the counter beside the coffeemaker, back to the door.

"What on earth is wrong with you?"

So much for the lecture.

"I'm sorry," Rita says, still facing away from him. "It's just, you've told me how competitive you two can get, and the way you turned me down earlier tonight because you were worried about her, I just"—she turns around, leans her elbows back on the counter—"I wanted to make you jealous, I guess."

Rita's rambling. She only does that when she's flustered, like when she finally came clean about her out-of-town *conferences*, or the first time she came into his office late at night after giving back her ring.

In fact, she was in this spot—this exact position—the last time he gave in.

"Look, it's not what you think."

"Then tell me what it is," she says, voice a notch above a whisper, "because I don't know how much longer I can handle this."

Rita knew he worked for the Agency. Eric tried to keep it from her, but when the salesmen he wanted made no sense, she tried enforcing the clause in their contract that gave her veto power on new hires. She freaked out. Everything she had was wrapped up in their business, but Eric told her building the business was integral to his plan, so making FAST a success was just as important to him as it was to her. After that, she took over the business side and he ran the covert side.

She hadn't asked for specifics until now. And she already knows more than Gates had ever intended.

"We talked about this. There are things I can't tell you. It's for your own—"

"Bullshit," Rita says, voice full of hurt rather than rage. "She's not one of your spies. You hired a woman you wanted to screw, did it, and now you're flaunting her it in front of me. That's about us, not your covert missions or whatever."

Eric hates it when she refers to them as a couple. It's hard to blame her, though. Their relationship was borne of proximity. He never acted on his attraction at OU, and their communications for the two-and-a-half decades after had never taken a romantic or sexual turn. But during that first year after she returned to Oklahoma from Silicon Valley, Eric and Rita spent eighty hours a week or more together. It might've been stranger if they hadn't started sleeping together.

As he watches Rita pout at the counter, Eric sees for the first time how much damage he'd caused. He'd seen Rita's jealousy grow and hoped it would get her to stop trying to fix what she'd broken. It would've been easier than confronting her.

I can't keep doing this. Rita's cheating had crushed whatever trust they'd built as a couple, but she's still one of Eric's oldest friends.

"It's complicated," he says, "but Lori *is* a part of my covert operations. What you've been seeing is me working her for information. I actually don't like her that much. But I need her."

She blinks, forcing tears to stream down both cheeks. "Like you need me?"

Eric steps to her. "No. I told you, it's not like that."

"So you haven't slept with her?"

Two more strides gets Eric so close Rita has to look up to meet his eyes.

"No."

Before he can react, Rita grabs the nape of his neck and presses her lips onto his. He kisses her back, grabs her ass and lifts her onto the counter. They only have a few minutes before the others will wonder how slow his coffee maker is. After that, there's Phase Two of MANIFEST.

As he unbuttons his jeans, Eric glances at his watch.

Forty minutes.

24
JEREMIAH

Love's Travel Stop, Guthrie, Capital Province
Republic of Oklahoma

Though INSTA rigs are outfitted with bleeding-edge tech advanced enough to protect nuclear material, they still require diesel. Diesel requires payment, which usually comes from the agency's gas card, which is usually somewhere on Mac's person—at her request and with approval from Daniels after Jeremiah lost one years ago.

Now?

"How're we paying for this?" Mac asks as all four hop down from the truck.

They have personal credit cards valid across the Divided States, but Jeremiah pulls out a sandwich baggie filled with a short stack of cash. The bills are American greenbacks, a pre-secession holdover deemed too costly to destroy and replace.

"Compliments of Novak. He said we need to use it for anything we buy this trip, so feel free to splurge."

Dom and Zeus give each other a *hell yeah* high five and wait to receive their share. Jeremiah smiles and tosses the bag to Mac.

"Sorry guys, she's still in charge of the money."

"Be nice," she tells them, "and I'll let you both get two packages of jerky each. The biggest ones they have."

The boys mumble under their breath and start for the glass doors below the red-and-yellow heart.

"Eighty bucks should top it off," Jeremiah tells Mac as he lifts the nozzle. "If not, it'll be more than enough to get us to Cushing."

Jeremiah usually got within half a gallon, especially now that the price of gas had stabilized across the Divided States. For a few months during and after the secessions, it swung so wildly and so often he needed a calculator. He was told the cost of a gallon of gas was related to the price for a barrel of oil, but that didn't always seem to make sense. When crude was worth negative thirty-seven dollars in 2020, gasoline didn't become so valuable that only the one-percent could fuel their limos.

The nozzle clicks off with the meter showing $79.18. Novak and his people—whoever they are—can afford to donate the balance.

Jeremiah feels odd in the moment. It's almost the same as a hundred others from The Before Times. He's never been to this Love's, but it's the same as a dozen others along his usual routes.

Except, it's not.

This one's in The Republic of Oklahoma. The exterior hasn't changed much, but as Jeremiah walks to the glass doors, he reads the loitering and alcohol consumption notices. They now cite Oklahoma national law, not state law.

Changes on the inside are just as subtle. The shelves and refrigerated sections are the same, but the composition of the items they display aren't. As part of their secession agreement, Oklahoma convenience stores can only sell items from companies based in Oklahoma or Texas. The selection is smaller, but only noticeable if you favor Brand A over Brand B. Take the jerky stocked in this store. Shelf space that would've been devoted to Slim Jim and Jack Link's now belongs to Edes Meats from Amarillo and Clint & Sons from nearby White Deer.

Zeus and Dom pick up a package of each to go along with their energy drinks, chips, and an assortment of travel snacks. They don't care about the new junk food lineup. What's the difference?

The changes were subtle enough that many folks in the plains states saw no major disruptions to their daily lives. Governments had never run as efficiently as when they facilitated the migration of unhappy residents and produced new citizenship documents for those eager for the separation. For most in these parts, everything's the same, save for a minor round of rebranding.

Except, it's not.

Jeremiah grew up pledging allegiance to the flag of the United States of America. One nation. Indivisible. He saluted that flag while serving the republic for which it stood and protected its liberty. But with the strokes of a few pens, those serving in his home state were now saluting the flag of the Republic of Texas. Anyone who wanted to keep serving under the Fifty Stars were allowed six months to move to the new USA. Few did.

Serving under one star means more time at home. They're not off fighting other people's wars. The Republic is now the most well-defended Allied Nation and is unable to be dicked around with.

Except, it's not.

Whoever Novak works for has found a loophole. Scratch that. They *think* they've found a loophole. But this war game won't work with Jeremiah and Mac at the wheel.

Well, not literally.

"Dom, take over driving," Jeremiah says as he and Zeus pile their purchases next to the register.

"Wilco," Dom says before asking the clerk to add four cheap stogies from behind the counter to their order.

Mac pays for them and for her Texas spring water. "Getting anything?"

"Give me the cash and I'll meet y'all out there."

Jeremiah expects her to balk, but she zips up the bag and tosses it to him. "Don't take too long. We're still trying to outrun the weather."

He nods and turns toward the aisles. There used to be a dedicated shelf space in convenience stores for trucker electronics like Bluetooth headsets, GPS systems, and prepaid cellphones. He finds the section, but it has everything a driver could want except the thing he needs most.

Jeremiah grabs a can of Sonic-brand cherry limeade and approaches the exhausted cashier. "You don't happen to keep any prepaid phones back there?"

She studies him for a moment. "Who's asking?"

Jeremiah's not sure how to respond, but the cashier reads the situation before he can ask a stupid question.

"You're not from here, are you?"

He shakes his head.

"How many you need?"

"Three."

The cashier nods and shuffles toward an employee-only doorway. Jeremiah's never bought a burner phone, but he never imagined it would be this much of a hassle.

She emerges a minute later with a cardboard box with the logo of a food distribution company. "Two hundred. They ain't new, but they'll get you out of a jam."

Jeremiah whistles at the steep price but starts counting the bills. "I take it burner phones are illegal in Oklahoma now?"

"The government says these aid drug dealers, and I tend to agree." She pockets the cash and sits the box on the counter between them. "And I don't sell to no drug dealers. Usually women escaping abusive men, that kinda thing. Now, you ain't that, but you ain't dealing, neither. Not round here, at least. Plus, with whatever's gonna happen after those shootings, extra cash sounds mighty good right about now."

Smart woman.

He crosses the parking lot toward Mac, who's standing beside Blue's passenger door, sucking on her vape pen. INSTA employees are given insurance incentives to quit smoking and all but Mac had done it, save for Dom's victory cigars, which even Daniels said didn't count. She lodged a complaint a few years ago, arguing she should get half-credit for switching to e-cigarettes, but they cited popcorn lung and other complications. She brought up the cigars, which were also deemed acceptable because the higher-ups were all former officers and refused to be denied the pleasure of fine Cuban tobacco.

Mac pockets the device when she sees him and flips her left palm skyward, pointing to the watch with her right index finger. He gives her a quick sorry and climbs up into the overhead with Zeus.

"Why don't I ever get to ride shotgun?" he asks.

The answer is nuanced. Were this a normal transport on a normal day, Jeremiah could joke and say it's because Zeus is smallest. A more neutral answer would be that Zeus brings no expertise in terms of driving ability or communications training.

But on this morning, with the team on edge and out of its comfort zone, Jeremiah picks the answer that'll feed Zeus's ego.

"Our secret weapon won't be very secret if he's riding down there."

Zeus's smile lets Jeremiah know he chose correctly.

"Thanks. And thanks for not sending me home because of the"—he mimics tipping back a bottle—"I'd've felt like shit, leaving you and Dom hanging."

"Hey, it was a selfish decision." Jeremiah slaps him on the shoulder. "Without you, I might be dead or in jail right now."

Zeus pats his rifle. "It was nice to let Roxie stretch her legs. Maybe she'll get to eat later."

Zeus had never fired her outside of the range, but Jeremiah put the chances of Roxie breaking her fast at sixty-forty.

With a pause in the conversation, Jeremiah had an opportunity to discuss something sensitive but necessary before they got there.

Just rip it off like duct tape.

"Do you have a problem with Mac?"

Zeus dismissed her earlier and didn't list Mac as someone he'd almost left hanging. Jeremiah hopes he's doing it on purpose. He could deal with a known problem. Ferreting out a hidden issue, however, isn't in his wheelhouse, and they don't have time for a therapy session.

"It's not her. It's my wife."

Jeremiah tries to piece it together, but after a few seconds he gives up. "I don't follow."

"Sarah Grace's pissed at me. That's why I came in even though I was hammered."

"But weren't you two …"

"We'd just finished when they called. Sarah Grace saw it was the plant and asked if Mac was coming in, too. It got pretty bad from there, so I called them back, chugged a few more and got out of there."

Jeremiah puts an index finger to his lips and leans in. "So she's jealous of Mac? You've been working together for almost a year now."

Zeus was the newest member of the team and the only one to serve under the Fifty Stars and the Lone Star. He'd been a military contractor until the secessions. They moved back in with Sarah Grace's parents and were in bad financial shape when Daniels finally hired him.

"Yeah, well, she'd never seen Mac until the Christmas party, and I never told her what Mac looked like."

"Oh."

One word rarely says so much. But, in this case, it says that, on the day Sarah Grace met her, Mac was wearing an elegant, emerald green dress with a slit up the side that was a few inches too high for a work function. It also says Mac was in high heels, which brought her height up to more than six feet, while Sarah Grace was five-four in hers.

And, though it has nothing to do with her looks, it also says Mac drank a bit too much and kissed a very married Dom below the mistletoe before stumbling out of the party.

But Jeremiah doesn't remember Mac making a move on Zeus.

"You've served with women," Jeremiah says. "Has she ever been jealous before?"

"Yeah. Calls it her crazy lady brain."

It's inappropriate, but the phrase strikes Jeremiah right and he chuckles. He expects Zeus to get upset, but instead they end up echoing and feeding off each other until Mac yells up at them to quit giggling like schoolgirls or share with the rest of the class.

Jeremiah collects himself and motions for Zeus to huddle up again. "We all bring our personal stuff to the job, I get that." He leans in just a bit closer and lowers his voice to a whisper. "But being shitty to Mac because your wife's jealous isn't fair to her, and it puts us all at risk."

Silence and a nod are apology enough for Jeremiah.

Time to troubleshoot.

"Sometimes," he whispers, "acknowledging another woman's beauty and the bond that comes with working together is a good first step. When you talk to Sarah Grace, let her know she's your wife and Mac is becoming more like a sister."

One corner of Zeus's mouth ticks up. "I probably shouldn't bring up sisters, either."

How messed up is his marriage? Then again, Jeremiah's not one to judge another man's matrimonial issues. Before he can respond, Zeus's expression turns to embarrassment.

"That came out wrong." He says, eyes wide. "I mean, Sarah Grace and my sister don't get along, so bringing up Lexi would just piss her off."

"Why's that?" Jeremiah's never had a sister-in law, so he's honestly curious.

"Sarah Grace hates Lexi. Thinks she's disloyal to me and our parents."

He probably wants to leave it there, but Jeremiah can't help but look confused, so Zeus continues.

"Lexi's always been an ambitious hot shot and pretty much disowned our parents a long time ago. She lives in Pennsylvania and could've helped me out when I lost my job, but she wouldn't. She got to keep her old cell number, so we still talk sometimes. We just have to keep it on the DL."

Jeremiah nods. He can infer the rest. It wasn't universal, but the policy of sponsoring relatives during the migration was a purity test for many families. Return to whence you came, and you were a member in good standing. Refuse the offer, and you were one of *them*.

Tension like that could fester and infect the rest of the team, so Jeremiah considers further discussion. Then he remembers where they're going. This may be everyone's last trip, one that was brought about by Jeremiah's complicated relationship with Lori.

They sit in silence for a moment, and in the quiet Jeremiah hears sleet battering the roof of their compartment.

Zeus looks up. "I know I just said I'd stop dissing Mac, but isn't it her job to steer us around this?"

Under normal circumstances, he'd be right. Jeremiah would be hollering down to ask if Mac needed help or get an explanation for their route. Instead, he's faced with a decision. Jeremiah and Mac can keep Zeus and Dom in the dark. Or, he can have Mac find a place to pull over, read everyone in, and use their collective brain trust to improve on the flimsy plan he's formed over the last two-hundred eighty miles.

He climbs down. "Guys, there's a turnoff for Old State Highway 33 coming up. Take that and pull into the first empty parking lot you can find."

Dom glances his way.

"What's wrong?"

25
LORI

FAST offices, Cushing, Northeast Province
Republic of Oklahoma

People think they can hide their affairs.

They can't.

Take Fowler and Clarke, acting like they didn't just have a quickie when everyone can smell it on them. That's why Lori and Jeremiah meet at one of their apartments. No dates. No taking each other as plus-ones.

Lust mimics romance when it escapes the bedroom.

Or when someone—Clarke, in this case—lets it out.

She was polite when handing Boudreaux his coffee, but the overt come-ons were gone. She was also nicer to Lori. Not quite pleasant, but far removed from the rom-com villainess she impersonated before her break-room release.

Fowler, meanwhile, entered unchanged. He didn't invite Clarke to stay. Didn't react when she announced her departure from his office a bit too loudly. Didn't watch her leave, instead choosing to engage with Boudreaux while her angry steps filtered in from the hall.

Then Clarke returned to Fowler's office less than twenty minutes later, asking to see something on his computer while leaning over him to see the monitor.

"Thanks again," she tells him. "I can't believe I accidentally deleted that phone number. We're lucky you know how to recover files."

What a load of crap.

"No problem." He backs his chair away from the desk and Clarke stumbles out of the way. "And since you watched me do it, now won't have to rely on me next time it happens."

Translation: *You're being transparent. Now go.*

She doesn't.

Instead, Clarke turns to Boudreaux. "I forgot to ask you ..."

Lori drifts away from the conversation while she waits for Boudreaux's modafinil to kick in. He'd said it was like washing down Adderall with an energy drink, then chasing it with a shot of epinephrine. He also gave her two pain pills courtesy of his pilot friend, which makes her thankful for the safe landing.

She still hears everything and will record the bad soap opera unfolding in front of her. But Lori can think over the conversations and find what's relevant in the background in the unlikely case she needs it. While Boudreaux and Fowler reminisce about an op in Brazil, Lori thinks about Jeremiah. She feels sorry for him. Truly. She never loved him and is 90 percent sure she's incapable of feeling that way about anyone.

But for him, she'd been willing to fake it.

Listening to Clarke act surprised at Fowler's tale of daring-do reminds Lori of Jeremiah the first time they dined out after hooking up post-separation. The way he couldn't forgive her but feigned interest in the new restaurant for the sake of maintaining a respectable, stable, married life. He was willing to push aside headlines about a homicide detective being put on administrative leave. Then fired. Then no-billed thanks to what the media deemed a corrupt DA's office bowing to a powerful police union that threatened a sick-out.

Jeremiah's one of only three living souls who know the truth. Lori's one of two who heard the sounds, the way they echoed, dueling screams fading into sobs and silence.

Lori's last sober day? The one before she confessed to Jeremiah.

For reasons she'll never understand, Jeremiah remained the dutiful husband, literally by her side on the Potter County Courthouse steps as the Houston lawyer announced how vigorously he would defend Lori in the family's civil suit. But Jeremiah only had so many vacation days, and soon he was back on the road. When she was a cop,

Lori filled time with extra shifts and studying for degrees and police exams. After she made detective, she worked her cases nonstop. When Amarillo wasn't deadly enough, Lori volunteered to help rural Panhandle counties.

Without the job filling her spare time, she reverted to pre-academy Lori, the one who hopped from foster house to foster house and experimented with sins her father wouldn't have allowed. The young woman who later realized being high—be it from alcohol, opiates, or another person's touch—didn't turn off her freakshow of a brain, but made her feel less alien.

After leaving the force, drinking away the spare time was easy. Though she'd switched to craft beer while on the job, Jeremiah kept a fun array of hard stuff in the house. It only took two trips for inhibition-less Lori to pull up her mental rolodex. She called dealers for Vicodin. Then Oxy. Lori could get as wild as she wanted when Jeremiah was away and knew how to hide it while he was home.

When he finally asked about her cash withdrawals, which were particularly noticeable without her half of their income, Lori thought about weaning herself. But it had been three months. Slowing down left Lori dope sick and, though she thought she'd hidden it well, Jeremiah isn't stupid.

He isn't rash either, so Jeremiah brought evidence to their inevitable blowup. The pill bottle underneath her side of the mattress. The emergency sandwich bag stuffed into the toe of a pair of shoes she keeps in their box in the top of the closet. The proof that sent him over the top? Her multivitamins, the ones she took in the mornings, sometimes standing beside him, that had been switched out for the opioids.

Jeremiah threw that bottle at her. She yelled. He screamed. She slapped, then punched, then kicked Jeremiah. When he went silent and started to leave, Lori jumped on his back. Jeremiah tried flinging her away, but Lori had the choke locked in, which is why she didn't blame him for falling backward onto their glass coffee table.

Jeremiah checked into a hotel that night and was on the road by six the next morning. Then, before he called or confronted her at their home, Jeremiah found a cheap apartment. He tried to forgive her during the separation. Asked her to go to rehab. Begged her to put their marriage, their love, above her depression. But when Lori told him she felt neither depression nor love—that she was happier alone and high than she'd been during their years together—he filed for divorce.

When Jeremiah contacted her again more than a year later, he was unwilling to forgive, but willing to forget. I know we don't love each other anymore, he'd said, but I can't keep you out of my life, either. Her first instinct was to warn him off, to tell him she'd already ruined one man who cared about her despite the flaws of character.

Now, sitting in Fowler's office watching his lips move, Lori wishes she'd done it. Then maybe Jeremiah wouldn't be trying to keep her out of harm's way, breaking every oath he'd ever taken in the process.

Clarke stands and Boudreaux follows—*Is he showing off or is his chivalry honest?*—and Fowler lifts his cheeks as she passes by on her way out. He's already seated again when an older man blocks Clarke's advance by filling the doorway. The man's barrel chest is bolstered by a thick winter coat, not the paunch and waddle of most men his age. She pictures Boudreaux in ten years, but New Guy's stare is colder.

For New Guy, unlike his ex-finance, Fowler jumps to attention.

"I didn't know you were coming, sir."

Sir? Fowler uses names with people he knows, never honorifics. Well, almost. He's used sir in her presence exactly once, when he took a call while she paused outside his doorway to look for breath mints in her purse. He might use sir and ma'am upon first greeting, but New Guy isn't new to Fowler.

"You didn't think I'd sit on the sidelines while we're under attack, did you sport?"

New Guy is originally from Minnesota but has lived elsewhere for a long time. They didn't meet as children. Maybe college, but probably in the CIA.

"Everyone, this is Randall Gates," Fowler says. "He's one of my oldest and closest friends."

Lori's never heard the name. After Fowler makes individual introductions, Gates inhales deeply.

"That coffee smells wonderful," he says.

Fowler turns to Clarke. "Would you mind?"

Though Lori expects her to look irritated by her continued relegation to barista, Clarke smiles and says she'll be right back.

"I'd love some vanilla creamer," Gates says. "And if you have it, just a dash of cinnamon."

Now Lori's awake.

26
ERIC

Gates can't be here. He designed MANIFEST, and per the protocols, he is to be nowhere near the op's moving parts.

Yet here Gates stands, shutting the door to Eric's office.

"They up to speed?" Gates asks, his back to the room. Eric recognizes Gates' tone, the one he uses during dangerous ops.

"Yes."

Eric wants to say more, but his presence and question means Gates is now in full control of MANIFEST. Eric's his deputy again, trusted with carrying out orders, not giving them. Asking why in front of the others would undermine the director's authority.

The first person he addresses directly is Boudreaux. "I need to thank you for saving this operation. From everything Fowler's told me, I expect you to be a hell of an asset for us today."

"I appreciate that."

Gates freezes for a moment. He's expecting a sir from Boudreaux. He'll never get one in this context. Maybe if they were having a drink, but not acknowledging a chain of command from someone who never served.

"As for you, Miss Young," Gates says before shifting her way. "I'm sorry we had to bring you in under these circumstances."

Lori's gears are turning, which makes Eric nervous. On one hand, she has a law enforcement background and understands, to some degree, how an op can go wrong if someone disobeys orders. Lori also has a history of not giving a damn about consequences.

If her give-a-shit's busted, this could get ugly fast.

"It's okay, Randall. I was in this the moment that asshole shot me. I know the stakes."

Gates nods. "Of that, I have no doubt."

They were passive-aggressive, but Gates must not have taken much offense. He walks toward Eric, who expects to be the next person he engages.

Instead, Gates pulls out the office chair and sits.

"Say Fowler, could you go check on—"

His thought is interrupted by a knock at the door. Fowler doesn't hesitate.

"Just in time," Gates says when Rita appears with a Yeti coated in orange with a purple FAST logo, their most popular piece of swag for sales calls. He takes a sip. "Perfect."

Gates reaches into Eric's desk and pulls out the satphone without having to be told which drawer. He's taken over the desk, same as he took over the room and the op.

Gates stands, looks at Boudreaux. "Hip and ankle?"

Boudreaux nods. "Plus a rifle in the truck."

"Get yours," Gates says as he walks past Eric. "And give him your keys. You're riding with me."

Eric tosses the keyring to Boudreaux and scrambles to the far end of his office. After Gates is out of the room, Eric catches Lori's gaze and tilts his head toward the gun safe. She tells Boudreaux to go warm up the truck while she uses the restroom again. After he's clear, Lori walks over.

Eric hands her one of two Glock 19s. "In case this goes sideways."

"Why would it?"

"Your ex got to bring three of his people in case Moore ambushed him on the way here. They're all armed, so we better be, too."

Lori nods and racks a round.

***

FRIGID WIND stings Eric's face as he turns toward the curb and watches Lori jog to the comfort of Eric's white dually with the vinyl FAST logo across its side. Gates has a black Escalade running, heat no doubt on full blast. Rita's new car isn't there, but she probably parked it under one of the covered spaces behind the building.

Eric wants to question him as soon as the door's shut. But he restrains himself. Gates will tell him what he needs to know when he needs to know it.

"You waited for her." It sounds like a statement, but it's really Gates demanding an explanation.

"I wanted to make sure she and Rita didn't start talking."

The excuse sounds lame, but it's true. Lori did need the restroom, so he stood out in the hall. Rita poked her head out once but ducked back in after Eric shook his head.

When Gates doesn't react, Eric wonders if he knows about giving Lori one of the pistols. His anxiety's already at ten and they haven't left the parking lot.

"It's not that I don't trust you," Gates finally says, eyes still on the road. "I'd've aborted if anyone else were in charge, but I knew you could handle it. You did a helluva job getting us here."

He shouldn't need Gates's approval anymore, but to ignore the satisfaction from getting an attaboy would be disingenuous. It's been this way since he joined the Agency.

"But," Gates continues, "I couldn't ask you to do this alone. You see my presence here as a lack of confidence, when really it's a compliment. We're going to be partners on this thing." He turns to Eric when they reach the one stop sign on the short route. "Work for you?"

Partners. Many leaders use the word as a carrot. If you perform well enough this one time, we can be equals. Eric knows better than to believe such nonsense. Then again, Gates, though never angry, has never blurred the lines between boss and underling.

Until now.

"Absolutely."

Smiling is also rare, but Gates wears it well as they near the meet.

"You remember the last time we were in the field together?"

Eric mirrors Gates and adds a chuckle. "Caracas. You were pissed."

"I was demoted to COS and sent to the most dangerous place this side of the Atlantic. You'd be pissed, too."

Demotion isn't a strong enough word for what happened. People joke about Siberia, but real punishment was going from running the Latin America desk to herding a team of edgy officers in Venezuela.

Eric should know.

"Well, I wasn't exactly thrilled when you stole my job."

Everyone assumes Gates is ex-military because of his demeanor and strength, but he was recruited while earning a Ph.D. in economics at Pepperdine. Gates is a genius and refused to pretend otherwise for the sake of office politics.

That's why Gates, in a briefing on the seventh floor in Langley, told the Director of Central Intelligence that he was being obtuse for what was later seen as an inconsequential decision.

He was in Venezuela by the end of the week.

"Well," Gates says, still smiling, "I'd say it worked out for both of us."

True enough. After working so closely for three months, Gates placed his new favorite officer in his hip pocket. All he asked was acknowledgment of his superiority, and Eric had never seen evidence to the contrary.

Daybreak is still a few minutes away, but night has lightened into gray in the final pre-dawn minutes. Gates flips around and pulls into a caliche lot near a colossal oil storage tank. Once white, the seventy-foot-tall behemoth is covered in a dingy film of hydrocarbons and rusty soil. It's just one of a thousand clustered into tank farms that stretch for miles south of Cushing.

Gates parks parallel to the road facing west so he'll see the semi coming. Boudreaux parks behind him, but Gates rolls down his window and waves the truck forward.

"Always keep the rifleman between you and the other guy." Gates loves finding teachable moments, whether his lesson was correct or not.

After a few minutes, Eric focuses on the lightening horizon, frustrated. "They're running late."

"Must've caught the edge of that storm. Nobody here knows how to drive in a little snow."

"Two feet is more than a little snow—even for someone who grew up in Minnesota and lives in Wyoming."

Cold weather isn't Eric's favorite, but heavy precipitation of any kind can mean a boost in sales and service calls for FAST. Not that he'll have to worry about that anymore. Rita will get controlling interest in the business when MANIFEST is complete, and Eric will serve as deputy to Director Randall Gates under Alexia Ramirez, president of the restored United States of America.

Phase One will be done as soon as Jeremiah Reynolds pulls up with his nuke.

Phase Two's timetable is a bit more fluid.

"What's China doing?" Eric asks.

Gates glances down to the clock on the dash. 7:32.

"I may have time to get a sitrep." He pulls out the satphone, dials, waits a few seconds. "Status? … Understood … Will advise when the payload …"

Eric follows his gaze to an eighteen-wheeler that's just pulled into view.

"The payload's here," Gates says. "Phase Two is a go."

He ends the call and replaces the phone. "Get the girl. I'll wait here."

Eric obliges and, for the first time all night, shivers as he steps out into the cold.

27
JEREMIAH

Columbus Petroleum Terminal,
6 miles south of Cushing, Northeast Province
Republic of Oklahoma

Jeremiah nods at Mac and pounds the roof of the cab. They're moving forward with the plan, which is simple in theory. The execution won't be.

He opens the door and steps down, gloved hands in the air. Mac stopped about twenty yards short of the white dually and black SUV, steam billowing from their tailpipes. Fowler is standing beside the Escalade and opens the door for Lori, who looks like a nine-year-old in her father's winter coat.

Novak and Robb briefed Jeremiah on the other players. The older yet imposing man who leaves the pickup is Randall Gates – the brains of their operation.

The guy holding a modified Heckler & Koch 416 rifle is the brawn.

Jeremiah's not naked, but his SIG Sauer and burner phone aren't much comfort as he steps toward Lori.

"You can put your hands down, son," Gates says over Blue's idling engine. "We're just playing a game of musical trucks here."

Jeremiah looks back. Dom has already slid into the passenger seat, so Jeremiah acquiesces. At least now he'll have a chance to pull his sub-compact before Boudreaux can raise his rifle.

"Before my team leaves the truck, Lori and I need to be in that Escalade and driving away."

"You don't expect me to agree to that, do you?"

No. But it was worth asking.

"Well then, I'm not sure where we go from here."

Gates purses his lips as though he's thinking and hasn't planned the whole scenario already. "Let's try this. Your people exit the truck without their guns, and we"—he jerks a thumb at Fowler—"drive away. Boudreaux can babysit you until we're clear, then you get in the Caddy and go eat breakfast in town."

Comebacks don't come naturally to Jeremiah, but this one's so easy he grins.

"You don't expect me to agree to that, do you?"

He expects Gates to react negatively. A frown. A clenched jaw, at the very least. Instead, Gates smiles right back.

"Let's game this out. You've got Ramirez positioned behind the trailer, waiting for a signal."

Dammit. They stopped before turning onto the straightaway leading to the meet and Zeus held onto the back for nearly a mile. Jeremiah doesn't react, but Zeus hears his name and moves away from the truck, flanking the group from the north, Roxie shouldered and hungry.

Boudreaux mirrors him.

"Welcome to the party," Gates says. "So, the two rifles cancel each other out. You've got a pistol on you, but so do I. Fowler's Glock gives me a one-man advantage if Hansen and MacLaughlin stay in the truck, which they'll do since their goal is to not give up the payload at all costs."

One problem with a simple plan: It's easy for the other guy to figure out.

Gates takes a step toward Fowler and Lori. "But, if I know my boy Fowler, he slipped Ms. Young a pistol, thinking she'd be on his side if shit hit the fan. He always trusts his assets too much. But if she pulls that gun, it'll be on him, which puts us at a stalemate again"—he nods to the stretch of road behind Jeremiah—"but only for a few more seconds."

Jeremiah turns and sees a silver sedan bearing down on them. When he swivels back, Boudreaux and Zeus have already retreated to the north sides of their respective trucks, shielding themselves from the car but keeping their rifles on each other. Fowler remains still, except for his eyes, which bounce between the car and Gates. Lori pushes up her coat sleeves, preparing for the chance to flag down the driver.

The high-end car flies past them—then shows off its braking system. The driver, protected by tinted windows and a gray dawn, whips into the lot behind the other vehicles.

Fowler spins and grabs Lori's arm when she takes a step backward, away from the sedan.

Gates winks at Jeremiah.

28
LORI

Lori didn't need the broken piece of her brain to figure out who's in the Mercedes. Yes, it matched the coffee orders in less than a second back at the office, but her prefrontal cortex pieced together the rest without much trouble.

Lori expects Clarke to make up an excuse for her presence. Instead, she exits with her pistol drawn, blonde hair streaming across her face.

"Stay calm," Clarke says in her natural voice, the one she used while talking to Gates in the hall.

Fowler releases Lori's arm, but only so he can walk toward his business partner and ex-fiancé. "What's going on?"

Fowler always pretends to be smarter than he is, but Lori's never seen him this dense.

"She's working with Gates behind your back."

Fowler whips his head to Lori, to Clarke, to Gates, and starts the pattern again before Gates puts a stop to it.

"Keep it together," he says. "She's on our side. Always has been."

"No," Lori says. "She's on *his* side."

Lori's not sure what the difference is, but liars never have the same objective as the people they're deceiving.

Fowler takes another step toward Clarke. "How long?"

Clarke still has both hands on the gun, though she's dropped it to hip-level. "Stanford."

"You mean—"

"Yes."

29
ERIC

Eric's a boxer in the fifteenth round. "A sleeper? This whole time?"

She parts her lips, pauses, closes them again before speaking. "Yes and no."

"That's a bullshit answer and you know it."

"Listen," she says, slowly advancing toward Eric and Lori. "I was recruited by a computer science professor at Stanford. They wanted to plant me as a financial analyst on Wall Street, but I loved California and refused to live on the East Coast. They eventually let me work in Silicon Valley and made sure I took frequent trips to China. But I was let go after the secessions. Then Gates called me."

She's less than five yards away, and Eric isn't sure if he can stand for her to get any closer. He raises his gun.

Rita stops but keeps explaining. "Yes, I moved back and reconnected with you for him. But I never lied about loving you." She glances at Gates. "He wasn't happy about that. Hell, he was trying to talk me out of marrying you."

Bullshit. Gates stares back, lips thin and flat, eyes unreadable.

"I never cheated on you, either," she continues. "I was getting intel back to Gates. When you confronted me, Gates saw it as an opportunity to put an end to our relationship."

Eric focuses on Gates, his face reddening in the freezing wind. "Why?"

"You know as well as I do that developing feelings—"

"Fuck off." The emotional outburst surprises Eric, but he leans into it. "You know what I meant. Why is she here? Why would you give me a babysitter?"

"You're a born tactician and a master manipulator," Gates says. "You're also the most loyal creature I know."

And?

"He couldn't trust you with executing MANIFEST's endgame."

Rita always could read his mind, even as undergrads. She was one of his first adult crushes—a fact he almost certainly told Gates at some point. That's why he chose her. Rita was a blind spot.

But why did Gates want to exploit it?

"I don't understand. Threatening a nuclear detonation here was my idea."

Gates nods. "And it was a fine plan. Almost perfect. I just had to tweak the ending."

No. Not that. Gates asked for Eric's red line in the early planning stages, just after Eric retired and not long before Rita re-entered his life.

"I know we discussed it, but you agreed not to ... we said we wouldn't ..."

Eric can't say it, won't say it, won't breathe life into the idea. He looks at Rita, runs to her, praying she'll tell him he's wrong.

"No matter what happens next," she says, "I want you to know that I still lo—"

30
JEREMIAH

The rig's diesel engine screams before anyone can react. A gunshot from Zeus was one of two actions Mac had been waiting on, the other being a *you'll know it when you see it* look from Jeremiah. Either would trigger the team's two-part plan. Step One is haul ass behind the truck's bullet-resistant glass and reinforced body. Step Two is driving until its tanks are nearly on E.

But based on the exit wound, the bullet didn't come from Zeus's rifle.

It came from Boudreaux's.

There'll be time later to figure out why. With Blue finally in motion, Jeremiah's priority shifts to ensuring Lori's safety.

Short bursts come from both rifles. He can't tell if Zeus and Boudreaux are shooting at each other or Gates, who was standing between them. Those three are occupied either way, so Jeremiah pulls his SIG and aims at Fowler, who's kneeling beside the woman's body, sleet now pelting them both.

He's about to squeeze the trigger when Lori steps in front of him and pistol-whips Fowler, who crumples onto the bloody mess he was cradling.

Jeremiah sweeps his SIG to the north. He sees legs underneath the pickup and SUV, but it's been a few seconds since he heard gunfire. Zeus is either on the south side of the trailer or already in the cab, which has pulled level with Jeremiah and is veering toward the road.

Time to grab Lori and jump in.

Jeremiah is nearly to her when the pickup's tires slip on gravel. The sound draws his attention. Jeremiah takes a moment to confirm Gates is the driver, but the distraction gives Boudreaux just enough time to emerge from his position and advance toward Lori.

Jeremiah raises his pistol. "Stop or you're dead."

Lori raises hers and aims at Jeremiah. "Don't. He's on our side."

That would explain why he shot blondie, but there's no time to verify his allegiance. The rig has passed them and is gaining speed as it nears the roadway.

Jeremiah rushes to Lori and grabs her arm, but she jerks away.

"You go take care of the bomb," She points to Boudreaux. "I'm going with him."

He could never reason with Lori, especially when she's jonesing for conflict. But Jeremiah can't abandon her, either. He pulls out the burner phone, meant to be Jeremiah's lifeline if he couldn't make it back to the rig.

Now it's Lori's.

"Call one of the saved numbers when you need to."

Lori and Jeremiah share a silent nod as she takes the phone. It's not exactly a plan, but it's the best he can do before they part ways.

Lori runs to Boudreaux.

Jeremiah runs to Mac.

31
LORI

Lori told Boudreaux about Clarke's connection to Gates on the drive over, so her appearance at the meeting shouldn't have surprised him.

That leaves her with one question as she slams the passenger door.

"What'n the Sam Hell's going on?"

Boudreaux's focused on the road ahead. "Gates turned right about a mile up. Where's he going?"

"How should I know?" she asks as the Escalade's back tires slip. "And quit ducking my question."

They ride in silence for more than a minute. Lori wants to break the awkwardness with a scream. They're going more than one-twenty when she finally speaks.

"Take your next right. He's heading back into town."

She falls half over the center console as Boudreaux fishtails around the corner, trading one single-lane road for another. He's leaning forward, gloved hands gripping the smooth steering wheel, still facing dead straight.

"Got you," he whispers.

Lori returns to the passenger seat and starts tracking the white dually on the horizon along a shoddily paved straightaway leading straight into Cushing. Fowler's beast is no snail, but the Cadillac should run him down before they reach the city limits. She wants to have Boudreaux's back when they get there. First, though, she needs to know what she's helping him with.

"Are you going to tell me what the hell's going on?"

"You remember what Moore said?" He curses under his breath and continues before she can call him a dumbass. "He didn't tell you everything. That's the problem with these intelligence assholes."

Moore said Fowler and his boss—Gates, she now knows—were going to park the bomb in the middle of the gas company terminals, contact presidents Ramirez, Cole, Anderson, and the rest. If they don't reunify under Fifty Stars, Cushing would be blown to hell. The economic fallout would be as bad as that left by the nuclear detonation—theirs and China's. More than 10 percent of DS crude would be wiped out and the price of oil would be an unknown variable, throwing every other economic equation into chaos. Markets crash. Breadlines form.

Fowler and Gates would paint a future the rich bureaucrats couldn't stomach. The Allied Nations would become the United States again, and the rest of the world would return to a path that didn't involve global nuclear war.

But Moore said Gates had a slightly different endgame.

Gates knows they won't all agree to reunify. So, instead of asking for that, he planned to declare himself the new American President and install his loyalists—including Alan Novak, a dishonorably discharged soldier turned extremist with a cult military following—into key defense and intelligence positions.

"So you're saying the guy trying to steal a nuclear bomb doesn't actually want world peace. Shocking," Lori says, the words dripping with sarcasm. "I didn't need Moore to tell me that."

Moore hadn't known whether Fowler was in on the true endgame or not. Neither did Boudreaux. They didn't tell Lori that, but it was obvious. Otherwise, Boudreaux would've gone straight to his friend, Fowler, rather than cook up this scheme to get the three of them together.

Of course, Boudreaux was probably supposed to get that information at Fowler's office—a plan that assumed Gates wouldn't be in the goddamn room.

"And now we know Fowler isn't on the same page as Gates," Lori says. "But that doesn't explain why you shot Clarke."

The white dually is within a car length, so she excuses Boudreaux for not responding right away. Instead, she clarifies one point before they take out Gates.

"Not that I mind. But on the way here you said the plan was to talk first, then shoot if that didn't work."

Boudreaux glances at her—a bit risky with the Cadillac nearly kissing the pickup. "You're right about Fowler. He thought he was on the right side of this. But that's not the piece of intel you're missing."

He puts on his seatbelt rather than filling her in. Her buckle snaps into place just before Boudreaux jerks the Cadillac onto the left shoulder. He gains another few feet and takes a breath before slamming the front end of the Escalade into the bed of the pickup.

The dually overcorrects and nearly completes a 360 before coming to rest on the shoulder, the airport a few hundred yards in the distance past a barbed wire fence and frozen lake of dead grass.

The Escalade speeds past and Boudreaux's door is open before the SUV is in park. He reaches into the backseat for his rifle and is standing outside before she's done checking her pistol. Special Forces training versus the police academy. Plus more than a couple years of rust. And she's fighting the ogre-sized coat. They're excuses, but she can feel sorry for herself later.

Lori rushes to Boudreaux's side, her leg throbbing but not incapacitating thanks to his field-medic work and the pills.

They're still twenty yards away when Gates bails out of the truck.

"Stop," Boudreaux yells over the still-advancing storm.

Gates turns as though he might run into the fields on either side of the road, but Boudreaux lets off a few rounds near his feet. Gates stays frozen for a few more seconds before turning, palms out, teeth bared in an expression that makes her shudder, though she'll blame it on the cold if Boudreaux brings it up later.

"I surrender," he says, eyes ablaze, likely picturing whatever evil he still plans to unleash. "You win."

Boudreaux takes a few more steps toward Gates. Lori lowers her pistol to her hip and crabwalks to the right. She's eighteen feet away from Gates. Boudreaux stops his advance five yards shy of the target.

"You're right." Boudreaux tosses a pair of white flex cuffs at Gates's feet. "And if you put those on and come quietly, you might get the needle instead of the noose."

Maybe he's from Texas? Either way, he knows the new laws. The Republic, which would likely assert jurisdictional control since it was their bomb that was nearly stolen, has two kinds of capital punishment. Those who don't confess and repent—or convicted of select crimes like possession of child pornography—are hanged outside the prisons for public viewing, weather permitting.

Gates doesn't budge. "Why not the firing squad like Clarke?"

Lori shifts her focus to Boudreaux. She has no problem with the fact he killed her—Lori's body count was higher than his for the year—but this explanation should answer her questions.

"She was more dangerous than you and had to be neutralized. You can't detonate that bomb. But she could've."

Gates's reaction is subtle, just a dropping of the smile and his hands, but it's enough to let Lori know Boudreaux is right. And though the word was already permanently logged, it takes a moment to get from her recorder to the prefrontal cortex.

Detonate.

That's the intel she was missing. Gates didn't want to threaten a nuclear blast. He wanted nuclear holocaust.

The thought is enough to lighten Lori's head.

"Normally I'd say you're bluffing," Gates says. "But you executed her as soon as you figured it out. If not, you'd've let her keep spewing that lovey-dovey shit because you have empathy."

Gates waits for an acknowledgement. All he gets is the vapor of Boudreaux's steady breath.

"But how? Only three people alive knew, and Fowler wasn't one of them."

Boudreaux points his muzzle to the cuffs, then returns it to center mass.

Gates squats and cries out, eventually drops to a knee beside the thick zip ties. He palms them, then pauses. "Daniels?"

"Our time in combat applications did overlap by a few years."

Wait. Is Boudreaux saying what I think he's saying?

Gates shakes his head. "Can't believe I didn't know you were a Unit operator, too. You people really do keep your lips tight. Except amongst each other, it seems."

Whoa.

"We kept in touch after I left. He even tried to recruit me for his transport team a time or two," Boudreaux says. "And yeah, he knew the bomb was supposed to go off, but I didn't know Clarke was here to arm the thing until you started running your mouth."

Lori's still stuck on Boudreaux's past. Her new friend wasn't just with the Rangers and SF while in the Army. And after checking, Lori's surprised to find that she's only heard one other person talk about being in Delta.

Her father.

He probably wasn't supposed to discuss his work—not even with his daughter—but the Colonel wanted to make sure Lori knew the men he brought over were *the best Capital-O Operators* in the world. Other SOF servicemembers might argue the point, but Delta operators do fight like hell, that much she can vouch for personally.

His status as a former operator may also explain how Boudreaux instantly knew she was the Colonel's daughter, though if her father ever spoke of Lori, he'd have used her full first name.

Gates winces as he stands, an awkward, painful movement that might've drawn sympathy an hour ago. "If Daniels told you, he must've gotten it from Robb. I knew his constitution was weak, but I couldn't figure a way to do this without him." Gates slips his right wrist into the cuffs and tightens. "Wish I'd known that before calling Novak. Would've told him to take out Robb, too."

He reaches the hand behind his torso to finish cuffing his hands.

No, he's not.

Gates isn't injured. He has a pistol hidden in his waistband.

Lori raises hers. "Do it and I'll drop you."

Gates finishes gripping the gun as though she hadn't threatened to kill him. Rather than whipping around to fire at her, Gates lowers the Glock to his thigh, index finger along the slide.

"Novak's a hell of a leader. Almost as smart as Clarke was. Almost as smart as me, if I'm honest. That's why he's in charge now." He smiles with his lips, but his eyes darken. "I can't believe you didn't think I had a contingency. Novak can execute MANIFEST from where he is. You've got till nine. Then you're screwed."

His right index finger moves to the trigger. Lori does the same, but before she can fire, the sound of gunfire drifts northeast with the wind. She rushes to Gates. By the time she gets there, Boudreaux's already kicked away his gun. Her next instinct is to check his pulse, but it would be superfluous. His left temple is gone and four GSWs are grouped tightly on his sternum.

"You heard the same thing I did, right?" she asks.

"Yeah." He checks the black watch on the inside of his wrist. "The bomb is detonating in seventy-three minutes, forty-two seconds. We need to contact your ex."

She pulls the burner phone from her coat pocket. "On it."

A gust nearly knocks her off balance.

"Go to the Escalade," Boudreaux says. "I'll be there in a minute."

Sleet stings Lori's face and she fights the wind for gulps of air. She's thankful for sanctuary when she closes the passenger door and swipes up on the phone's screen.

It wants a six-digit passcode.

Jeremiah didn't give her one when he handed her the device, but there are a few likely choices. Before their divorce, he yelled it to her when she demanded to check his phone in a moment of projecting her own secrecy onto him.

She taps in the numbers.

The phone shakes.

She used to constantly tell Jeremiah her code. Maybe he made it easy for her.

Nope. *Shit.*

All phones lock after a string of incorrect entries, and the max number of tries for this phone could be three. Lori needs to think before entering another code.

She'd been assuming the phone was programmed with either Jeremiah or her in mind. But it could be one of a batch, meant to serve as walkies for his team. Giving her one might not have been planned. If that's true, the passcode would be easy and universal.

Had Jeremiah ever mentioned that? Yes. Once, when they were discussing INSTA contingency plans. It was early in their marriage. His job scared Lori and she demanded to know every safety measure. That's when she got details of *Big Blue* and every other eighteen-wheeler INSTA uses. She also got a promise that if a transport felt off, he'd give her a way to communicate.

The passcode would be all ones.

She presses the digit rapid-fire. The screen lights up with a few square icons in front of a bright blue background. She taps contacts and finds three—the card for her phone and two labeled MAC and DOM ZEUS. Before dialing, Lori turns and looks out of the back windows. They're dark and wet, nearly opaque, but she can still see Gates's body. One of the pickup's doors is open, Boudreaux half inside the cab, searching for something.

Lori takes a few more moments to open the contacts and read the numbers aloud before calling DOM ZEUS, knowing he'd let Mac keep her phone.

"Lori?"

"Where are you?"

"Driving north on the eighteen, just out of town. You?"

"Still south of town. We caught up to Gates and—"

"What's he saying?"

Lori chokes down her urge to lay into Jeremiah. Since their falling out, Jeremiah rarely lets her finish a sentence. It's annoying enough in everyday conversation, but right now he's making her want to reach through the phone and break his jaw.

"Nothing," she says instead. "He killed himself before we could interrogate him."

A pause. "I guess we can rule out money as his motive. Only a true believer eats cyanide rather than give up intel."

"It was a bullet to the head, but yeah. Gates did mention a guy named Novak"—Boudreaux lifts the rear hatch, so Lori puts the phone on speaker—"And apparently this Novak guy's in charge now."

"Oh Jesus," Jeremiah says. "That's bad."

Lori starts to ask for details, but she's interrupted by a loud grunt from Boudreaux. She turns to find him hunched over and sucking wind behind the Escalade.

Lori tells Jeremiah to hold on and mutes her end of the call.

"You okay?" Lori asks.

He waves her over. "Come help."

When she gets around the SUV, Lori yelps despite herself. Gates's body is laying parallel to the back bumper, what's left of his graying face staring blankly at the storm overhead.

"What the fuck, man?"

"If we leave him here, the cops'll be all over us. But if it's just a dented truck and some blood on the side of the road, they'll think a drunk hit a deer and fled."

Lori's skeptical. "What about the deer? Where'd it go?"

Boudreaux straightens and breathes deep. "Maybe it survived and limped away. Or the guy's buddies decided they wanted venison tonight. But if we don't take him, the sheriff's are guaranteed to be up our ass while we're trying to keep the world from bombing itself into oblivion."

Fair enough. Lori's not sure why she was being so bitchy. She thinks about apologizing for questioning him, but right now she has to focus on the task at hand because Gates is a big man. His dead weight is almost too much, but Lori and Boudreaux manage to flop him up and roll him in. She's still trying to catch her breath after returning to the cab and unmuting the phone.

"What's wrong?" Jeremiah asks.

"Nothing." Another labored breath. "We had to take care of the body."

"Oh."

Boudreaux opens the center console and drops in Fowler's satphone and Gates's Glock.

"So Novak's in charge now?" Jeremiah asks.

"Yes," Boudreaux says. "And Gates said he's capable of detonating your payload."

"Remotely?"

Lori looks at Boudreaux and points to herself. She should deliver the news.

"He didn't get into specifics," she says. "But we think so."

Silence.

"And Jeremiah," she says, delaying it for a few moments longer. "He's going to do it at nine o'clock."

"You mean an hour from now?"

"Yes."

Lori and Boudreaux wait a moment to let Jeremiah—and anyone in his truck who might've heard—process the information. Lori has no idea how she'd handle knowing the moment she'll die.

"I'm so sorry," she says. "I know you're only in this because of me, and—"

"In the movies, they always try to send the bomb into water," Jeremiah says. "We can make it to Sooner Lake in time."

Jeremiah wasn't contemplating his imminent death. He was finding a way mitigate the damage.

Problem is, he's wrong. She thinks.

"If you do that—"

"We'll still die. I know."

"Will you let me talk for once. I was going to say, if you do that, the fallout might be worse."

Lori watched a documentary about Operation Crossroads several years ago. The government detonated a pair of nuclear bombs in the Marshall Islands in 1946. The second test, Baker, was detonated about 90 feet underwater—a close approximation to detonating at the bottom of a lake.

"Bullshit," Jeremiah says. "The water will dampen the explosion."

He may be guessing, but Jeremiah's right about that part. The thermal radiation that burns everything around ground zero will be absorbed by the water.

"But the fallout will be worse if it detonates in the lake," she says.

According to the documentary's smooth-talking narrator, the Federation of American Scientists concluded fallout from a detonation in shallow water would spread over a larger area than one on solid ground. But a nuclear explosion in the lake would be better than Cushing, not to mention a major city.

"And how would you know any of this?"

An old documentary is flimsy evidence. And there's a possibility the information's out of date or if she misunderstood the documentary since her audio recall is perfect, not her comprehension. But he's no more a nuclear physicist than Lori. The disbelief is rooted in his mistrust of her, not the information.

Boudreaux must know it too because he picks up the phone. "She's right. You need to drive to a rural area without many towns to the northeast. Let me pull up maps on this phone."

He doesn't have time to open it before Jeremiah speaks. "I know a place."

"Haul ass," Boudreaux says. "We'll go back and get Fowler, see if he knows how we can stop Novak. We have to retrieve the woman's body anyway."

"Copy."

Boudreaux ends the call before Lori can say goodbye.

"Hey—"

"You'll say goodbye later. Right now, I need you to get your shit together and help me keep more people from dying."

Nobody's spoken to her that way since she wore a badge. Back then, she'd just grind her teeth because making detective seemed like the most important thing in her life.

Not anymore.

"What the fuck did you just say to me?"

Goddammit. She hopes he doesn't catch it, but the corner of Boudreaux's moustache rises so she cuts him off.

"It's a figure of speech, asshole. You know what I meant."

Boudreaux punches the ignition button and puts the Escalade in reverse. "If we're going to survive this, I need the Lori Young who killed those boys in New Orleans with nothing but a letter opener."

He may be right, but Lori won't give him the satisfaction of a response.

"You were a step behind just now, and it wasn't your leg. Then there's Fowler, who you knocked out instead of shooting—"

"Are you fucking kidding me?"

When he's done turning, Boudreaux stops. "Yes, we're lucky you left him alive. But that doesn't mean it was the right tactical decision. I need the woman who'll pull the trigger. The one who'll beat an evil sonofabitch to death because the world is better for it."

Angry is Lori's default. But now, confronted with her past, Lori feels something else. Her face, already hot from rage, begins burning. Stomach acid crawls into her esophagus, leaving in its place a knot that nearly doubles her over.

Alcohol and opium have kept it at bay for so long, Lori had almost forgotten the visceral nature of self-loathing.

"You don't know everything." The words are weak, barely audible over the engine and chassis jostling over the crumbling road.

"I don't need to," he says. "What I need is for you to turn back into a badass. Now."

I can't.

"And don't tell me you can't."

How does he do that? But he's just reading her. He doesn't know her. Lori's not a vigilante, righting wrongs and cleaning the streets one shitbag at a time.

"It doesn't work like that." She's still mumbling and won't look him in the eye.

Boudreaux pulls over as they approach the intersection that leads back to Fowler and Clarke's body.

"What are you doing? We don't have time for this. What if Fowler wakes up?"

"I know, but I need to say something." Boudreaux's tone is no longer antagonistic, but matter-of-fact. "I thought pissing you off would help get you where you need to be for this. It was an assumption based on your past, but I was wrong. For that, I'm sorry."

Thank you. "Whatever."

"But I'm not taking you into a volatile situation if you're going to keep hesitating, which I completely understand. So, if you can't handle this, it's better if I drop you off now and come back after I've secured Fowler." Boudreaux tells her to think it over while he's taking a leak. "But if you come, be ready to do whatever it takes."

Everything he said makes sense. She'd been off since they touched down and had no clue why. The information was still there. The instruction she'd been given. Muscle memory from ten thousand hours of hand-to-hand combat.

More than half of that HTH training—especially when it involved sharp objects and other improvised weapons—came courtesy of her father, who realized Lori's afflicted brain was an asset when combined with her inherited athletic ability. In addition to having an elite soldier with no empathy on one side, Lori's mother was a world-class mixed marital artist who would've gone to the Olympics were it not for her schizophrenia. Neither lived to see if Lori also inherited their psychological defects.

Then there was the academy, where she kept her combat skills sharp and improved with her pistol. And even after years off and nearly a quarter of her life spent treating her body like shit, Lori had still disposed of two trained intelligence officers with nothing but a letter opener and a GSW to her leg.

What had changed in the intervening seven hours? It wasn't exhaustion. That go-pill Boudreaux gave her was every bit the miracle drug he claimed. She hadn't felt this clear in years, which may explain why thinking about that night hit her so hard.

Had Kevin Ryan Booker deserved to die? Absofuckinglutely. He raped four women in downtown Amarillo over the course of two months. The first two didn't report them until after the third was found unconscious in a parking lot. The next ended up spending a month in the ICU. He was escalating so quickly, SVU briefed her and the three other homicide detectives.

The guy was white, approximately six-three and two-forty with brown or black hair, green or brown eyes and no visible tattoos. He acted after three in the morning, when even the hardest partiers had found a place to rest—except the women who'd gone home with someone else but didn't want to leave their car overnight.

Booker had used chloroform at approximately 4:05 A.M. and shoved the fourth victim into her own Jeep, keeping her inside for more than an hour as he raped her, beat her unconscious, then woke her up and raped her again. SVU's canvas turned up two witnesses.

Neither approached the vehicle, assuming it was just a couple screwing in the back. Patrol had increased downtown after victims one and two came forward, but none were on that block during the sixty-eight minutes of brutality.

In her official statement, Lori said she'd happened upon Booker and his fifth victim, Angela Jazmine Collins, after leaving a bar on Polk Street and walking across downtown to take in the cool night air. All of that was true, but she left out the fact she'd started doing it every time Jeremiah left town, hoping to run into him.

Lori said she heard a scream as she walked south on Pierce Street, prompting her to engage with Booker. In truth, she'd seen Collins walking to the car from one of the second-floor lofts that had become popular with the city's young, single professionals. She stayed low and hid behind a hedge half a block away until Booker sprinted to her Bronco from the other side.

The first scream belonged to Collins. Lori showed up before he could apply the chloroform, so she knocked her out of the way. She took about ten frantic steps before stopping.

The second round of screams were Booker's. After he lost consciousness, Lori's voice provided the acoustics as she grunted and screamed obscenities at his battered face while dropping knees into his torso, which was filling with blood. The medical examiner in Lubbock said Lori displaced several ribs on both sides, causing Booker's abdomen to fill with blood and puncturing his left lung. She also bruised his liver, broke his jaw, and snapped his left radius.

Collins started sobbing and asked Lori to stop. But Lori was still working him over. Collins went silent before it ended and pulled away when Lori tried to console her. Collins didn't let anyone touch her until a sympathetic EMT led her toward an ambulance.

Lori has no choice but to remember the sounds. But for this memory, all five senses will forever remain in sharp focus.

She's not sorry Booker's dead. That's not why it makes her gut clench.

Lori hates how it happened.

She was armed that night and could've pulled on Booker, got him to stop, maybe even called for backup without laying a hand on him.

If he attacked Lori in the process, she wouldn't have hesitated to shoot. But her prolonged, unnecessary beating brought back a truth she spent decades avoiding.

Not everyone she'd killed deserved it.

***

SNAPPING FINGERS send Lori into a panic. That wasn't just thinking over the noise. She'd gotten lost in thought. That's never happened, not even when she's loaded. If she ever sleeps again, it'll require noise-cancelling headphones.

"Tunnel vision's another side effect," Boudreaux says. "But it helps me find clarity sometimes."

She tries slowing her heart but can't. "How long were you out there?"

Boudreaux narrows his eyes. "Less than a minute. Why?"

Lori hits rewind. The muted slam of a car door. Then nothing. Forty-six seconds of silence until Boudreaux snaps in her face.

"What did you say?" she asks.

"I said it helps me find—"

"No, before that. Before I came out of it."

Boudreaux's eyes widen. "I told you constant pit stops are one of the modafinil's side effects."

What in the actual fuck? No drug's ever pressed her mute button, prescription or otherwise. But if modafinil can do this every time, if she has a way to shut out the noise, maybe Lori can escape this miserable existence.

"Has this ever happened before?" he asks.

Lori shakes her head.

"Okay, here's what we do. There are a few tanks half a klick east. I'll drive down and park behind one, then hoof it." He reaches into the console and pulls out the satphone. "I'll call when the threat is neutralized. What's the number?"

A solid plan—if Lori were helpless. But she's not. In fact, though she'll process the implications later, she's never felt more in control. "No. I'm good."

He leans over, grips her shoulder in that caring way Jeremiah did after her confession. "Your mind's literally not in this. And there's nothing wrong with that."

If he believes Lori about her jacked-up brain, maybe Boudreaux can also believe her now. "I know it sounds that way, but that's not what's happened."

Boudreaux studies her face like the answer is tattooed on her forehead. "Tell me what did."

"I found clarity."

A slow nod. "Copy that."

Lori spends the short drive silently recalling tactical procedure until she sees a human-shaped mound through the slush and windshield wipers. Boudreaux parks and they exit in synchrony.

It takes her two steps to realize there's only one body and no silver sedan.

Fowler's gone.

32
ERIC

Unknown location

Eric gave up yelling after a few minutes. Whoever's driving the car knows he's in the trunk and has only stopped for what he assumes were intersections. The car's turned twice, but he can't be sure where they were when he woke up, the base of his neck cut and swollen, wrists zip-tied behind him.

Eric's eyes are closed as he remembers kneeling over Rita, his friend for decades and his lover for years, the most constant presence in his life while he worked to keep bad men in check.

The most accomplished liar he'd ever met.

But even in her final minutes, spent trying to explain away her deceit and insist she only betrayed *some* of his trust—that she only manipulated some of his actions and feelings—Eric wanted to move forward with her. In the moment before Boudreaux's bullet tore through her hair and skin and bone and brain, Eric was formulating an argument that would bring her back to reason.

Though he'd seen people shot, Eric had never been close enough to feel the spray, warm flecks on his frozen cheeks. It wasn't real. Couldn't be real.

His last thought before waking up in this rolling coffin?

Maybe I can still save her.

Eric's eyelids flutter open when the car begins to slow. Another stop. The roads have been too rough to be Provincial Highway 18—not that it kept the driver from hauling ass—but the precipitation was lighter, which meant they'd been heading north. He prepares for the car to start moving again, but the car rocks forward and stops.

Park.

The trunk pops open, and though storm clouds are blocking what little light has made it over the horizon, his eyes are barely adjusted when the driver's face comes into view.

"What the hell are you doing here?"

Eric was prepared to see Gates, thinking he'd loaded Eric into the trunk of Rita's car after escaping the firefight. Boudreaux wouldn't feel the need to cuff Eric, even if their goals no longer aligned. The INSTA team would've put him down, and Lori deferred when given the chance.

The other logical option was an unsub. The plane that landed just after Lori and Boudreaux had been carrying Gates. But perhaps he'd brought someone unknown to everyone but him. Having an ace up both sleeves would fit Gates's MO.

Hell, the way this day was going, Eric had even considered one of his officers turning on him.

But never Robert Moore.

"You always had more heart than brains," Moore says. "Roll over."

"Screw you." Eric tries spitting at Moore, but his mouth is dry and the spittle barely clears the trunk.

Knowing he won't live to see the world burn gives Eric some comfort. But that doesn't mean he has to make it easy on the sonofabitch.

"If you're going to shoot me, you'll have to look me in the eyes."

Moore's hand shifts, and Eric starts the Lord's Prayer. He's on *hallowed* when it hits him—Moore's holding a blade, not a pistol.

"I just want to take off the cuffs so we can talk."

Eric doesn't want to comply. Moore's just as deadly with a knife, and turning that metaphor into reality is his brand of gallows humor. But even if Moore's plan is to cut Eric loose, part of him would rather die in this truck than take orders from this traitorous piece of shit.

Then again, if he can get his hands free, maybe Eric can exact some personal revenge before his nightmare comes to fruition, so he rolls over and grits his teeth. When Moore cuts the plastic, Eric takes a moment to let his muscles relax. He flexes both hands twice. Rolls his shoulder. Breathes deeply.

But he doesn't roll over.

"All right," Moore says. "Let's go."

As Moore reaches for him, Eric flexes his right arm and swings the elbow back. The timing isn't perfect, but it connects solidly enough that Moore's out of the frame when Eric rolls over. Eric bails out and lands on top of Moore.

That's where his plan falls apart.

Eric was a skilled operations officer and always passed the required physical and combat training with no issue. Moore, on the other hand, is an ex-Marine who contracted with Ground Branch in the Special Activities Center. Eric eventually talked Moore into applying for a paramilitary operations officer opening. Becoming a PMOO meant Moore could lead GB but also climb the company ladder with Eric.

But Moore always preferred wartime ops and never lost his edge.

In fighting Moore, Eric had hoped to get lucky, maybe land within reach of the knife or knock the wind out of Moore. But, just like every other time Eric had felt froggy, Moore spends about thirty seconds wrestling with him before ending the fight with a rear-naked choke.

"You done?"

***

"LET ME get this straight." Eric's in the passenger seat, where he sat and looked for weapons as Moore drove like hell and explained his version of the last week. "You were on the flight that landed right after Lori and Boudreaux?"

"We were supposed to be a few hours behind, but our pilot wanted to make sure we missed the storm. I was pissed we were so close, though. I froze my balls off for twenty minutes waiting for my local team to pick me up and get to your offices without raising suspicion."

Eric had made so many assumptions over the last nine hours. For instance, he'd been positive Gates was in that plane. It made infinitely more sense than the truth: Gates had already been nearby, messaging him from a hotel room. Or the house Eric and Rita used to share before he moved out to give her space. The thought made him equal parts furious and ill, though some of that is from the massive headache.

"And you didn't know Gates would show up?"

"You think he'd've made it in the building? We were caught too off-guard and too far away to intercept him. Annie was still in her case, so we couldn't neutralize him, either."

Eric glances in the backseat to check again. Yes, the long gun is still in its case. More interesting are the two pieces of technology. Directly behind Moore sits a new laptop, its screen open and buzzing with lines of code and scrolling numbers. The other looks more like the first computer developed in Bill or Steve's garage, but the screen's missing and the keyboard's not quite right. The power cable is also wrong and looks more like the thick coax cable.

Neither will work as a weapon. The Ka-Bar and at least one handgun are somewhere on Moore's person, but wrestling them away would be futile. At this point, Eric's only move is lunging at the wheel when Moore's defense is soft.

So Eric keeps him talking.

"And Boudreaux didn't alert us to the tail because he knew your team would be back there."

"Bingo."

Moore had already told Eric about climbing on top of a nearby storage tank and watching the meet through Annie Oakley's scope.

"Why didn't you just take us out? You had clean shots."

But Eric does understand. His objective wasn't just stopping Gates. It was stealing the bomb for himself and the Federalists. Reynolds and his team would've fought Moore just as hard as Gates if he'd started shooting.

"Young was supposed to tell her ex we were coming to secure the payload, but we hadn't accounted for the blonde woman. Then Boudreaux screwed the pooch by starting a firefight." Moore glances at the car's nav. "My team said the truck's still driving north on the eighteen, just outside of Ralston."

"Why aren't you with them?"

Moore must know he won't get any information from Eric. Their history is too long and strained for building new rapport, and enhanced interrogation would be too emotional to be effective.

"Because you're no longer an enemy combatant. You're an asset."

Good. Keep thinking that.

"When I saw the blonde was aiming for you and not Reynolds, something didn't add up," Moore says.

"Her name's Rita. We have a rocky history."

"Oh I could see that, even from up there. But you didn't see Gates give her the kill sign"—Moore takes his right hand off the wheel and slashes it across his throat—"just before you ran toward her."

Whatever happens next. That's what Rita said just before Boudreaux's bullet tore through her face. Had she and Gates planned to kill him all along?

"That's when I knew you didn't have the full picture. I told my guys to follow the truck while I retrieved you. I'm glad you're not eating your way through retirement like Gates."

"Where is Gates?"

"Don't know. He took off in your dually. Boudreaux and Lori chased him in the Escalade, but my team hasn't seen either vehicle."

Three missing. One dead. Another taken. How had a simple trade gone so wrong?

"You trusted Gates too much," Moore says.

All this time, and they're still in sync. Sometimes they'd jinx each other at work and catch shit from everyone else in the room. Then the ball-busting would stop and they'd get back to the business of keeping America safe. He and Moore were a hell of a team once.

Stop it.

"And you're capable of offering an objective opinion on Randall Gates?" Eric asks.

Moore's smirk is infuriating. "You always said you're better at reading people, but I've known Gates was a psychopath since Venezuela."

Eric clenches his jaw. "That wasn't his fault."

It was mine.

Two months into Gates's three-month timeout, counterterrorism obtained human and image intelligence suggesting Russia had shipped a cache of nuclear warheads and ICBMs to Venezuela, a doomsday scenario on par with the Cuban Missile Crisis and whatever history books call this cluster.

Gates charged Eric, who was still an acting Deputy COS, with confirming CTC's intel. The weapon was being stored at a secret military installation south of the Orinoco River in the state of Delta Amacuro. Satellite images confirmed an encampment there, so Eric brought in a team from GB for recon.

As they prepared for the op, Eric and Moore each recognized a fellow Texan. By the end of the first night over arepas and rum, they'd calculated the odds of having tackled each other on the gridiron at 100 percent. Eric played quarterback and corner for Longview and Moore was a wideout and strong safety for Marshall.

The next morning, Gates got word that the HUMINT had been right about the location of the military camp but wrong about the shipment. Russia used the shipment disinformation to identify an asset, who was presumed dead.

Gates should've sent GB home. But the encampment was new information and the acting COS decided it was worth the risk despite knowing the intel was tainted. They're already here, he said. And they're soldiers. They can handle it.

His presence in Caracas was the result of a bureaucratic pissing contest, but Eric had been COS for nearly a year and knew he could get the intel another way. There was no reason to risk it.

But Eric wasn't COS. And even if they reverted to their previous positions, Gates was still his boss. What was Eric supposed to do? Go to Gates's immediate superior? The DDO? Sure, he demurred, but jellyfish show more spine than Eric did when he sent Moore and five other GB operators into the Venezuelan jungle.

Two survived.

Gates called them and the rest heroes while explaining his actions. In private, he told Eric they were contractors, not Agency officers, and therefore expendable pawns for those charged with protecting America and her democracy.

Eric believed him, and for years he and Gates did that.

Didn't we?

"And Even if you put Venezuela on Gates," Eric says, "That was a tactical mistake. An op gone sideways. That doesn't make him a psychopath. It's not like he sent you to go butcher women and children."

Moore shuts his eyes for so long Eric nearly reaches for the wheel. They're red when his lids lift, and Eric realizes the second toughest SOB he's ever met is holding back tears.

"You really can't see it, can you?"

Can't see what?

Then it clicks. The New Year's Eve attacks.

No. For the love of God, please, no. Eric chokes on his tongue. His fingers tingle. When his heart rate increases past 150 beats per minute, Eric thinks he's having a heart attack. But he tries polygraph countermeasures and calms down in less than a minute.

"Why?" It's all Eric can manage, and even that barely slips through his sand-dry throat.

"I'm sure you know China's been revising its nuclear strategy since Taiwan, focusing on our new centers of power over here."

Eric nods, his breathing still irregular.

"Well, I got intel last week that they'd recalibrated their ICBMs and upped the readiness level. I'm sure Gates did, too."

Except for MANIFEST, Gates monitored all the nuclear activity overseas and updated Eric with the intel he needed to know—like, say, if their largest geopolitical adversary had its nuclear arsenal aimed at them with its index finger curled around the trigger.

"When Boudreaux called—on my encrypted line, and I'm still trying to figure out how that happened—he said the timetable had moved Destiny's timetable up. You were still slow-playing the asset, so Gates found a more direct way to use her. Put her in danger and keep her from making contact, knowing you were tracking her and would call Boudreaux for an extraction. If you hadn't thought of bringing her here for the exchange, he'd've told you to."

Played like a fiddle.

"In addition to the shooter in New Orleans," Moore continues, "Gates had someone else there, waiting to kidnap her. But thanks to Boudreaux's warning, we took him out and my team secured her. They weren't supposed to ditch the watch, but I suppose that's not important now."

The weight of it all seems to stop Moore there.

"MANIFEST," Eric says, only a bit shaky now that the panic attack has mostly passed. "We called the operation MANIFEST, not Destiny. And Boudreaux has buddies everywhere, including guys who still work at the NSA."

What Moore said makes sense, but there are a few lingering, horrifying questions. "Why stage shootings in so many cities? Why all that carnage just to secure one asset?"

"Boudreaux's guy didn't say anything about that. In fact, he didn't know there'd be a shooting in New Orleans. He just knew she'd be in danger and taken. My guess? Gates figured you'd question everything if he tried to make it look like a random kidnapping or mugging or whatever. But if she were just caught up in a massive international terrorist plot, you'd be too focused on her safety to sniff out his plan."

Would Gates really kill hundreds of innocent people—once and future Americans, he'd hoped—just *in case* Eric was smart enough to stop his grotesque plan?

And what about the gash in Lori's leg? "The guy shot her, though. What if she'd died?"

"Look, I don't know everything. She probably wasn't supposed to get shot, but she was one of only a few survivors in New Orleans."

Eric's not sure he buys that. Especially when he considers the source.

"I still don't understand where you fit into this. Why would Boudreaux, who's always been more my friend than yours, cash in a chit with his NSA contacts to call your backstabbing ass instead of warning me?"

Moore pauses, probably so he can come up with a convincing lie.

"Boudreaux didn't know how deep into this you were," he says. "Apparently the whistleblower was told you'd have to be manipulated into getting Young here because you're soft when it comes to your assets. But as far as Boudreaux knew, you knew the plan was to detonate the bomb."

How could Boudreaux think I'm capable of that?

"But Boudreaux knew I wasn't part of it," Moore continues. "His source said Gates and that fruitcake Novak think only *they* can restore America's military power in time to stop worldwide nuclear war, but they need a show of strength to prove it. They think detonating the nuke will convince Anderson, Cole, and the Western governors to take control of the nuclear stockpiles in their countries, forcing Ramirez and the other leaders to concede. If nothing else, Boudreaux figured I'd want to keep Anderson in power."

Everything fits together so far, which Eric hates to admit. But this is all thirdhand information from an expert liar with almost no moral code.

"Did Boudreaux name his source?"

"Yeah. Guy by the name of Daniels. Said they served in the Army together. And apparently Daniels was given the plan by his boss, Robb something. I guess he wanted to recruit this Daniels to be in the new regime, but told him not to tell Novak. Boudreaux said Daniels got as many details as possible to pass on before telling Robb and Novak to go screw themselves."

Lori's mentioned Jeremiah's bosses, Greg Daniels and the head honcho, Logan Robb. So, it's all true. Eric is partially responsible for the hundreds who were already dead. He's also to blame for the countless more who will be vaporized or burned or die slowly from radiation poisoning and famine.

Unless I can stop it.

"We can still salvage the op," Moore says.

"Who's we? You and Annie Oakley back there?"

"Dammit Eric." He's screaming, which is deafening in the confines of the sporty sedan. "You don't want that bomb to go off and neither do I, so we need to put our shit aside and work together."

Moore's right. But how's Eric supposed to trust him again? "And what happens after? We go back to our corners? Go back to playing spy versus spy because it's so much freaking fun?"

"Let's hope we get to cross that bridge."

"Fine." Eric will have to work with him—at least until an alternative opportunity presents itself. "So what's your plan?"

As Moore purses his lips and puffs out his cheeks, the reality sinks in.

"Well?" Eric shouts. "What were you going to do after getting control of the truck?"

"I don't know, all right." He's matching Eric's volume. "That's why I grabbed you. You were always better at strategy. You plan, I execute."

He's right. But still. "Don't you oversee intelligence for a whole country now?"

He grips the steering wheel tighter. "I delegate."

Moore hates office work. He would've stayed in GB another ten years if not for his family. After his first daughter was born, Moore told Eric he was thinking of going to work for a paramilitary contractor so he could make bank while still in his prime.

But Eric knew Moore's safety would be his family's priority, so he promised a desk job and every promotion he could swing.

Then Eric left, leaving Moore to deal with Gates and the weakening Ramirez administration.

"Why did you do it?" Eric asks. "I know your career in the Agency wasn't going anywhere, but why would you betray everything we stood for. Everything we fought for."

Saying the question out loud is at once painful and joyous, a release years in the making. Eric has fantasized about the day he would confront Moore. Put him in his place. Shame him. Kill him.

"It's where I wanted to raise my children."

Eric has no comeback. In all the times Eric has rehearsed this conversation, Moore never gave that answer. So he sits, venom meant for Moore now pooling in his own mouth, poisoning his own blood.

All this time, it had nothing to do with the Agency or the government. He doesn't believe the Federalists have the best form of democracy. Doesn't believe in states' rights. Doesn't believe in a decentralized government or unfettered capitalism or the abolishment of welfare.

Moore doesn't believe in anything.

He's not a traitor.

"You're a coward."

"That's not how I see it," Moore says, a smooth lawyer making his case to the jury. "The secessions were going to happen whether I wanted them to or not, and I never blamed anyone involved in the process. Our situation was toxic, and sometimes leaving's necessary because staying together is worse. So I picked the place me and mine would be happiest. I couldn't go work with you because I knew what Gates was capable of. I thought about moving us back to Texas, but Levi Cole is worse in his own way. So when Anderson approached me at one of the last secession summits, I accepted his offer."

It all sounds nice. But there's a dark truth to his speech. "And what about those Urban Zones in your cities? How do you live with shit like that?"

"How were you planning to live with stealing a nuclear weapon and overthrowing the governments of eight sovereign nations?"

Eric's indignation is righteous, but he realizes Moore just wants to get through this life with a happy, healthy family. They may never agree about a lot of things. Maybe that's Moore's point.

For now, Eric has little choice but to focus on the one issue they do agree on.

And he has an idea.

"Would Anderson help us get control of the bomb?" Eric asks.

"Maybe. I've made him aware of the situation in China. Right now he thinks I'm still in Shreveport briefing the officers at Barksdale. When Boudreaux called and said your asset was in New Orleans, I told Anderson it would be better if I was on-site."

Smart. Not only did that get Moore close to Lori, but putting Barksdale on high alert is a prudent move. It's one of only two old Air Force bases with both munitions storage facilities and B-52 Stratofortress bombers. The other is in North Dakota, where the governor won't know anything's wrong until after a first strike.

Eric is about to suggest Moore contact his boss when the satphone receives an incoming call from Moore's team trailing the semi. It's short, and all Eric hears is *copy that* twice.

"The truck just turned east on Highway 60," Moore says. "They're heading for a town called paw-hooskah."

Eric's not intimately familiar with the highways north of Cushing, but they can't be more than fifteen minutes from that turn toward Pawhuska.

But where are they going? The town is surrounded by a million and a half acres of Osage Reservation, much of it uninhabited. There are small towns to the south and east, but virtually nothing but plains to the north until you reach The Frontier.

"They also said an Escalade is behind them and coming up fast."

33
JEREMIAH

Oklahoma Highway 60,
17 miles west of Pawhuska, Northeast Province
Republic of Oklahoma

Either someone is tailing them, or some poor sucker chose the worst possible morning to travel through northwestern Oklahoma.

Either way, the black car is stopping.

"This should do it," Jeremiah says from the passenger seat.

Dom hits the jake brake. The obnoxiously loud sound is followed by furious cursing in Spanish and English from the overhead.

"You were supposed to warn us, dick," Mac calls down, but it's hard to hear over their delirious laughter.

It's all they can do now. They've already said their goodbyes. Zeus and Dom used up one of the burners talking to their wives, though Dom had to finish his conversation using Mac's. Both will survive, but they wanted to do it just in case.

When she got the phone back, Mac immediately went to work, determining exactly where they should park and wait.

Oklahoma's Internet is open enough to access one of the more reputable sites that map blast and fallout scenarios. Novak wouldn't tell Jeremiah what they were transporting, but one of the haggard workers said they were loading a B83, the baddest gravity bomb they have. Though the yield can be set lower, Mac calculated using the max of 1.2 megatons. The wind took a bit more guesswork, but the latest radar indicated gusts up to 50 mph and the storm was moving northeast at almost exactly 45 degrees.

The website spit out a model with a blast radius that ends a mile or so east of where Dom has stopped across both lanes of Highway 60. They can't help who drives into ground zero from the east, but they can help this black sedan set up a perimeter and save a few lives.

It's a quarter till nine and their optimal spot is ten miles down the road, so they'll have to make it quick.

Jeremiah, Zeus, and Dom jump down and jog around the tractor. Mac stays in the cab and will move behind the wheel. There's no reason for the whole team to die, and those two have families. Jeremiah didn't want to burden them with breaking this awful news to whoever's in the car. He gave Mac the choice, and she said she'd rather wait behind the wheel in case the car's occupants come out shooting. If all goes smooth, Jeremiah will relieve her in less than two minutes and be at the optimal detonation zone with at least one to spare.

The sedan is parked about thirty yards away but nobody's gotten out, so he gives the universal *come on out* arm swing. When that doesn't work, he tells the boys to stay back and alert. As he jogs toward the car. He clocks a black SUV parked on the shoulder in the distance.

He gets within twenty feet before the driver exits. He's wearing tac gear, as is the passenger and another man behind him.

"I don't know who you're with or how much you know," Jeremiah says, "but there's a nuclear bomb in that truck and it's set to go off at 0900."

The driver's cheeks redden below disappearing irises. "That's only fifteen mikes from now."

"Exactly." Jeremiah points a thumb over his shoulder. "These two are going to help you set up a roadblock. They can handle the Suburban parked behind you and will walk back to you, but y'all need to drive to the intersection with Highway 18. Stop anyone going north or east. All traffic needs to go south or west because it's against the wind."

"Are you sure? I mean, how do you know—"

"Look, if I'm wrong and you stay, we have a fourteen-minute lead on you. If I'm right and you follow us, you're dead too."

"Yeah." He looks at a spot between them. "Yeah. Okay."

Jeremiah spins, then jogs toward the truck, passing Dom and Zeus. He's halfway there when the driver calls after him. The man is waving wildly at the SUV on the shoulder.

"What the hell are you—"

"Your wife's in there," he says.

As it gets closer, Jeremiah recognizes the Escalade. He sprints toward the car, where the boys have stopped, unsure what to do.

"How did you …" Jeremiah stammers. "I mean, nobody else—"

"We were there. We saw what happened."

Jeremiah wants details, but there's no time. The SUV screeches to a halt and Lori hops down, Boudreaux a step behind her. Jeremiah and Lori embrace with a ferocity he's never felt. Will never feel again.

He's lost in it until he hears the rig's engine. Time's up, and Mac's threatening to leave on her own. He releases Lori and extends his hand to Boudreaux.

"Take care of her."

He nods toward the rig. "You too."

Jeremiah turns and jogs toward the truck, which is revving and starting to pick up speed. He does the same and veers wide until he can see Mac's face in the sideview mirror.

She makes eye contact.

Then shifts into a higher gear.

She can't be serious. Jeremiah ducks his head and hopes for the adrenaline of a mother lifting a car off her kid. He gets it and is level with Mac's door in about ten seconds. He can't sustain this speed for long, though, so he jumps and grabs the mirror.

"Stop," he yells through the window. When she doesn't, he tries pulling rank. "That's an order."

She turns to face him but doesn't say anything, so he yanks the doorhandle.

Locked.

They're going at least twenty at this point and if she doesn't stop he'll have a choice—break the glass with his SIG or bail and watch her commit suicide in his stead.

The staring contest lasts a few seconds before Mac jerks her head around and downshifts. She doesn't roll down the window until the truck has stopped.

"Get down from there," he screams. "And I mean right the fuck now."

"The guys need you. Plus you're sober and have an ex-wife you love. I'm just—"

"We don't have time for this. I have to get this rig going or they'll die, too."

"Well I'm not leaving this seat," she says. "You can shoot me or get in the passenger side. Your choice."

Jeremiah reaches for the inside door handle. He's confident he can outmuscle her until his back hits the pavement.

"Don't do this," he screams in anger and passion and disbelief at the fucked-up situation they're in. "I can't watch you kill yourself. I just can't."

Mac leans out the window, the corners of her mouth pulled lower than he's ever seen. "Well neither can I," she screams back. "So get in here already."

The engine revs again before he can get to his feet, and as Jeremiah runs to his death, he smiles. Even in their last few minutes together, Mac won't let him treat her like anything but the badass she is.

But after slamming his door and catching his breath, reality sets in. There are no more missions. No transports. No sparring sessions. No hundred-dollar bets on the range.

Just eight more minutes by her side.

"I'm glad you got to see her," Mac says.

"Yeah," he says, realizing he was, too. Things were bad between him and Lori at one point. Terrible, actually. But lately they could be around each other and talk like old friends and lovers without opening the bottle of poison that killed their marriage.

"Do you regret divorcing her?"

Why's she asking that now? Jeremiah wasn't prepared for deep conversation. He'd planned on singing *It's the End of the World as We Know It,* then cracking jokes about his age and her terrible taste in music. Anything to avoid discussing the fact they were about to die while unleashing the full power of humankind's worst creation.

Or that other thing. The way he saw it, there was no use discussing something they'd never get to act on.

"I don't know," he says. "Never really thought about it like that."

"Don't do that," Mac snaps. "Our atoms will literally split apart and disappear into the ether in seven minutes." She throws the rig into high gear. "That's how long we have to make up for seven years of not talking about it."

She doesn't elaborate, but Jeremiah knows what *it* is. The whole team knows. Lori knows.

Hell, even Boudreaux seemed to know.

"Well?" she prods. "Do you wish you hadn't left her?"

"No," he says. "Our marriage was one of the best things that ever happened to me. But so was our divorce."

Mac's next breath is sharp on the inhale, relaxed on the exhale. "So you still hate her."

"No." He doesn't feel like elaborating, but the calm that flooded Mac's face a moment ago fades instantly. "I never stopped loving her. I stopped liking her, yes, but our divorce was never about hate. Our situation was toxic, and sometimes leaving's necessary because staying together is worse."

Mac nods, seems to accept his answer. "So you love her, but you're not *in* love with her."

"No, Shaye." She turns and their eyes meet. Hers are wet, and his are filling. "I'm not in love with her."

Five more minutes.

* * *

"WE WON'T make it in time to stop for a real goodbye," she says.

"And who's fault is that?"

Mac snortgiggles and wipes away wet streaks with the back of her hand. Rather than vomiting their feelings and living the rest of their lives in emotional agony, she and Jeremiah chose to sing the song and make the jokes, to keep their shit together and make one last on-time delivery.

But now they're sixty seconds away from reaching their optimal detonation point going 88 mph, just like that old time-travel movie.

Jeremiah scoots over to her, intertwines the fingers of his left hand with her right.

Then his chest starts pounding. Jeremiah would ordinarily rely on the gesture to communicate the words. It's how their relationship works. It's what they do.

But as their final minute ticks away, he knows that won't cut it.

Just say it. "So, uh, do *you* regret anything?"

Pussy.

"I regret a lot of things." She squeezes his hand. "But the answer to your question, Jeremiah, is yes."

Twenty seconds. He can't catch his breath. *You literally have nothing to lose.* "Shaye, I ..."

She turns to him, eyes brimming with hope and tears.

"I just wanted to say thank you," he says.

Asshole.

"Okay." She takes a ragged breath and closes her eyes. This time she doesn't wipe away the tears, just nods and grabs the wheel with both hands, elbows locked. "Okay."

Ten seconds.

"No. I mean ... What I meant to say is ... Shaye, I—"

Mac leans over and pulls his face to hers, fingers digging into his scalp. The kiss starts rough, frenetic. But then they melt into each other, salt flowing onto each other's lips, heartbeats falling into rhythm, skin thrumming until they're not two but one, exploding together into the pure, unbridled energy that has burned through everything in existence, now and forever.

34
LORI

Intersection of Oklahoma Highway 60 and Provincial Highway 18, Northeast Province
Republic of Oklahoma

Lori's standing with Boudreaux beside the Escalade, which is parked in the eastbound lane of Highway 60 where it crosses the 18. Both of her arms wrapped around his left, face turned west and half buried in his coat sleeve. She shivers, cold and anticipating the explosion while every scream she's ever heard plays on a loop.

When Boudreaux shifts, she knows the sound and the heat are coming. She hyperventilates for a moment, then holds her breath.

"I'm sorry," he says.

She exhales and turns her face. But when there's nothing but gray on the horizon and a wintry mix in the air, she looks up at Boudreaux.

"Maybe my watch is off."

Lori lets ten more seconds pass before allowing for a sliver of hope. She finds the moment just before Gates raised his pistol. *I can't believe you didn't think I had a contingency. Novak can execute MANIFEST from where he is. You've got till nine. Then you're screwed.*

"He never said the bomb was going off at nine." The words have little separation as she blurts them out. "Gates said he had a contingency. We assumed Novak could detonate it remotely, but what if he can't? What if the contingency is something else?"

By now a minute has passed and Lori's convinced. She lets go of Boudreaux's arm and pulls out the phone.

He answers on the third ring. "Your intel was off."

Lori laughs despite herself. He's okay. She knew the bomb hadn't detonated, but Lori had imagined Jeremiah offing himself beforehand or having a heart attack as the moment approached.

"Hey," he says, "will you send someone to help us? We ran off the road and blew a tire."

She agrees to send Ramirez and Hansen in the car, leaving the Escalade for her, Boudreaux, and the three other men who say they're with Moore—splitting the group in case the detonation has only been delayed seemed pragmatic, if macabre.

"What's the plan after you get rolling again?"

"I have an idea, but I need to run it past my guys first. I'll call back when it's solid."

Lori ends the call and relays the information to Boudreaux, who jogs south across the highway toward Jeremiah's team. Moore's men leave their post to the west to meet them. Lori's fine where she is, content watching Boudreaux give out orders and have the others hop-to.

Her perspective allows Lori to see the silver sedan first.

She knows who's in the car. The guys in the black tactical gear explained the situation, though Lori can't imagine Fowler being of any use to them. He's a creepy liar who uses people. Does he want to watch the world burn? Maybe not. But if it does, it'll be his fault. Moore thinks he can keep Fowler in check, which is bullshit.

Lori hopes Boudreaux's on the same page as she limps toward him. The adrenaline is gone, and she'll need some Vicodin or Oxy soon. If he doesn't have any more, the new guys might.

But that'll have to wait. Moore and Fowler are opening their doors, and they don't look relieved by the absence of a mushroom cloud on the horizon.

"We've got a problem," Moore says.

"What?" asks one of Moore's men, a younger guy with a neck as thick as Lori's waist and the same West Texas accent.

"It's bad, Soddie. He has a B-52 in the air loaded with LRSO cruise missiles."

"Sweet Jesus," says Soddie, who she now suspects is also from the Amarillo area based on his nickname. "Who does?"

35
ERIC

Eric hasn't had time to process it all yet. At the roadblock, Moore's mercs had relayed the awful news. Even though Boudreaux had killed Rita and Gates, the bomb was set to go off in less than ten minutes.

Then, when they didn't see a flash or cloud at one after, he and Moore cheered. They high-fived and yelled so loud they almost didn't hear Moore's phone ring. Not the satphone, but his government-issued cell whose screen filled with the name PRESIDENT ACE ANDERSON and a Birmingham phone number.

Moore was on the phone as they approached the roadblock. Though Eric only heard one side of the conversation, he got the gist. He hung up as they parked and said he'd explain it to everyone at once.

"Alan Novak," Moore tells the thick kid, one of three former Branch guys he hired for the op. "It just left Barksdale en route to Rick Husband in Amarillo."

The tallest GB steps forward. "Who's Rick Husband?"

Lori beats Moore to the answer. "It's not a who," she says. "It's the airport. They named it after an astronaut who died in a shuttle crash."

Boudreaux shakes his head. "That can't be right. Novak's followers are batshit, but there's no way he talked a crew into loading nuclear cruise missiles onto a B-52 and got landing clearance from a civilian airport."

"You're right," Moore says. "The Federalist and Republican presidents did."

"Good God," the third of Moore's men says. "Anderson and Cole are in on this?"

Moore shakes his head. "I don't think so. Everyone here knows China was already a short hair away from pressing the button, right?"

A round of nods.

"Well, I provided that info to President Anderson last week. And as you probably know, he and President Cole go way back."

Eric's a little fuzzy on the details. "He was on Anderson's staff once, right?"

Moore nods. "From his second term in the House until he left to run for governor of Texas. So when President Anderson found out about the threat from China—"

"He shared the intel with his old friend in Fort Worth," Boudreaux says.

"Bingo," Moore says. "And after the mass shootings this morning, Cole wants to make sure he can strike back at China, so he consults his resident nuclear experts in Amarillo."

Novak and Robb.

"President Anderson just told me that Cole asked to borrow a plane with cruise missiles that's also capable of utilizing The Republic's cache of B83s," Moore continues. "It took off at nine."

"That's the contingency plan," Lori says, excited she solved the puzzle despite its implications. "Gates didn't want to work with any of the governments. But since we stopped him from detonating his own bomb, he has to."

Eric starts to panic. "If the plane's already airborne, he can nuke Cushing any minute now."

"I don't think that's the target anymore," Moore says.

"Why?"

"When all they had was a gravity bomb and no plane, Cushing was a great target," Moore says. "It was easily accessible and has major global economic implications. But now they have a plane and more than a dozen Long Range Standoff cruise missiles. Wall Street's in play. Pennsylvania and San Francisco are in play. Hell, Novak could take out Durango just for fun."

Everyone's silent for a few excruciating moments until Eric finally says it. "We can't stop him, can we?"

36
JEREMIAH

Oklahoma Highway 60,
7 miles west of Pawhuska, Northeast Province
Republic of Oklahoma

He's still holding Mac's hand as the car pulls into view. They were scared shitless when the front driver's-side tire popped, thinking it was the beginning of their end despite knowing they'd get no warning. They celebrated being alive by kissing and grabbing and licking and gasping, stopping for a few minutes when Mac's pocket started buzzing, then resuming until it was time to get the spare into position. Jeremiah pushed her against the door for a few more private moments before hearing the car carrying Zeus and Dom.

He releases her hand and walks to meet the car as it stops. "I've never been so happy to see someone so ugly," he tells Dom as he exits the passenger side.

"What happened?" he asks, all business.

Shit. Jeremiah hadn't come up with an explanation for running off the road. "Ask the driver."

He expected Mac to be smooth and shit-talk her way into a laugh. Instead, her eyes widen as she stammers something about a deer running in front of them. Zeus shuts his door and seems to accept the answer.

Dom doesn't. "Bambi was going to die anyway."

"Look guys," Jeremiah says. "We thought we were smoked just now, so our nerves are a little shot. We just need y'all to do this for us, okay?"

Zeus gives a halfhearted *Roger*. Dom watches Mac as she shuffles toward the back of the trailer.

"Why's your shirt untucked in the back?"

Mac lowers her head and jogs out of sight. Jeremiah wants to follow her. To comfort her. He also knows it'll make things worse. Zeus and Dom gave them shit because they knew nothing is going on. He wasn't giving her special treatment, which meant they didn't have to. But now the team's ecosystem has been disrupted, and to Dom and Zeus, it's now two kids against a united Mom and Dad rather than three against a commander.

Jeremiah's only move is to let Mac disappear for a few minutes while he explores the possibility of their next move.

"Your family's from Colorado, right?" Jeremiah asks Dom as he lifts the new tire into place.

"Nosir."

Jeremiah doesn't understand. He knows they are. In fact, he was banking on his having at least one uncle or cousin still living in La Plata County.

"Most of my relatives currently reside in the great and noble Free State of Southwestern Colorado," Dom deadpans. "That is very different from the Colorado Territory, which is beholden to the overlords who established the confederation of America's Western Territories." He looks up from the tire, smiling like a toddler attempting his first joke. "Citizens of Southwestern Colorado are the only truly free people on this continent, so to say they're from Colorado is like saying someone from The Republic lives in The South."

Jeremiah didn't think he'd laugh so soon after his … should he call it a near-death experience? The nuke was never armed, so the threat was only perceived, not real. Either way, the release is incredible, second only to the one Mac provided less than fifteen minutes earlier. "Near Durango, right?"

"My cousins live in the foothills near there. Took over the compound from my crazy uncle Edwin after he became sheriff. I've told you about him, right?"

"The one who built that underground bunker big enough to drive a Mack truck into."

Dom nods, then stops tightening the lugnuts. Zeus gives him shit for being a dumb oaf, but Dom's one of the sharpest tools at Jeremiah's disposal. "And you want to know if a Peterbilt will fit, too?"

Jeremiah doesn't get to confirm Dom's theory because Zeus comes strolling over in a mouthy mood. "Damn, you're still not done? Everything else is put up but the four-way."

"It's not even a four-way, moron," Dom says. "You ever going to learn English?"

"You wanna go, motherfucker?"

Dom stands with the torque wrench and Zeus reaches for his knife.

"All right assholes, that's enough," Jeremiah yells. "What the hell's gotten into you two?"

He knows the answer, but so do they, and it has nothing to do with them. Zeus walks to Dom and holds out his hand. "Here, I'll finish up. My bad."

Dom flips the wrench and hands it to Zeus handle-first. "Me too."

Jeremiah puts his arm on Dom's shoulder—an awkward feat considering the height difference—and walks with him. "So, if we were to drive to the border, do you think they'd let us in and store the rig in your uncle's bunker?"

"Maybe. Uncle Edwin's the county sheriff, but we'd have to convince the border militia of my bona fides."

"Can we call and give him a head's up?"

Dom sucks in through his teeth. "They're not big on technology anymore. Especially him. It's mostly CB and HAM radios, so it's best if we wait to use that when we get close. But they'll be happy we can make them a nuclear state. Especially since Colorado Territory has what's left of NORAD."

"Sounds like a plan."

They round the trailer's corner to find Mac cursing and pounding on her vape pen. Jeremiah reaches into Dom's chest pocket and pulls out one of the cigars and a butane lighter.

"What the hell?" Dom protests.

"You can have mine," Jeremiah says before tossing the pilfered contraband to Mac. "Trade you for the phone."

She fishes out the burner and underhands it to Jeremiah, but Dom intercepts it. Jeremiah looks up to Dom, who stares, defiant.

"Don't make me say it, Dom. You know it makes me feel like a d-bag."

Dom doesn't move, and Jeremiah refuses to pull rank and order him to drop the phone. Jeremiah knows it would take him and Mac together to make Dom comply if he goes there.

It doesn't come to that, though. Dom smirks and tosses the phone onto the ground between them and Mac. Jeremiah's pissed and wants to knee him in the balls, but decides instead to pick up the phone and walk to Mac as she turns to block the wind and light up. He pulls up the contact card for his own name and taps the green receiver, his hands shaking with anger at the slow-moving insurrection and excitement at being near her.

"Lori, it's me."

Silence.

"I'm calling with the plan we talked about," he says, wondering why he'd have to remind her.

"Yeah. Right."

"One of my guys has contacts in Southwestern Colorado. He has a deep drive-in bunker. It would mitigate a detonation, at least to some degree, and at the very least it'll provide some security from Novak and his crazies."

Lori's sigh comes through the phone's cheap speaker as static. "That's a great plan," she says. "I just wish yours was the only nuke in play."

What the fuck did you just say? "Pardon?"

"Novak talked The South into giving him a bomber with some long-range nuclear missiles, or something like that. It's heading to Amarillo right now, where they're going to load up more bombs like the one in your truck."

Our father, who art in heaven … "What can we do?"

"We're working on it. For now, you and your team should—"

An electronic voice tells Jeremiah he's out of prepaid minutes. He pulls the phone away and reads a similar message on the screen. He heaves it across the highway, yelling like a shot-putter at the Olympics.

"What'd she say?" Mac asks, smoke leaking through her nostrils.

"Novak has a plane with nuclear missiles now."

Mac coughs. Dom turns and calls to Zeus. "Load up. We're going back to the plant."

"Dom," Jeremiah yells. "I'm this team's commander, dammit. You don't give the orders, you hear me son?"

Zeus rounds the corner, eyes wide. "What's going on, chief?"

"We've got an ass to kick back home," Dom says. "That's what."

"I wasn't talking to you, Shrek."

"Guys, enough," Jeremiah says. "Our mission hasn't changed. We have to secure the payload, which now means getting the rig to Southwestern Colorado. Dom's family has an underground bunker there strong enough to withstand a nuclear blast from the outside, which means it'll at least help if it blows up on the inside." He turns to Dom. "Right?"

The big man's nostrils are still flaring, but he nods. "Uncle Edwin says it's a thousand feet deep and reinforced with ten feet of concrete."

"Bullshit," Mac says. "You know how expensive that would be?"

"Cost like a hundred mill. Pretty much every rich asshole across the DS agreed to invest after the secessions. Didn't hurt that my cousin worked for Berkshire after stints with a few Fortune 500s." He turns to Zeus. "She's a genius. Runs in the family."

Zeus's face cracks and he slaps Dom on the ass. "No doubt, man. No doubt."

Mac laughs out her final puff of smoke before stubbing out the cigar on the trailer. "What about this Novak guy? What are we going to do about him?"

"I have a feeling Boudreaux and that team of contractors can handle him," Jeremiah says.

"You think so?" Mac asks. "Novak must be a major player if he's stirring up this much trouble."

"Hey," Zeus says, "who is this Kojak, anyway?"

The team laughs, and Jeremiah hopes the tension is gone. "Y'all know about those people that follow K, right?"

Snorts and cackles serve as a collective yes.

"Didn't the Martians tell them the United States have to reunify or they'll invade Earth?" Dom asks.

"Don't they also say The South is perfecting a virus that can turn their leaders into vampires, and the only way to stop them is killing them all pre-emptively?" Zeus asks.

Mac nods. "I can't believe they all listen to their Supreme Leader crackpot. What does he call himself? Captain something?"

"Corporal," Jeremiah says. "Corporal K."

"Right," Mac says. "So what does Novak have to do with them?"

The words are barely out of her mouth before Dom pieces it together. "Novak's K."

"To be more specific," Jeremiah says, "Alan Novak's a soldier who was discharged for having a mental breakdown. What they used to call a Section Eight. When he went on social media to air his grievances under the pseudonym Corporal K, hundreds of thousands of people started following him, including a lot of active military and police."

Jeremiah's brother, Jedediah, was one of them. He killed himself a few years later, after the country split apart.

"When they wanted corporate sponsorship for the streaming shows, a group of K's acolytes started a nonprofit," Jeremiah continues. "I forget the original name, but Novak came out as against the split, so it changed to the United Intracontinental Coalition. It was supposed to stand in opposition to the White Hats and other fringe groups, but it just became another one."

Jedediah's suicide note asked his wife to send hundreds of pages of scribblings to his *fellow UNIC brothers and sisters for inspiration in the war against civility*. If Lori's life hadn't hung in the balance, Jeremiah would've tried killing Novak as soon as he found out he was K.

While Jeremiah stews in rage, Mac begins laughing uncontrollably. "I'll bet you a hundred bucks Corporal K is really short for Corporal Klinger."

Jeremiah chuckles despite himself, but the boys look at them like they deserve a Section 8. "You've never even heard of M*A*S*H?" he asks.

Dom and Zeus don't even bother shaking their heads.

"Christ we're old," Mac says.

"Anyway," Jeremiah says, "Novak and his followers can't be taken lightly. They've organized a few times and killed at least a few thousand people since the secessions. So if the guy who's flying with those nukes is one, or if his commander is, that's the ballgame. But we can't worry about that right now. We need to refocus and get to Southwestern Colorado."

"I figure the best way right now is heading north into Kansas," Mac says.

Jeremiah nods. "That also means we can swing by the roadblock and borrow a satphone from Boudreaux or the others."

Mac starts walking to the cab and looks at Dom. "Your turn to drive."

"Sounds like you two have it all figured out," he says. "Sure you even want us to tag along? Or would we just be a couple of cock blocks."

Mac flips him the bird. "Blow me, Dom."

He looks at Jeremiah. "I'm not into sloppy seconds."

Jeremiah stares at Dom until he gives in and walks away.

It worked this time.

But Jeremiah needs to fix this.

37
LORI

Provincial Highway 18, 3 miles south of Farefax, Northeast Province Republic of Oklahoma

With Jeremiah's plan set, the only move for Lori and the rest was a retreat to Fowler's offices, where they had access to better communications equipment for monitoring the situation. An optimist might even give them a shot at preventing a nuclear holocaust.

When the phone cut off, she assumed Jeremiah's phone ran out of prepaid minutes. Lori hated leaving without a direct line. But he and his team were more than capable of handling themselves. Plus, the nuclear device in his truck was now the least of their worries.

So she and Boudreaux dumped the decomposing bodies out of the Escalade and loaded in with the taller of Moore's men, Road Runner, and Soddie—a small-town kid saddled with the shortened version of Amarillo's old Double-A mascot, the Sod Poodles. Meanwhile, Fowler joined Moore and the oldest of his men inside the silver car after putting a rifle and some odd computer equipment in the trunk.

Both vehicles were now southbound in a hurry. The B-52 would be flying over them soon. From there they'd look like a tiny convoy cutting through green and brown squares, racing toward an inevitable fate with the delusion of control.

"Hey, I need to pull over again," Boudreaux says.

"Again?" Lori asks.

"I told you, it's one of the side effects."

"Modafinil?" Road Runner asks from the back in his Appalachian dialect. "You have any more?"

"Not for you, bud."

Rather than make small talk with the new guys as Boudreaux sidles up to the front tire just outside his door, Lori focuses on the sideview mirror. Moore has pulled over about twenty yards behind them, and the oldest of his soldiers is taking the same opportunity.

But instead of pulling down his fly, he raises a pistol.

"Holy shit," she says and turns to the men in the backseat. "Your friend just pulled a gun on Moore."

They turn to look through the tinted back window.

"You sure?" Soddie says.

"Looks to me like he's just taking a piss," Road Runner says.

Idiots. Boudreaux is still holding himself, so she crawls over the center console and throws the Escalade in reverse, cutting it sharply until she's facing Fowler, Moore, and the car's taillights hauling ass in the other direction.

"Oh shit," the kids say in unison as though they share one brain.

Lori peels out for all the good it does because three seconds later she's slamming on the brakes as the back doors fly open. As they run north on the highway squeezing off rounds at the car, Lori runs to Fowler and Moore.

"What happened?" she asks, as though the answer wasn't obvious.

The guy wasn't really with Moore.

"He got out like he needed to go," Fowler says, "then pulled a gun on us, said something about a lighthouse, and told Moore all he wanted was the car. Sounded like a hell of a deal to me."

We are the lighthouse. It's the derivative slogan of that ridiculous UNIC cult of Novak's, developed as an answer to the other side's lunatics. Out of any ten people, four are insane now, the only difference being the letter of the alphabet they worship.

Though Fowler looks relieved, Moore's pissed. "Speak for yourself. Annie was in the trunk."

"Who?"

"His rifle," Fowler says. "But if it's between me and Ms. Oakley, I'll give up the keys every time. Besides, all that prick's getting is her, a fast car, and some old computer equipment."

Boudreaux pulls up behind her, a bit out of breath from the run. "What's that about old computer equipment?"

"Well, one of the laptops was new," Moore says. "It had a program running in the background. But the other looked like something out of a museum. Just a keyboard and some weird cables."

"And they were already in Clarke's car when you took it?"

Soddie and Road Runner come racing back before Moore can answer. They say one taillight is out and the back window is cracked, but the car's still heading north.

Boudreaux looks like he's about to get sick in the middle of the highway.

"Tell me exactly who that guy is and what he told you."

38
ERIC

The Branch guy's name is Grady Levine. Moore tells Boudreaux he gave them the lighthouse line and said he just wanted the car. Eric can't believe they're wasting time talking about something so irrelevant to the big picture.

"Guys, can't we solve this riveting carjacking case while we drive back to the office?"

Moore shrugs. Boudreaux ignores him and turns to Lori. "When we were assigning vehicles, did Levine ask to ride in the car?"

Lori shifts her gaze to the horizon and freezes, lifeless. Eric rushes to her, mind swirling with thoughts of standing seizures and strokes.

"Lori," he screams, grabbing her shoulders. "Are you okay? Can you hear—"

Boudreaux knocks Eric away. Eric raises a fist and prepares to find out just how much of a badass his friend really is.

"Yes," Lori says. "He said he wanted to ride with Moore and opened the back door of the car before anyone could say yes or no."

"What was that?" Eric asks her.

Boudreaux responds instead of Lori. "You've never seen her do it?"

Fatigue mixes with confusion and Eric stumbles backward into Boudreaux. "Easy buddy," he says. "We'll let you lay down in the back. It doesn't stink too bad."

"No, I'm fine. I just need to get back to the office."

"You're half right," Boudreaux says. "We need to move, but not back to Cushing. We have to catch up with the car."

He starts leading Eric to the escalade. The others follow suit, but Eric jerks away.

"Why the hell would we do that?"

"Because he's with Novak," Boudreaux says. "That's what he meant by *We are the lighthouse.*"

"So?"

"So," Boudreaux says as though explaining bedtime to a three-year-old. "He figured out what was in Clarke's car and is driving toward that eighteen-wheeler right now so he can arm a nuclear bomb."

Moore speaks up before Eric can fully form his question.

"The computer stuff?" Moore asks.

"I killed Clarke because Gates all but said she could set off the bomb. She must've brought the equipment with her."

Moore mumbles something. When all eyes turn on him, he elaborates. "It's called a permissive action link, a physical safety measure that plugs into the bomb assembly. I knew about PAL systems in concept, but never seen one. Obviously."

The laptop. "She was decrypting something to get the code," Eric says. "That's why Gates put her in charge of setting off the bomb. She was literally a computer genius."

"Correction," Moore says. "That program's still running. So if it finishes, and Levine puts the PAL together with the bomb ..."

Eric opens the rear passenger door. "Get in. That car's fast and has a head start."

39
JEREMIAH

Provincial Highway 18,
9 miles south of Kansas Territory Border Crossing
Republic of Oklahoma

They were cut off from the rest of the world again, which pissed Jeremiah off to no end. Lori knew his phone had run out of minutes, and still she'd left. So had Fowler and the rest, leaving them with the option of buying more burner phones or turning on their comms and alerting INSTA to their empty quiver.

To make matters worse, they were now dealing with traffic. Not much, a few other truckers and some flatbed pickups, but enough to make the rig stand out by going almost ninety and forcing them half onto the shoulder. If one of them decided to call the national, provincial, or local law enforcement, they might have a disastrous standoff waiting at the border.

After passing what looks like a pipeline welder, Dom turns to Jeremiah after nearly twenty minutes of the silent treatment. "You know you screwed up, right?"

"You don't know what you're talking about," Jeremiah snaps back. "And even if what you think happened did happen, so what?"

Jeremiah knows he's wrong for being confrontational. He's also loud enough for Mac and Zeus to hear. But he's tired and emotionally spent, not to mention angry that he led four of his closest friends into an impossible situation.

"You're our commander, J," Dom says. "You have to make decisions based on what's good for the mission and the team as a whole, not the one of us sucking your dick."

Suppressing his urge to correct him—hurried as it was, they'd made love—Jeremiah concedes the point and tries to make headway. "Under normal circumstances, I'd recuse myself from the mission until we figured out a more permanent solution. But that's obviously not an option right now."

Under normal circumstances he'd point out that Mac would sooner shoot Jeremiah than let him treat her like a damsel in distress, but the mood's still a bit too tense, so Jeremiah's content listening to classic country. After a hit each from Garth, Toby, and Blake, Dom stares at his side-view mirror and shakes his head.

"Check out this moron."

Jeremiah leans over to get a look. It's a silver car. Scratch that. It's *the* silver car, the Mercedes blondie drove to the meeting.

Dom recognizes it a moment later, along with the driver. "That's one of the mercs who helped us with the roadblock. Guess they didn't hang us out to dry after all."

The sedan passes the rig like it's standing still, and as it drifts back into the northbound lane, an arm appears out of the driver's side window, motioning for Dom to follow.

"Looks like we're getting an escort to the border," Jeremiah says. "And some backup if shit hits the fan."

***

THE KANSAS TERRITORY doesn't have the same trade agreements with Oklahoma as The Republic, so the border crossings—even a small one on a provincial highway surrounded by nothing but dead fields—looks more like the Berlin Wall than a Metroplex toll booth.

The solid concrete structure is taller than Big Blue by several feet and stretches well beyond the two lanes of Highway 18, though Jeremiah can see the ends. He can also see overwatch guards with scoped rifles posted each side. At the end are fire escapes with UTVs at the bottom for crossing the plains to outposts along the border. He wonders how many guards it takes to man them and why anyone would try sneaking across.

Unlike I-40, which widened to six lanes on each side at Texola, there is only one lane open in front of them. He can picture traffic backing up for hours on a normal day, but it's still before nine after one of the biggest drinking holidays of the winter.

The car, which looks to have sustained heavy rear-end damage during the tank farm shootout, pulls up to the armed guard. Jeremiah wonders what kind of ID the guy has and how he'll explain it not matching the car's registration. The encounter is brief enough, and the car disappears past the gray barrier.

Dom has his paperwork ready, along with his story. He tells the guard someone at *the main office* messed up big time. The ubiquitous *powers that be* had told him to deliver the foodstuffs to Shidler when they meant Ponca City and, well, it was just going to be easier to keep driving North and make two lefts than try and turn this big boy around. Plus he has a girl in Arkansas City and has a chance to get him some.

"You can cut a poor trucker some slack, can't you?"

The guard eyes him one more time. "Your name can't really be Dominic Torretto, can it?"

"My folks loved those old racing movies. Plus, it's not spelled the same. But when they find out I basically drive for a living, they had themselves a big laugh."

Jeremiah's having a hard time keeping a straight face while Dom defends his imaginary parents in an awful accent and nearly sighs in relief when the guy waves him through.

Concrete pillars force him to creep right, then left, then right again until he's in a large, partially enclosed lot beside the silver car, which is empty. Another guard, this one armed with an M4 automatic, waves them forward then holds up a fist. Dom stops and waits as the guard approaches, talking into his shoulder radio.

"Morning sir," Dom says. "What do you need from us to get us on the road again?"

"We'll need all of you to step down while we search the truck."

Dom, terrible actor that he is, starts breathing harder. "Is that really necessary, sir?"

"We know your situation, and I'd be fine just letting you move along. But they have cameras everywhere, so we have to make it look right. So, if all four of you can exit the vehicle, we'll get this done as quickly as possible."

How's he know about Mac and Zeus up top? But Jeremiah knows asking that will only complicate matters, so he opens the door, and everyone piles out.

Four other guards are at the rear, preparing to open the trailer. Jeremiah looks around absentmindedly until he comes up with another question. *Where is Moore's guy?* He walks around the front of the truck and sees the car still sitting empty, but now the trunk is open and one of the guards is bent over while another looks inside. Jeremiah takes a step in their direction when a noise distracts him.

It's Dom shouting, followed by Zeus cursing and Mac calling Jeremiah's name. He turns to see every firearm in the place drawn but his.

"What's going on?" Jeremiah asks the guard closest to him.

"We have orders to detain you and release this truck to Mr. Levine."

Mr. Levine? "Look, I don't know who's giving you that order, but—"

"All I need is the truck." The voice is behind him. When he spins, the car's driver is walking toward him, the muzzle of his PDX short-barrel aimed at Jeremiah's chest. "There's no need for anyone to get hurt."

"And what do you think happens when this thing detonates?"

This guy—who must be Levine—takes a moment to think, seems to go back and forth in his pea brain about the consequences of setting off a nuclear bomb. "Fine. There's no reason for any *good* people to get hurt."

Jeremiah knows this guy will drop him before he can draw his SIG, let alone fire a round. He also can't live with himself if he gives him control of the rig.

He's frozen and starting to panic when Levine's focus shifts. Jeremiah hears gunfire behind him but doesn't turn to find its source. With Levine distracted, Jeremiah sprints to him and grabs the weapon. Their tug-of-war only lasts a few seconds before he hears more gunfire, this time much closer, followed immediately by Zeus crying out in pain.

Now Jeremiah's distracted, pulling on Levine's PDX while spinning his head. Before he can find Zeus, the barrel slips from his hands. Metal crushes his temple a moment later, and Jeremiah crumples to the asphalt.

It's a brownout, not a blackout, so he's still conscious and can hear voices talking behind him and closing Blue's doors. He's nearly back to his feet when the diesel coughs to life and the trailer moves, revealing Mac and a shirtless Dom leaning over a pair of writhing legs. The rest of the guards have faded into the background, weapons pointed not at Jeremiah's team but at the border, where war has broken out.

Jeremiah stumbles forward, holding the side of his head. "What the hell happened?"

Dom rips a sleeve off of his shirt and presses it into Zeus's lower abdomen. "They turned their rifles on us and tried telling us to back away." His words are getting harder to hear over Zeus's screams. "We were trying to talk them down when someone started shooting back at the guard station."

"One put a round into Zeus's hip," Mac says. "He'll bleed out if we don't get him to a hospital."

Jeremiah doesn't know much about Kansas, but there's a hospital thirty miles south of them and the Mercedes can have them there in fifteen minutes. "We're going to have to clear these guys out and haul ass back the way we came." He pulls out his pistol and hands it to Mac. "Go give'em hell. Dom, help me get Zeus to the car."

He and Dom each grab an arm and they duck under Zeus's armpits. As they lay him down in the backseat, Jeremiah notices a rifle case in the trunk. He unzips it, then smiles.

"You still good with the long gun?" he asks Dom, who leans over from the other side.

"Oh hell yeah."

40
LORI

Provincial Highway 18,
100 feet south of Kansas Territory Border Crossing
Republic of Oklahoma

She's already fired twelve from Fowler's Glock 19, which means she has three left in the magazine. Lori has no idea if she's hit any of the border guards, but three are dead less than thirty yards in front of her. Two more fell from the top of the concrete barrier after Moore picked them off with a rifle borrowed from Soddie.

They've all taken shelter behind the Escalade because bullets from overwatch guards are ripping through doors and cratering the ground near their feet.

"I'm out," Soddie yells.

"I've got a few left," Road Runner says.

She's leaning against the treads of the left rear tire facing south, Fowler doing the same on the passenger side. He's all but crying. "I'm so sorry, Lori. I can't believe this is how we're going to die."

"Speak for yourself."

She knows it's true unless something changes, but Lori will be damned if she'll admit it. She spins to her right and fires at the overwatch nearest her.

Miss. She spins back just in time to see sparks jump from the pavement a few feet in front of her.

Two rounds left.

She's recalculating for her next shot when the sound of another rifle enters the mix. This one's a larger caliber and meant to be fired from farther away. There's also a few more pistols from farther away.

Lori leans over and doesn't see the shooter until she scans the ground near the base of the border wall.

Jeremiah and his team have joined the party.

Boudreaux and Moore give the other two orders while she and Fowler take better positions behind the open back doors. The four former operators leave their sanctuaries and begin firing the rest of their ammunition—one final flurry of pops until Boudreaux shouts a definitive *clear*.

Lori moves into the open and scans. Boudreaux and Moore have made their way past the border, while Soddie and Road Runner are kicking guns away from bodies. Fowler's shaking. She's not, but only because she's focused on her breathing. She'd been half in the bag in New Orleans, and that didn't last a third of the time.

What she would give for a shot now, be it booze or a narcotic.

Lori walks on her aching leg toward the guard station when a blaring horn makes her jump.

Moore comes jogging out from behind the barricade. "Move the bodies," he yells to his men. "We need to clear a path."

Fowler joins the other four. Lori hangs back, not wanting to anger her wound any further.

The Mercedes creeps along as the guys pull corpses out of its way. When a path is clear, the car's engine whines. As it races toward her, she sees Jeremiah in the driver's seat with Hansen leaning over Ramirez's body in the backseat.

In the background, MacLaughlin is walking toward them, rifle case in hand.

"Looks like we have a stowaway," Boudreaux says.

"If they didn't put a round through the engine block," Moore says.

Boudreaux punches the ignition, and the seven of them exhale collectively when the Escalade turns over. All four tires are still inflated, too, so they pile in. Soddie and Road Runner take the back row. Lori slides to the center of the middle row. Moore sits as gently as he can in the seat to her left, careful not to jostle her.

MacLaughlin loads the case into the rear, then plops down to Lori's right.

"They're headed to a hospital thirty-three miles south of here," she says. "Town sounds like one in Virginia. Not Langley, but another one."

Lori catches her use of Jeremiah's first name, which she knows isn't common on his team. She opens her mouth to say something, then thinks better of it and smiles in what probably comes across as a *bless your heart* expression. Screw it. She's in pain and her nerves are shot. Everyone'll just have to put up with her being bitchy until she can talk someone out of an Oxy or two.

Road Runner leans over so his head's beside MacLaughlin's. "How bad is he?"

"Took one high on the right hip," she says. "They packed it, but he's lost a lot of blood. Right now they're hoping he doesn't go into shock."

Boudreaux puts the SUV into gear and starts for the border crossing. "Did you see a couple of computers in the trunk of the car?" he asks MacLaughlin.

"Negative," she says. "Just the rifle. Good thing, too. That's how we got the advantage. Why?"

"Not only does Levine have your bomb," Fowler says, "he now has the means to detonate it."

"Dammit," she says. "Well, there's a layer of cargo stacked in the back of the trailer keeping people from getting to the payload. They'd need a fork truck to get the pallets out. That or stop to cut open the cellophane and toss out a bunch of boxes with food and stuff."

Boudreaux weaves through the last of the barriers, then groans. "You mean those boxes."

Through the windshield, Lori sees cardboard squares littering the highway, a trail of breadcrumbs leading to the end of the world.

"Even if it's armed, it won't be going off immediately," Moore says. "Unless all they're looking to kill is livestock, we have time to catch up before it detonates. But how do we stop the truck?"

"The rig's all but bulletproof," MacLaughlin says. "I guess we could crash it. Shoot out its tires. Maybe cross its path and make it T-bone us."

Lori's been on board with saving the day since getting on the plane with Boudreaux. But there must be a better way than crashing an eighteen-wheeler with a nuclear bomb in its trailer.

"Moore," Lori says. "I think it's time you used that cellphone to call your president and tell him what's going on."

"I can do that on the way," he says, "but we still have to stop that bomb from getting near a major city."

Lori can't argue that logic, so she doesn't.

* * *

WHEN THEY GET a visual on the truck, Lori starts arguing.

"So, what's our plan for the two Humvees?"

The two tan vehicles are sandwiching the semi, straddling both lanes like they're on their way to stage a military coup. Because they are. As the Escalade gains on the follow vehicle, Lori makes out the letters KTG on the back—for Kansas Territory Guard, she assumes—and turret on top. The gun's not pointing their direction.

Yet.

Boudreaux's the first to offer a strategy. "We need to get Moore up front with the sniper rifle."

"Wouldn't do any good," Moore says. "We'd be stuck fighting off two crews, which we have to assume are fully armed. Even if we could take them all, there's no chance this vehicle's drivable after. Taking out the tires and engine's the first thing they'll do."

As if on cue, the barrel of the Humvee's cannon swivels their way. Boudreaux hits the brakes in time to keep any bullets from hitting the Escalade, then puts it in reverse and backs up until the shooting stops.

"We can't just turn tail," Boudreaux says.

"Maybe not," Moore says. "But we can't stop them, either. I'll make the call. We can follow at this distance to keep track of the bomb's movement."

Boudreaux looks like he wants to rip the steering wheel from the column, but he doesn't push back this time. Neither does anybody else.

"Mr. President, we have a situation. The Republic has an … Good God. Sir, I don't believe that's what's happening. If you'll just give me a moment to—"

Moore takes the phone away from his ear and eyes the screen. A moment later, Moore hits the button on the side, turning everything dark.

Their eyes meet.

PART III: NUCFLASH

41
ERIC

Kansas Highway 15, 8 miles north of Oklahoma Border Crossing
Kansas Territory

Eric shifts in his seat and finds Moore in the rearview mirror. Though he knows what news Moore just received, Eric needs to hear the words. "What did he say?"

"There's been a nuclear detonation above downtown Los Angeles," Eric says, eyes still on the floorboard.

The Escalade fills with gasps and whispers from everyone but Eric, who knows it could've been worse. He knows it's a horrible thought upon learning of the first nuclear attack on the Divided States.

Horrible, but true.

A few years ago—if his quick math is accurate—an airburst nuclear detonation over LA would've killed at least a quarter million and injured another three-quarters from Hyde Park to South Pasadena. And that's being conservative.

But the greater Los Angeles area is mostly abandoned now. The death toll will be in the thousands, not millions.

"Did your president have a casualty estimate?" Eric asks.

"No. Most people have already written off anyone who still lives there."

Again, horrible, but true.

The Southern California population began leaving after the state's wildfire season refused to end, though the masses didn't leave downtown and Hollywood until fires threatened to burn the city a few years into the crisis. After that eventuality came to fruition, flames left almost nothing but the H, W, and one O on the sign and ruins below it. Eric knows because every year a new documentary is made about the hangers-on in neighborhoods nature spared and the residents who live like survivors of an apocalypse.

That's going to be all of us. Eric shudders. "I take it he thinks China launched a first strike?"

"Yeah." Moore finally looks up, eyes red. "He had an incoming call from Cole and cut me off before I could tell him it's a Nucflash."

Lori clears her throat. "I apologize for being out of the loop, but what's that?"

"It's a DOD term," Boudreaux says, still facing the windshield. "In this case, it means an unauthorized detonation that creates the risk of nuclear war."

Moore brings his phone back to life. "I'll contact my asset in Beijing and tell him what's happening. MSS agents are fixing to start reporting on the military forces gearing up for a retaliatory strike." He hands the satphone to Eric. "Who can you call to get intel on Novak's next move?"

"Other than Novak himself?"

Boudreaux turns to Eric, taking his eyes off the horizon for the first time since the Humvee fired at them. "Gates said someone named Robb is weak and that he didn't get the chance to put out a kill order on him."

"That'll work." Eric pulls out the phone's antenna. "While I do that, get us headed back to Cushing."

"And drop me off at that hospital in Arlington."

Eric had forgotten the other woman was back there. He's fairly sure Gates called her MacLaughlin before everything went to shit at the tank farm. Novak must've called Gates with the intel before Reynolds's team left Amarillo—a courtesy he hadn't extended to Eric.

"It's Farefax," he says and tells Boudreaux it's on the way.

Boudreaux agrees to the plan and executes a hurried three-point turn, forcing Eric to grab his oh-shit bar. After recovering, Eric calls Robb's office, which served as the backup in case Novak wasn't available on his phone.

"Hello?" Robb answers, his voice shaky.

Good. "Don't react. It's Fowler. Is Novak in the room with you?"

"Affirmative. I have everyone here busting their ass to get everything ready." Novak's distant voice asks who's on the line. "Just one of President Cole's staffers."

Quick thinking, but it still might not buy much time. "Is the plane still going to land and load up on gravity bombs?"

"Yessir, we're on schedule. And you said the President wants four, two each for China and Iran if we're able to coordinate an attack with The South, right?"

Iran? They don't have ICBMs and even the Libs would notice an incoming Russian-built bomber. Novak tells Robb to quick jaw-jacking because they're already running late. Eric's running out of time, but he needs more answers.

"Novak's going to detonate the bomb we stole from your plant and say Iran snuck one onto the continent?" he asks.

"Uh-huh. Well, we appreciate the call, but I have to let you go. If anything changes in the next ninety minutes, the president can reach Mr. Novak on his satphone."

"They're detonating the bomb in ninety minutes?"

"That's correct." Robb pauses, presumably to make sure Eric understands. "You take care now."

Eric ends the call, folds down the antenna, and waits. When nobody speaks, he assumes the collective question.

"He said yes."

After a round of loud exhales and choice words, Lori points out the obvious. "We're in the middle of Bumfuck, Oklahoma. What's he going to blow up that's only an hour and a half away?"

"Wichita?" Moore offers.

Eric knows the area better than anybody in the Escalade, and he can only think of one target that close with enough potential impact.

"No," he says. "They're going back to Cushing."

Boudreaux tells Road Runner to duck down. "He's right." Eric turns with the rest and sees a tan square in front of a blue eighteen-wheeler. "They must've turned as soon as they found a place wide enough."

Of all the nightmare scenarios he helped game out, the one being faked by Novak and his army of mouth-breathers was nearly the worst.

Iran and China hated the old United States, albeit for different reasons, but two things turned the problem into a powder keg.

First, America turned the attention of its foreign policy away from Iran. It wasn't for long, but the pause gave the Islamic Republic's scientists enough time to jumpstart its nuclear program. This shift was one of the many divisive political strategies leading to the secessions.

Then Iran increased the frequency and severity of its cyberattacks on the American government.

China had been doing the same for years. When the nations learned of their synergistic goals, they aligned. Iran supplied its true-believer energy to the cause, while China brought superior digital infrastructure and nuclear knowledge.

When the Chinese unleashed the fury of man's deadliest engineering feat, targeting the Divided States seemed natural, though an unprovoked attack was unlikely. But if Iran were to take the leap, an emboldened China would almost surely back their play. And vice-versa.

That alone was enough to justify MANIFEST.

Now add Russia to the equation.

Russia and Iran had been strategic partners since before Eric was a tadpole stirring his father's loins. But Russia's relationship with China blossomed late, despite how natural it seems now. Both were experts in the art of cyberespionage, remained nuclear threats to America, and had military might that most other nations feared. As the Union degraded, the bond between China and Russia strengthened.

It makes him ill to think about Gates, but Eric remembers the chess metaphor his former mentor favored while planning—and justifying—MANIFEST. When Iran and China threw in together, that was check. If Iran, China, and Russia coalesce into a Tehran-Beijing-Moscow Axis?

That's mate.

None of that has happened, but appearances are what matters now. The Divided States will react to the bad intel, and someone will launch a real first strike. Soon.

Like everyone else traveling south on the endless gray line that is Kansas Highway 15, Eric knows they have to mount a counteroffensive to the impending assault on Cushing. First they'll have to get past the border crossing again. And, though they weren't gone long, a fresh batch of guards have taken up the post.

They're a few minutes away from a turkey shoot with no escape. Well, that's not entirely accurate. Eric has something percolating. But it has to be a last resort.

"I hope one of y'all has a good idea," he says, "because all I have is a really bad one."

42
JEREMIAH

Community Hospital, Farefax, Northeast Province
Republic of Oklahoma

The pavement is slick with visibility approaching whiteout, so it's little wonder the car slides into one of the brick pillars at the hospital entrance. The conditions also cause Jeremiah to lose his footing and grip while trying to open the back door. After a quick recovery, Dom prepares Zeus.

"This'll hurt like a bitch, but you'll feel a lot better after we get you inside, I promise."

Zeus growls through a nod.

"On three," Dom says. "One, two—"

He doesn't wait until three. Zeus is screaming bloody murder as Dom slides him across the leather seat until he can stand on the slick asphalt. Jeremiah's on the other side and steadies his footing, then slips his arms underneath Zeus, who's writhing in pain. Dom and Jeremiah lift Zeus until he's vertical enough for them to pull his arms over their shoulders.

They walk him to the front door like an injured football player. When Dom opens the door, it flies open in the wind as though it might sail off. It does, for all Jeremiah knows. The three are through the entrance before he can check its status, Jeremiah and Dom yelling for a doctor. They look around and see … nobody.

Dom continues to rage until Jeremiah convinces him to shut up. Even Zeus suppresses his screaming enough for them to listen.

Talk radio. Strange talk radio, the voice low, somber. It's interrupted by a gasp from one hospital staffer and an expletive from another. Jeremiah and Dom get Zeus to one of the chairs.

"Stay here with him," Jeremiah says. "I'll go kick someone's ass or get a gurney myself."

He leaves them and runs toward the radio. After barreling through a set of double-doors, he gets a bead on the sound and turns left, where he finds a crowded nurse's station.

"Hey assholes," he screams, causing several of the men and women to jump. "I've got a dying man out in the lobby." He waves for them to follow, but nobody moves. "What kind of backwoods-ass hospital is this? I said a man's dying—"

A tall man in bright Hawaiian scrubs finally reacts, wiping below his eyes as he walks toward Jeremiah. "Sorry, I think we're all still in shock."

Radio. Somber voice. Highjacked nuclear weapons.

Good God.

"Where?" is all he can muster.

"Somewhere over Southern California," the nurse says. "Guy on the radio says the power and electronics are screwed near LA, but people saw and heard the explosion from farther upstate."

That information doesn't compute. "What station are you listening to?"

"NPR from California."

Nurse Hawaii reads the confusion on Jeremiah's face and heads off the question. "Hospitals have their own radio networks since we have to transfer patients internationally. Right now everyone's daisy-chaining a report from the Bay Area."

INSTA has a similar network, so Jeremiah believes the information is relatively accurate. Assuming that, two things are immediately clear. The blast came from an LRSO, not the bomb for which he's responsible. Also, from what he knows about Southern California and nuclear electromagnetic pulse blasts, Novak's still going for a military coup, not a nuclear holocaust.

But Novak will have to act fast to ensure nobody on this side of the globe fires back at … "Are they saying where the missile was fired from?" Jeremiah asks.

"Nobody from any Allied government's commented so far, but the reporter's saying it was probably China. But hell, I think it could just as easily be Russia or North Korea. The guy does think it's weird that nobody's taking credit. He also said it's strange that whoever it is dropped the bomb there rather than New York or one of the capitals."

Smart reporter. Using a B-52 stocked with cruise missiles, Novak could've maximized casualties and taken out all those cities at virtually the same time. But even with his one-strike strategy, Novak and his UNIC cultists chose the most desolate *metropolitan* area in the nation. He'd have done more damage blowing up the oil in Cushing.

He also declined to unleash the worst-case scenario: a high-altitude nuclear detonation. Those produce electromagnetic pulses capable of knocking the continent back to the 1860s. Instead, Novak maximized blast and heat damage to an already devastated region of California.

Jeremiah hears the double-doors open and snaps back into focus. Nobody here can help California.

But they can save Zeus.

43
LORI

Kansas Highway 15, 50 yards north of Oklahoma Border Crossing Kansas Territory

Lori can't believe she's about to do this.

It's not Fowler's fault, though if anyone asks that's who she'll blame. He did ask for better ideas, though. Episodes of MacGyver didn't help, nor did any action movie she's ever watched or heard in the background.

So here she sits, busted leg tense, fingers wrapped around the doorhandle, waiting for the signal to open, tuck, and roll as the Escalade speeds down the highway.

"You got the child-lock disabled?" MacLaughlin asks Lori and Moore.

They answer in the affirmative. MacLaughlin will follow whoever gets clear first, followed by the guys in back. Everyone will bail paratrooper-style when the SUV is so close the six ground guards will be preoccupied with not getting torpedoed. The two up top will see everything clearly, but the overwatch on one side will have three moving targets, the other four. If they all do a little zigging, maybe throw in a few zags, one in each group is bound to make it around the edge of the wall.

Whoever's still mobile will get in the nearest UTV and drive like hell across the fields.

After that?

Survive.

"We're going seventy," Boudreaux says, "so this'll hurt like a sonofabitch."

Fowler starts to take the Lord's name in vain, but catches himself just in time. "I really could've done without that knowledge."

"Hey, this is your plan," Boudreaux says. "Plus you only have a few more seconds to think about it."

He's wrong. Bullets start smacking the Escalade in less than two.

It takes everything she has to push the door open, and she only manages a half-assed tuck before her left side is smacked with a Lori-sized tenderizer. After rolling a few times, she gets to her feet and gimps as quickly as she can toward the edge of the border wall. Fowler pulls into view, taking an angle closer to concrete barrier. He's moving faster than she is, though he wasn't shot in the leg less than twelve hours ago.

"Coming up on your six," MacLaughlin yells.

She's there after two more steps and ducks her head under Lori's right arm while securing her waist. They move like that for a few seconds before Lori realizes it's not helping enough.

"Go on without me. Better only one of us gets caught or killed."

"Negative," she says, quickening their pace as bullets nip at their feet. "If I survive and Jeremiah finds out I left you behind, that's not going to work. For either of us."

Lori wants to argue the point, but they're only a few yards from the edge of the wall. She finds enhanced motivation as the UTV sputters to life, assuming Fowler's chicken-shit enough to leave the women in pursuit of his own salvation.

But as they turn the corner, the side-by-side is advancing toward them, the passenger doors open and waiting. MacLaughlin hip-tosses Lori into the back and grabs onto the front-side grip with her left hand. After securing her left foot in the vehicle, MacLaughlin pulls a pistol and fires at the overwatch, who's been spraying wildly in their direction. Fowler kicks up freezing clods and dead grass as he spins the UTV south, then takes off as MacLaughlin empties her magazine.

Lori's body aches, but she sits up and looks behind them. The gunfire has stopped, but a green Humvee—from the Oklahoma Guard, she assumes—is giving chase. Though their souped-up dune-buggy can haul ass, the Humvee is rugged enough to chase them and comes equipped with a .50-cal. She spins around as MacLaughlin leans toward Fowler, likely telling him about their tail.

Lori screams when they dip into a shallow, dry creek bed. But on the other side there's nothing in front of them but the flat, frosted plains and a roiling blizzard. There are trees in the distance to the right, but they're at least a mile away.

She has two rounds. MacLaughlin's out.

Lori leans forward and slaps Fowler on the shoulder. "Hand me your pistol."

He cocks his head her direction. "I emptied it earlier and tossed it."

Lori shoves herself back, disgusted with him. With herself. With everything. Her 9mm rounds won't do any good unless one miraculously found its way through the turret's shield and into the gunner's face.

They need to get to the trees and split up.

Lori leans forward again. "Take a sharp right and head for the trees," she screams into Fowler's ear.

He nods, but MacLaughlin joins the conversation. "No, we'll be an easier target. They can just park and aim."

She has a point, and Lori knows it. But rather than concede, she fires back. "Well what else can we do?"

McLaughlin points 45 degrees to the right. Lori follows her gaze to an embankment. The drop-off can't be far based on the terrain, but it might provide just enough cover for them to set up a last stand. If she's accurate with the two bullets, the rest is likely to be one-on-one combat. Lori's in rough shape but can handle her man. She doesn't know much about MacLaughlin, except that Jeremiah always talked about her like she was one of the toughest SOBs on his team. Fowler's not a fighter, but maybe he can hold off his guard long enough for Lori to help.

"Yeah, that'll work," Lori yells.

Fowler turns the wheel.

Two seconds later, an explosion.

She jumps and covers her ears. It's just the .50-cal, but Christ is that thing loud. The shots get closer, but Fowler avoids them as dirt kicks in the air. The embankment's only ten feet ahead when she sees what they're driving into.

A pond.

Are you fucking kidding? It's the middle of winter, but somehow a body of water the size of a small caliche pit has appeared in front of them. Fowler turns the wheel, then a real explosion lifts her from the back seat. No. Not lifts. The seat fell half a foot because the rear passenger tire blew after being hit by a round from the Humvee.

Fowler tries to correct but can't. She can feel the UTV tilting as though in slow motion. The rollbar has a gap wide enough for her to jump through, so she leaps from the falling vehicle into the water.

44
ERIC

Approximately 30 yards southwest of Kansas Territory Border Crossing
Republic of Oklahoma

Eric can't breathe. He's broken the surface of the pond, but the cold sent his body into shock. When air finally fills his lungs in short gasps, Eric starts paddling toward land. His feet catch ground after only a few seconds, and he slogs out of the water.

Only then can he comprehend the absurdity of what just happened. The trees Lori pointed out were almost surely on the banks of what was once an Arkansas River tributary, but that's more than a mile away. This pond is just a divot in the Oklahoma plain that happens to be filled with water.

Lori and the redhead have gathered under the steep embankment near the toppled UTV, where they, like him, shiver almost uncontrollably.

"She has two rounds," MacLaughlin tells Eric as he squats beside them. "She's going to take out the first two who show their faces, then hopefully it'll be one-on-one." She blows into her hand and pulls a combat knife from a sheath on her leg. "You have a weapon?"

"No. Hand-to-hand's not something I prepare for much these days."

Lori shushes them and points east, past the drop. Voices approach. At least two men, one giving orders, though Eric can't quite hear what they are. Lori crawls a few feet to her right and raises her pistol.

Her hands are shaking. She was a police officer and has survived more in the last day than most people will their entire lives, but the chances of her taking out any of these paramilitaries while hypothermia sets in are slim.

Eric clenches his shaky fists and posts up near the north edge of the embankment, anticipating a flank maneuver. He tells himself watching Lori won't help her aim, so Eric turns his back and prepares for the assault.

The next thing he hears is Lori's Glock. He turns to find her aiming at a man in fatigues advancing on her. Eric runs toward them but is tackled from behind. Another shot rings out as he thrashes and kicks wildly. His attacker's strong, though, and Eric can't escape.

The women are screaming as Eric's face is pressed into the ground, arms twisted behind his back. He's getting restrained by flex-cuffs for the second time, and though he's awake this time, there's little he can do about it. The man pulls the ties tight around his ankles before standing, allowing Eric to roll and see the others. Lori's similarly restrained, but two men are still working on MacLaughlin. Eric doesn't see any bodies, which means he was right—Lori couldn't shoot straight enough to take any out.

After MacLaughlin stops struggling, the oldest of the men walks to the embankment so everyone can see him, all the swagger of Patton but no Fifty Stars in the background. "Listen up, shitbirds," he says. "I got orders to detain you, then drive us all to a transport vehicle waiting on the highway. But right now, you got a choice." He spits, leaving a string of tobacco-laced saliva on his stubbled chin. "You can let us cut the ankle restraints and walk calmly to the truck. Or you can resist. Do that, and we leave y'all here to freeze. I's you, I'd take Option One." He smiles, revealing jagged, dip-stained teeth. "That'll make K good'n happy."

45
JEREMIAH

Community Hospital, Farefax, Northeast Province
Republic of Oklahoma

The doctor's somber as he walks through the double doors. Jeremiah hopes it's the looming threat of nuclear war, but experience tells him otherwise. He and Dom are the only two in the small lobby, so the doc walks straight to them.

"Good morning, gentlemen, I'm Dr. Patel." Though Jeremiah can't place it, the doctor's accent isn't the Indian English he'd expected. "I'm afraid my news isn't as good as I would like. We extracted the bullet, but Mr. Ramirez lost a significant amount of blood. We used our available blood stores, but he still slipped into a coma. He needs another transfusion soon or he will die."

Dom sticks out his arm. "Take all you need."

"Your blood type, sir?"

"A-positive."

Dr. Patel shakes his head. "Your friend is O-positive, which is one reason we had enough compatible blood to keep him alive for now. Blood banks stress getting O because it's the universal donor, meaning anyone can receive his blood. But O-positive is not a universal receiver. Mr. Ramirez can only receive Type O blood."

"Bullshit," Dom says. "Any blood'll keep his heart pumping."

"Sir, if you'll let me finish, please," the doctor says, clearly annoyed. "As I said, blood banks keep Type O on hand, and we already have some coming. He's in a coma, but stable. Assuming the blood gets here in time, Mr. Ramirez will recover with only some permanent organ damage. But if we introduce large quantities of incompatible blood, the possible complications become much worse."

Jeremiah knew most of this already, which is why he didn't volunteer his rare AB-negative. "Thanks, Doc. We know you're doing everything you can."

Dom walks away in disgust. Some of his foul mood is Jeremiah's doing, but some of it probably has to do with his bad experiences in the Middle East.

When Dom's out of earshot, the doctor leans in. "Are you Mr. Ramirez's captain?"

"His commander, yes."

"I won't ask whose military you're with or what your mission is, but I do take it you're traveling internationally, correct?"

Jeremiah nods. The doctor mirrors him.

"I am confident he will survive," Patel says. "But you may want to alert Mr. Ramirez's family. International travel can be complicated, and if they want to ensure being here in the event something goes wrong, starting the process now would be prudent."

That's not something Jeremiah expected a doctor to think about, but Patel's right. "Do you know where his personal effects are?"

"I believe the nurses put them in the room. There are drawers where we store patient clothes and other items. Why?"

"He had"—Jeremiah searches for a phrase other than *death notice*—"emergency contacts written on a piece of paper that should've been in one of his pockets."

"Excellent news. Mr. Ramirez is in Room 5, through the doors and on the left."

When he gets there, Jeremiah is pleased to find Zeus resting peacefully. He knows the man's not sleeping, but he's also not feeling any pain. And as the monitor reminds Jeremiah with each beep, Zeus is still alive. The world may be about to end, but at least he'll get to spend Armageddon with his family.

A Bible's all he finds in the top drawer of the small dresser on the far-right wall, but the middle section holds Zeus's clothing, sans flack jacket. The olive undershirt has a chest pocket with nothing inside.

Same for his pants. Stowed in the bottom drawer are the tactical gear and objects, including house keys and tri-fold wallet.

The wallet contains about fifty dollars cash but no licenses or other identifying cards, which everyone had left behind as part of this terribly conceived op. He's about to fold up the worn leather when he sees a piece of white paper sticking out from one of the empty credit-card slots.

He unfolds the paper to find two sets of names and numbers: Sarah Grace and Lexi.

Jeremiah reaches for the bedside phone, then realizes he doesn't know how to dial out, let alone if there are any extra steps to call internationally. He walks out into the hall and orients himself toward the nurse's station, where Patel and Nurse Hawaii are discussing a patient chart.

Patel looks up as Jeremiah approaches. "Did you find what we discussed?"

"Yes, but I'm not sure how to get an outside line and all that."

"Silly me, of course." Dr. Patel points down a corridor to the left. "Follow me. It'll be easier on my office phone."

As they walk, Jeremiah notes the rooms. There were four down the hall that led to Zeus—numbers 3 through 6—and he just passed patient beds 1 and 2. They brush by an open door to a small conference room to the left, opposite one marked CLEANING, then two office doors at the end.

They walk through the one with a slide-in nameplate stamped with DR. R. PATEL. His office is cramped and the desk is overflowing with scattered files, except where medical texts tower over a laptop and a landline.

"Which countries will you be calling?" Dr. Patel asks.

"His wife lives in The Republic." The doctor looks confused, so Jeremiah clarifies. "Texas, I mean. I guess we're kind of full of ourselves over there."

Dr. Patel grins and nods. "You have much to be proud of."

"Maybe. At any rate, then I'll need to call his sister in the United States."

Jeremiah had known calling Lexi might be a problem. Rural Bloc nations didn't ordinarily allow for those calls free of government oversight.

"I see," the doctor says. "Fortunately, hospitals have an exemption from the Oklahoma laws governing communications with the United States, LSA, and Free States. All you need to do is dial nine, one, the country code, the area code, and the number. My mobile phone has the same capability, but reception in this weather may not be ideal."

Jeremiah grins. "Is that all?"

As they share a laugh, Jeremiah is convinced the good doctor isn't from India. The nature of SEAL Teams and DEVGRU meant never staying in one country for more than a few months, but he'd heard enough English-to-Farsi translators to differentiate that from native Hindi speakers living in the West, even ones as fluent as Dr. Patel. That got his brain noticing physical features like skin tone and facial construction. Not that any of it matters, but he's curious why a doctor would feel the need to hide his identity and take a job in the middle of nowhere. And if Jeremiah's going to make a dangerous phone call—which he wants to do, for Zeus and for his sister—he needs to know he can trust the man telling him it's fine.

"Well I'm really glad that's the case, Dr. Patel. You see, my friend's estranged from his sister. Can't really go see her or talk to her. It's pretty tough on him."

That may or may not be true of Zeus, but Jeremiah bets it's true of the doctor.

"I understand Mr. Ramirez's situation completely. That's why I suggested you call now, while it's safe."

"About that," Jeremiah says, shifting from the building rapport phase straight to interrogation. "You wouldn't be trying to convince me to tie my own noose, would you?" Dr. Patel clearly doesn't get the metaphor, which means he hasn't lived in the heartland long. "What I mean is, have you alerted the Oklahoma government that I'm here? And are you talking me into a suspicious phone call to incriminate myself, with the intention of getting me and my team detained?"

The doctor's eyes go wild with panic. "Sir, I would never do that. As I said, I understand being estranged from family and having to be careful about contacting them."

Now they're getting to it. "Is that because you are lying about your identity, Dr. *Patel*?"

Jeremiah knows he sounds like a bigot, like Dom pretends not to be. But that's his intent. If Jeremiah's right and this guy's Iranian and moved here not long ago, there's at least a fifty-fifty chance he's part of the coup. And if that's true, he'll more than likely get angry and cagey.

The doctor hangs his head. "Yes," he says, shoulders slumped. "My name is Doctor Sasan Hosseini, not Doctor Rahul Patel."

"So, you're not Indian then."

"I never said I was."

He has a point. The doctor let Jeremiah—and everyone else here—assume his nationality based on the fake surname.

"You're Iranian," Jeremiah states rather than asks.

"Yes. I lied to get this job."

The doctor's either guilty or deserves an Oscar. But the best terrorists usually do. "And that's my problem," Jeremiah says. "Why lie your way to get what I'm sure is a low-paying gig for a doctor?"

He sighs. "You're going to think it's silly, mister"—he looks up, embarrassed—"I'm so sorry. I never got your name, sir."

"Call me Jay for now."

"Jay," he says, as though committing it to memory. "Like I said, you're going to think I'm silly. I had a practice in Los Angeles but was forced to flee like most people there. When my wife and I talked about where we should go, she wanted somewhere wholesome where we could raise a family one day. And I—and this is the silly part, Jay—I suggested Oklahoma because I saw the musical at an LA theater and loved it. When I researched further, I noted how impoverished the state was and knew I could help people here."

Jeremiah suppresses a smile. Yes, it's silly. But if Dr. Hosseini is being truthful, it's also charming as hell.

"But no hospitals were granting me privileges. Not as a man from the Islamic Republic of Iran with a last name so closely resembling Saddam Hussein."

That seems far-fetched, but Jeremiah's willing to believe the man *thinks* that's why no hospitals wanted him to work there.

"So why not try other places? Forging documents is pretty extreme to get into a place like this."

"The heart wants what it wants, Jay. And who's to say any place other than a major city would've been more tolerant. Plus, the documents were so very easy to get with the money at my disposal, and the rural hospitals started calling almost instantly."

Jeremiah's far from convinced, but he tells Hosseini to continue.

"I am extremely fortunate I took such drastic measures. After the secessions, the Oklahoma government outlawed travel into the country by those of the Islamic faith, and many of the Muslims here were forced to leave."

Jeremiah knows about the travel ban. The Republic did the same after seceding. Hell, the USA had one when he was a younger man. But forcing Muslims to relocate? "I don't believe for one minute that the OBI or any other government entity forced anyone to leave based on their religion."

"My apologies, Jay, you misunderstand. The government didn't force them to move. Our neighbors did."

That, Jeremiah believes.

"But as I said," Dr. Hosseini says, "I was fortunate. My wife and I had been keeping my faith a secret. And it helped that she is white and protestant. When some of our less-tolerant neighbors began asking questions about whether I worship Jesus or Mohammed, I simply began attending her Baptist church."

"Sounds like you have it made here," Jeremiah says, his comment not entirely insincere. "So why all the angst about not being able to contact family?"

"My sister, Yasmin," he says. "Jazzy, as she's known on this side of the world. We both grew up in Tehran dreaming of coming to America. I studied medicine in Shiraz and she studied clothing design. She had to either stay on the West Coast or move to New York to stay working as a fashionista and social media influencer. Jazzy chose New York and therefore never had to hide her nationality or faith. I haven't seen her since moving here, not even on United States social media sites since those are blocked in the republics. But I do get to call her during downtime here at the hospital."

Dr. Hosseini moves around his cluttered desk and presses a few buttons. "See, here are the call logs. Notice the country code for two of the last five. All to the United States."

Not only that, but the calls are spread out over several days. Jeremiah tries to come up with a way he could've faked that, but can't. Not in the short time he's been at the hospital. Not even if Dr. Hosseini somehow had the help of either republic's government. And why would they help a suspected terrorist?

No, Hosseini can call out to the USA without being monitored. The rest is probably true, too.

Jeremiah holds out his hand. "My name's Jeremiah Reynolds. It's a pleasure to meet you, Dr. Hosseini."

The doctor's face lights up like a pitmaster receiving his blue ribbon. "An honor, Mr. Reynolds. And may I thank you for your service."

"I never said I served."

Dr. Hosseini smiles, wryly, like they're old buddies now. "Surely you're joking."

Jeremiah winks and takes out the piece of paper with the phone numbers.

He's halfway through Sarah Grace's when the screaming starts.

46
LORI

Outside of Farefax Community Hospital, Northeast Province Republic of Oklahoma

A few people remain in the green Expedition in front of her. Its rear window is tinted—just like the identical SUV she's sitting in—but there is movement inside. Two paramilitaries exited the lead vehicle a few moments ago, joining the two from hers.

The yellow-toothed UNIC who led their extraction remains in the passenger seat in front of Fowler, MacLaughlin, and Lori, so she hopes the lead vehicle also has one guarding Boudreaux, Moore, Road Runner and Soddie.

"Building's secure," says a voice from the guard's radio. "All clear to deliver the packages."

As she tumbles out of the Expedition and slides on the icy parking lot, Lori sees Boudreaux and Moore do the same from theirs. She stays focused on the SUV, expecting to see the others. When they don't appear, Lori eyes Boudreaux, who shakes his head.

Lori hopes neither had kids and that Moore can honor them with some tin if he survives.

If any of them survive.

The guy leading Moore and Boudreaux isn't familiar. But as they fight the harsh wind and approach the entrance, Lori realizes something about the scene is familiar.

Clarke's car. It's damaged in the front and back and partially covered in fine snow, but there's no doubt. Jeremiah and Hansen are somewhere inside, and there's a chance Zeus wasn't too hurt and can help, too.

Lori smiles. The dickless mothers must've missed them.

Two of the paramilitaries are standing in the middle of the lobby, rifles leveled at the hospital staff, including one white coat and Ichabod Crane in a Hawaiian shirt. They're huddled in the far corner, sitting and sniffling, glancing at Lori and the rest as they walk past.

Things get eerie past the double doors. Twin heartbeats beat out of sync, echoing through the T-shaped hallways. They turn left at an empty nurse's station and hear murmurs as they approach the end. The younger of their guards stops at the sturdiest-looking door and opens it for Yellowteeth and the rest.

Oh fuck. Two more guards are inside, holding a pair of hostages sitting at a conference table.

Jeremiah and Hansen.

Both have been stripped of their Kevlar and, she assumes, their weapons. Their faces are bruised to shit—though the sentries are sporting a shiner and split lip—which means they tried brute force and failed. Lori wants to know how the hell that could've happened, but that'll have to wait until they either figure a way out or are out of hope.

With the addition of Yellowteeth and his partner, there are now four guards. The good guys are seven strong, though only five have military training, four of whom still train regularly.

Yellowteeth takes charge and tells the new crop of hostages to take a seat around the table. Fowler, MacLaughlin, and Moore comply. Lori and Boudreaux, however, don't budge.

"Did you hear me, missy?" Yellowteeth says. "I said sit your ass down."

One of his minions shoves a rifle muzzle into her side. "You heard Sergeant Taggart. Sit that fine ass of yours down."

Lori's pulling up instructions from her father. She's fourteen and the Colonel is telling her to spin left and hit him with the back of her fist. Follow that with an immediate right cross, then sweep his legs.

She's about to execute when Boudreaux levels the guy with a fist from above. He gets a rifle to the jaw for his trouble, but Lori appreciates the chivalry.

"You two're trouble." Taggart flashes his jack-o'-lantern grin. "That's all right, we know what to do with trouble."

Taggart nods to one of his minions. Lori tries to turn in time, but the butt of a rifle smashes her side, penetrating deep enough she feels it in her liver and doubles over onto the carpet. She rolls over and catches a glimpse of Boudreaux in the fetal position, two more of Taggart's henchmen digging the toes of their boots into his sides. The soldiers at the table are standing, but the *sergeant* and another guard have their automatics trained in their direction.

"Get'em up," Taggart says. When they get Lori and Boudreaux to their feet, arms held behind them, Taggart walks to her and leans his face so close she can smell his minty dip. "You and your boyfriend are going to the hole."

Taggart takes a step back and punches her. His knuckles connect with her left eye socket and she collapses into the arms of the man restraining her. She's not sure what the others do to Boudreaux, but before Lori can reorient herself, both are being led out of the conference room and across the hall. Someone opens a door and she's tossed into a closet. It's dark, but she hears Boudreaux behind her and something rolling near their feet. She feels a dowel dig into her back. Those elements combined with the smell of ammonia tells Lori she and Boudreaux have been stuffed into a cleaning supply closet.

"You okay?" he asks.

No. Lori needs a hit of something. She'd settle for a swig of cough syrup at this point to help ease the pain. "Yeah, I'm okay. Hurt, but okay. I don't suppose you have any pills on you?"

"No, they searched us."

"Same here. What happened to the other two?"

"The tall one, Road Runner, he landed on his leg wrong. Pretty sure he broke it. His buddy stayed behind and tried to get them to safety, but they were picked off pretty quick."

Soddie should've been with Lori, but he followed Road Runner and Moore. A team never wants to split up. Perhaps there's a bit of poetry in them going out together.

"How far did you and Moore get?"

"Not very. The overwatch on our side had already blown out the tires on our ride. We surrendered, and Moore asked to go back for his men. We both went, but they were already dead. The guy who led us in here said the sergeant and K still had plans for us."

"We got a similar message. Any idea what they're talking about?"

"Not a clue. You?"

Lori shakes her head, then realizes they're in the dark. "No. But why don't we ask." She stands and feels her way to the door. The handle's made of cheap aluminum, and the door doesn't feel sturdy, either. "I bet you can kick this thing down in one shot."

Boudreaux stands and shuffles toward her. His hands accidentally grope at her aching side.

"Sorry." His hand moves from her to the door. "Look, you're probably right. But what good'll that do us? We're unarmed and outmanned. The longer they think they're in control, the more complacent they'll get. They'll put us back in the room, and eventually they'll leave just one or two of them in charge while the rest go piss or smoke or whatever. Then we have a chance to overpower them, take the guns, and start fighting our way out."

Lori reaches over, finds his arm, and grips it like she did at the roadblock. "What do we do until then?"

Boudreaux leads her to the middle of the room and helps her sit.

"We rest. It takes a lot of energy to take out a team of heavily armed soldiers, especially when they're fighting for a cause and not a paycheck."

Normally she'd call someone out for pretending to know what it's like to fight their way out of a situation like this. Almost nobody tries that and lives.

Almost.

"Have you gotten out of a situation like this before?"

"I have."

She waits for him to start telling the story. When he doesn't, she leans against him. "How'd you do it?"

"You sure you want to know?"

Lori nods into his arm.

"Okay, but a story like that's something you can't un—"

They both laugh, softly at first, but then it grows, louder, wilder, until she's crying and he can't catch his breath. It's not just the absurdity of Lori's condition and how Boudreaux can't help but bring it up every few hours. It's that with nothing left but their own ghost stories as distractions, Lori and Boudreaux have finally started contemplating the one, true thing that unites the whole of humanity.

They're going to die.

47
ERIC

Few things are as difficult as knowing you're about to die. One of those things—for Eric, at least—is knowing you're about to be tortured.

"You know none of us will talk, right?" he says. "No more that you four would. And I'll tell you this up front—if the pain gets too bad, I'm lying. I'll tell you I'm best friends with the Easter Bunny if it gets you to stop."

That gets a chuckle from two of the guards, so he keeps going. "Once, during SERE school, I told a guard my sister's phone number. Of course, what I really gave them was the number to the Dairy Queen back home." The laughs get louder. "Hell, I don't even have a sister."

None of that's true. Eric was given anti-interrogation training at The Farm, but not any of the formal Survival, Evasion, Resistance and Escape training programs. Moore did as a PMOO and probably as a Marine before that. In fact, other than the jokers holding them hostage, everyone else in the room has probably survived SERE school.

Eric also has a sister who lives in The Republic's Capital Province, though hopefully these guys now believe otherwise.

"You're full of shit, son," says the one they keep calling Sergeant Taggart. "Know how I know?" His smile is gross. "Because you're the only one talking about it."

Eric scans the room. Moore won't meet his gaze. Neither will Reynolds or his crew.

Busted.

"Of course, I already knew you're the softest one in the room," Taggart says. "Well"—he nods to MacLaughlin—"Not that it's not her fault, though. Military never should've expected girls to do men's jobs. Not even in the Air Force."

This gets the other guards going again. Eric also sees Hansen crack a smile.

"See, K gave me files on all y'all." This seems to impress the guards, which in turn makes Taggart puff out his chest another inch. "Perk of leadership in this here mission. For instance, Eric Fowler, I know you're a traitor. You helped plan MANIFEST, but Novak knew you'd turn coat as soon as you were told the truth by Gates, may he rest in peace."

Sgt. Taggart and the three guards bow their heads before he continues. Eric's never heard of this character, but the sergeant has heard of every top-level officer involved in planning and executing the op.

This is going downhill in a hurry.

"That's why I have a file on you," Taggart says. "Novak also knew your history with Robert Moore and figured you'd seek him out when your more feminine instincts kick in." Taggart turns to Moore. "Now you, you ended your career with the CIA, but you started out in the Marines, which I can appreciate. Never met one who wasn't a tough sonofabitch."

Now it's Jeremiah's turn. "Master Chief Special Warfare Operator Jeremiah Reynolds." Taggart takes an exaggerated breath. "Boy, that sure is a mouthful. At any rate, you and yours were my team's original targets."

Eric's still in the dark. Never in his adult life—maybe never in his entire life—has Eric's future been so out of his control. He was second in command of MANIFEST. How are two morons like Novak and Taggart getting the better of him?

"You're so full of shit," Eric says. "If you were really a part of this operation, I'd've known about you."

"Did you know about Rita Clarke?"

Eric feels the heat rise from his chest to his cheeks.

"That's what I thought," Taggart says. "You didn't even know your woman was playing you. Oh wait, that's right. She wasn't even your woman."

He steps around to Eric and leans down. Eric gets a heavy whiff of snuff and nearly gags as Taggart speaks.

"I mean, you knew she was screwing Gates, right? I'm pretty sure he needed the little blue pill, though. She wasn't quite pretty enough for him to get it up."

Something about the image and the smell and the knowledge he's been made a fool makes Eric puke.

"And you wanted us to believe you'd survive torture without giving up the goods. Pathetic." Taggart returns to his position near the door. "Clarke was a true believer, though. She was supposed to be driving that truck right now, not my man on the inside." Taggart looks at Moore. "Way I see it, y'all owe me something for Levine's death, heroic as it's gonna be."

Eric hocks some vomit out of his throat. "You can have me."

Taggart smiles, and Eric's not sure if one of his bottom teeth is missing or just covered with dip. "Much as I'd like it, Mr. Know Nothing, I can't kill any of you. Crime scene technology being what it is these days, all y'all have to die right when the time comes. Injuries have to be consistent and all that. But that doesn't mean me and my boys can't have some fun while we wait."

He nods to his chuckleheads and two of them leave. "See, I know doctors can detect water in the lungs. But you know what? Even if they find it, it'll just be in one of you, and it won't be a cause of death. Given the horror show they're gonna find, I'm willing to risk it."

He's going to waterboard someone. If ever there was a time for God to intervene, now would be it.

Eric stands. "It should still be me. Just tell me where to go."

"You're missing two things, boy. First, it ain't gonna be you, no matter how badly you want your death to be anything more than a product of your own retardedness."

Eric wants to tell this guy there's no such word, but he refrains. As he's talking himself down, the door to the conference room opens, and Eric understands the second thing he's missing.

One of Taggart's guys is carrying a full, orange bucket. The other is gripping bleach-white hand towels and carrying a gray pitcher normally used to provide patients with ice water.

"Second, the fun's happening right here. But the question remains, who's it gonna be?" Taggart walks around the room like he's playing a perverted game of duck-duck-goose, the kind Lucifer might play. "It ain't you, Fowler, because you'll cry too easy. It's not any of the other men because they won't break."

He stops behind MacLaughlin. "But for me, fun's gonna be proving my theory that women make inferior servicemen." He wraps a strand of curly red hair around his right index finger like a phone cord he once saw in an old movie.

"My apologies, hon." Taggart leans down and sniffs. "Inferior service*people*."

48
JEREMIAH

Dom was right about Jeremiah and Mac. Kind of. His decision-making was compromised, but he was overcompensating to disprove the favoritism. That's how he ended up sitting six feet away from Mac rather than beside her with a twisted freak like Taggart in the room.

Mac's sitting beside Moore with about three feet between them. Dom is to her left, while Jeremiah is at the head of the table. He'd have to be locked out of the room with Lori and Boudreaux to be less effective.

But dissecting his prior movements will have to wait until a debrief—if any of them survive. For now, Jeremiah must assess the situation.

Taggart has lingered behind her, and now he's tugging on her hair. He was obviously a sixth-grade bully who grew into an incel. If he was ever a sergeant, Taggart no doubt harassed the women with whom he served. In all likelihood, he raped some.

It sounds like Mac will be spared that fate, though. Taggart is more interested in pleasing Novak than his own sexual desires, so he'll find a way to exert power over her in the form of torture. He hates using the term, and waterboarding is interrogation in many theaters. But Taggart has no mission-critical information to extract from Mac.

Taggart releases her hair and starts walking around the table again. "Question is, how will I know if she breaks? I need to question her for intel. Verifiable intel. And something she desperately won't want to give up."

He's justifying his actions. To himself. To his team. Maybe even to Jeremiah and the rest. He probably sees them as men who've done—or wish they had done—the disgusting things of which he takes great pride.

Sicko. But it's also telling. Taggart won't just turn into a horror villain in front of them. He'll take steps and explain himself along the way.

That gives Jeremiah time.

And hope.

Hope that Mac can hold out long enough for Jeremiah to move into position. Or give signals to Moore and Dom. Hope that she'll engage with Taggart long enough for Jeremiah to rush him and break his neck.

"But who here dislikes this spicy piece of tail enough to let me know when she's given up the goods?" Taggart stops behind Dom. "You smiled when I talked about her earlier. The joke about being in the Air Force. You work with her, but you don't like her. Must be your upbringing in that cult. The one up in the Rockies."

Taggart isn't entirely wrong. Dom had to get through a lot of psych testing to get where he's at, especially when it came to getting TS security clearance. He even agreed to be tested more regularly than required, according to the documents Daniels was slipped thanks to his connections in the old White House. He shared them with Jeremiah as a courtesy. After all, Daniels never had to be out on transports with someone who once lived at a compound that called itself the Divine Order of Grace and Serenity—but Jeremiah did.

Dom is stone-faced, but Taggart presses on. "You know the acronym for that place spells dogs, right? You a dog, boy?"

The irony of a K-following UNIC like Taggart shaming Dom for his childhood years in a cult isn't lost on Jeremiah.

The Divine Order rose to fame after a streaming docuseries revealed its leader—known by his DOGS as Grand Messiah—considered the dozens of women his wives. Though that was par for most religious cults, the selective murder and breeding of the children he fathered were much more disturbing.

Boys who didn't mature to a certain physical size, like Dom, were deemed too small to work the land and protect the compound. The punishment for their genetic deficiencies was death.

The same fate awaited girls deemed unattractive by Grand Messiah. The children who remained were going to be forced to procreate on the mountain, but the documentary aired in time to prevent that awful act. Public and media pressure were put on the FBI and ATF, and they risked another Waco by raiding the compound. Nobody was hurt, though the number of human remains found within two miles of the Grand Messiah's house was enough to turn anyone's stomach.

Like the rest, Taggart likely knows all of this, which makes everyone wait for his next question.

"Did they make you"—Taggart pauses and gestures, apparently human enough to not just come out and say it—"up on that mountain?" When Dom doesn't respond, Taggart gets a bit more direct. "What I'm asking you, boy, is did you come down a virgin or not?"

Dom bolts upright and turns on Taggart, hands still secured behind his back. Still, Dom towers over the older man and looks ready to rip out Taggart's throat with his teeth.

Taggart doesn't flinch.

"Finally," he says. "Now that you've joined the party, I'll tell you what I know. You don't like women, or other races. You were raised that way. Can't help it. And Lord knows I won't judge you for it. Not like everyone else does." He pats Dom on the butt. "I'm with you on all of that. So why don't you help me out here. Let me prove to them what me'n you already know."

As Dom's features soften, Jeremiah thinks the worst. Of course Jeremiah knew Dom held those beliefs. But it never interfered with the work. Jeremiah was never going to be friends with Dom, but he couldn't argue with his efficacy as a member of his team or the value he added to INSTA.

But now Dom looks ready to join Taggart in his torture of Mac.

Dom leans down, nodding as he does, not yet making eye contact with Taggart. When their faces are level, Dom jerks his head to face Taggart.

The loogie is large and wet as it hits Taggart's face.

Dom headbutts him for good measure, and Taggart falls to the ground as his men take out Dom's knees. Dom's grunts are loud, but so is his smile as Taggart's sycophants kick and drop the butts of their rifles into Dom's torso and temple.

Taggart wipes away the veneer of control with Dom's phlegm, and by the time he's standing again, he's the personification of rage. "Enough with the dog, get the woman ready."

One of the mercenaries keeps a knee on Dom's neck while the other two lower Mac's chair so her head is near the carpet but her feet and hips are elevated. Taggart walks to the bucket, dips in a towel and the pitcher, then walks back toward her.

Jeremiah looks at Mac, ready to stand and rush the lot of them with his hands tied behind his back. Instead, she looks his way, corners of her lips curled, eyes twinkling. *Hold my beer and watch this shit.*

Jeremiah knows he'll have to rescue her soon. But first, she wants to make a point.

And if they're all about to die, he can give her that last bit of satisfaction.

Mac's still looking at Jeremiah when Taggart settles over her, legs spread.

"I'll start off with an easy one," he says. "You ever screwed a commanding officer? Keep in mind, I already know the answer. Split-tail like you'd never get as far as you did without it. But it'll take you a round or two 'fore you cop to it."

Mac rolls her head so she's facing the ceiling, but she keeps the grin.

"I am an American fighting man." Her smile widens. "I serve in the forces which guard my country and our way of life. I am prepared to give my life in their defense."

Taggart lets her finish. Then he drops his right knee into Mac's sternum and puts the towel over her face. One of his mercs tightens it over her face as he pours the water. The room falls silent, save for the splashing of water and her wet screams. Everyone, except perhaps for Fowler, has heard it. Hell, some units used to waterboard themselves to blow off steam overseas. They'd make a contest of it. Pool their money and bet on who could go the longest and how many seconds the winner would hold out.

When Taggart runs out of water, he tosses the pitcher and rips off the sopping towel. Mac coughs out what she can, though she'll die with liquid in her lungs.

"You think you're funny, bitch? First, Reagan changed that sacred code to accommodate your kind, so you ain't even saying it right."

The words *fighting man* were dropped from the official Code of Conduct for Members of the Armed Forces of the United States in 1988, along with a few other edits toward gender neutrality, but Jeremiah's sure some cocksucker of a CO made her memorize President Eisenhower's original 1955 Executive Order.

As she continues sucking in air, Mac opens her eyes and stares at Taggart.

"I will *never* surrender of my own free will. If in command I will never surrender my men while they still have the means to resist."

The guards don't have to be told. They stretch the towel over her face while handing him a full pitcher.

"I knew I's gonna make you scream from the second I got your file with that picture," Taggart says. "I just figured it'd be a different kind of screaming."

Jeremiah knows she won't make it to part VI of the code. He also knows she'll die trying.

He doesn't know how to make Taggart stop before then.

49
LORI

Boudreaux yanks Lori down to the floor. Her body's already aching. She may soon start calling it what it is—withdrawals—but for now, Lori's too consumed with ending the torture across the hall.

"I can't believe you can just sit here," she says. "You heard what those two pricks said when they came in."

Lori's eyes have adjusted to the dark, and thanks to the thin crack below the closet door she has enough light to make out shapes. She still can't see Boudreaux's eyes, though, and his voice—which must've been altered in an unnatural way—isn't giving her much. Lori thinks he's upset, but she's not sure.

"I know they're in there waterboarding her," he says. "But we can't do anything about that right now."

Lori punches where she thinks Boudreaux's chin should be. She connects, but nowhere near hard enough.

"I hate you right now," she says. "Do all men get off on hurting women, or is it just the ones in my life?"

"Lori." She's irate, but somehow her name coming out of Boudreaux's mouth calms her. "You have to wait with me. It's the only way any of us'll make it out of here."

Lori can't stand getting told to stand down. But with little choice in the matter, she scoots away from Boudreaux and takes a few deep breaths.

"Thanks," he says. "I know you think she's dying in there. And believe me, so does she. But I don't think this Taggart prick will kill her. Not in there, anyway. His men are younger and, from what I could see, not as depraved as their so-called sergeant. No matter how stupid and loyal, they'll never follow through with kill orders after watching a woman get waterboarded to death."

The logic is sound, but that doesn't keep her from grinding her teeth, thinking about her impotence. She's sitting on the floor next to a mop while someone else—probably another woman, albeit one whom she's long suspected as coveting Jeremiah—is drowning, simulated or not.

If Boudreaux would just help her break down the door, Lori has the knowledge and at least some of the skill left to beat the holy hell out of Taggart and at least one of his guards before getting taken out.

"You might get three of them," Boudreaux says.

How does he always know what I'm thinking? He can't even read her face—unless his night vision borders on superhuman.

"That fourth one would kill you, though," he continues. "That's why I need you to control your impulses. I know you've never really been able to do that in the past. But if you don't now, we die."

"And how the hell would you know what I have or haven't been able to do in the past?" It's a legitimate question. Boudreaux's seen her IA file and knows some of what she did to Kevin Ryan Booker. Boudreaux also knew her father, which means he understands more about her than most.

But Boudreaux can't know everything she's done. The Colonel would never discuss her training with anyone other than the participants. Her father's secrecy is the reason he's buried in Amarillo instead of locked up in Leavenworth.

"Here's what I know," Boudreaux says. "Your father was in command when I joined CAG. I wanted to be a shooter, but he said my file indicated I was best suited for advance force operations based on my time in the Ranger Reconnaissance Company."

"That *aptitude for intel* you talked about."

"Affirmative. But I was less enlightened as a slightly younger man and didn't want to work in the girl squadron, so your father and I didn't start off on the best of terms."

Nobody was ever on good terms with the Colonel, except maybe those who shared his special brand of psychopathy. "I thought you were going to tell me something I didn't know."

She can't see it, but Lori pictures Boudreaux smiling. "I was young and headstrong, so I told Colonel Young I'd only sign up for G Squadron if I was given a fast track to commanding my troop and a chance to lead the squadron."

"Ballsy. Even for an operator."

"I figured I had SF waiting for me. Or private security if he got me booted. Of course, your father had the last word in our negotiation."

Sounds right. "And what was that?"

"Colonel Young said he had a daughter that he was training to be a unit Operator. She was going to be the first woman shooter, but he'd have to use her in G Squadron first, then have someone else recommend her for operator training."

"And you were going to be that someone."

"He said he'd get me to command sergeant major if I helped him make history. And yes, that's how he phrased it."

Boudreaux had once again revealed nothing.

Well, almost nothing.

The Colonel told her from the time she hit puberty that his goal was to raise the first female operator. Women had worked with the Unit as combat and service support since before her father took over command. Most were on base, but the best had been used in the field, posing as wives and girlfriends as part of covert covers and preparing the battlefield in advance of operations.

But if her father got his way, she'd be the first woman to even attempt Delta's Operator Training Course.

She'd known all of this for more than twenty years.

Boudreaux's existence as her future mentor and ticket into OTC was the fresh intel.

How much does he know? "Yeah, the Colonel was something else. He and my mother—"

"May she rest in peace."

"Yeah, thanks. Anyway, they were teaching me hand-to-hand and MMA from the time I could walk. It started because I was cute, but then my"—she points to her head, then realizes that won't do any good—"my genetics started showing. Then training got serious. And after my mother finally cracked all the way up, my father could operate without resistance."

At this point, Boudreaux either knows who Lori is, or he thinks daddy was tough on her as a teenager.

"I know about them."

She doesn't say anything. Boudreaux could leave it there and she'd assume he put together the news reports about two missing soldiers found dead near Fort Bragg in North Carolina. Those facts are part of what led to Col. Wyatt Young's discharge from the United States Army for reasons other than honorable.

But the story gleaned from those stories and other gossip on base are far from what Lori would call the truth.

"I know it took two people to bury those bodies."

Well, of course it did. Anyone privy to the crime scene analysis would know that. If it's true.

"I know the first operator died nearly twenty minutes after the fatal blows to the head and neck."

Okay, so he's also seen the medical examiner's report.

"I know the second died much more quickly after taking a railroad spike to the neck. He bled out despite his killer's attempts to stanch the bleeding by shoving small thumbs inside the wound, though he probably wouldn't have survived the blunt force trauma to his head and face."

Pretty damn close. But he's guessing. Not only is he a little off, but there's only one way he could know the stuff he has right.

"I know she thought someone was calling a medic, but instead he was calling me."

No. There's no way that's right. But if it is… "I need you to know something." Her voice is shaking, stomach lurching. "Look … I didn't know … the first kid, he was alive when my father loaded him into the truck. I didn't know he died until after the Colonel was back from burying the second guy."

"You can't even say their names." Boudreaux's voice has lost its rounded corners. "And it's not like you could've forgotten them."

Boudreaux knows a lot—much more than she could've ever imagined—but her father didn't read him in all the way. He knows their manner of death, but not how they died. In this case, that's a distinction with a hell of a difference.

"I knew those men," Boudreaux says, his voice angry. "So now, even if it's the only time you do it, you're going to address them by their name when speaking of them."

"I never knew their names. And they didn't know mine."

"What, did they know you by your nickname? I'm sure they didn't tell you their real names, either. Doesn't make things any better."

"Screw you," she says, her voice now matching his. "Don't pretend you know everything about me. You have no idea what happened."

He doesn't speak, but Lori can hear Boudreaux work to control his breathing. "Then you better explain it."

"Why should I? You've had your mind made up about Gloria Young for decades, and you started projecting that onto me since the plane ride from New Orleans. What on earth can I say now that'll change your mind?"

"Two things." His volume's lowered, but Lori can't tell if he's any less furious with her. "First, Gloria Young has been a victim of a sadistic piece-of-shit father since I first heard her name. Second, as far as I can tell, Lori Young has been a victim quite a bit in her life, too."

She takes umbrage with being called a victim. But, perhaps arguing semantics and feminism with a man in the middle of a monologue won't do any good.

"But until a minute ago, I assumed you were remorseful for killing those men. Now I wonder if your memory takes up space that should've been reserved for empathy."

You and me, both. Psycho father. Schizo mother. A brain that scared her way before she knew what either of those things were. Yeah, Lori's questioned her actions before.

"Why do you think I'm a drunk and a drug addict?" It's the first time she's said the words, though the thought's been infecting her for years. "You've wondered if I'm a monster for two minutes. I've wondered that my whole goddamn life."

He scoots over to her. "If you're asking the question, the answer is no, you're not." Boudreaux's voice is back to his standard cement-mixer growl. "Their names were Dennis and Scott, and both'd just finished OTC. They were young, but they were operators. How'd you get close enough to kill them without introductions from your father?"

Lori's the only person alive who knows those details. It won't help her to tell Boudreaux. The weight of those memories won't lift if they're spoken aloud. It'll double and leave him as heavy as Lori's been since she was fifteen.

"My shoulders are load-bearing," Boudreaux says. "I can handle it."

"Okay," she says, excited, hoping she's not coming off as confrontational. "How do you do that? My screwed-up memory is one thing, but you've been reading my mind all day and it's starting to freak me out."

"I'm not telekinetic, I promise." Anger may be difficult to make out in his voice, but Lori has heard the smile in his voice and has a match.

"That's exactly what a mutant mind-reader would say, Professor X."

Boudreaux's laugh comes from deep in his chest. Lori would join him if she didn't feel so terrible.

"Lori, I've been thinking about you and your family for a long time now. I've had every conversation imaginable with you, and even a few unimaginable ones since we've been together today."

Yeah, but –

"And as for the weight and memories metaphor, your father used to use that one on us. I bet if you check, he did with you, too."

Lori does, and Boudreaux's right. He's not as smart as he thinks, though. And if it takes hearing the rest of this to get her point across, so be it.

"We both know a woman my size can't hope to take out someone like you without the element of surprise," she says. "Let alone a fifteen-year-old version of me."

"It's happened, but yeah, you'd never want to go in on equal footing."

"Now, me at fifteen with makeup and a dress, picture me as the Duchess Meghan, not your little cousin on her way to church. How do you think my father got his men to engage with me?"

"You don't mean …"

"The Colonel was friendly with the bar owners near base, as one has to be when corralling knuckle-draggers like—"

"Watch it." He's mostly playful, with just a little bite. "I bet I'm the most well-read man you've ever met."

"I wasn't going to say *you*, but obviously you've heard that one before." She lets him stew in embarrassment for a moment before continuing. "And I didn't know when it might be coming, so I had to always be on guard when he sent me out to one of his favorite places. I won five barfights and broke seven pool cues before it became a problem for the owners, so my father took his game to the streets."

Boudreaux shifts away from her. It's less than an inch, but the chasm between them will be the Palo Duro Canyon after she's done talking. "He made you pretend to be a hooker?"

"Yes."

"That's the most disgusting thing I've ever heard."

Just keep listening. "Anyway, the first guy …"

"Scott."

"Scott." She says the name, and Boudreaux's right—there's more meaning to the story now. More guilt. "Scott thought the Colonel had him on a solo training exercise. I was the ubiquitous bad guy's favorite working girl, and his mission was to get out of me the location of our favorite rendezvous spots. He was then supposed to get me to set up an appointment. Scott was told to use any means necessary. He wasn't told I was Colonel Young's daughter, and I think you'll agree, there's not a ton of resemblance other than our eyes."

Boudreaux doesn't speak, but his breathing grows more rapid as she continues.

"I knew Scott's playbook, but I have the best countermeasures for a man's training that nature's ever produced. All I had to do was tell him I was under constant surveillance, and my *manager* would kill me if I didn't earn. Scott offered to fake it, but I said I was too scared and that a blowjob in the cab of his pickup would suffice."

The shaking and nausea have returned. It's been years since Lori's dried out, and she's never talked about this. She's surprised Boudreaux isn't holding her hair over the remaining mop bucket already.

He sounds ready to use it, too. "At fifteen? Did you even know … I mean, Colonel Young didn't make you practice …"

"Oh God, no. I'd done all of that with boys at school already. The Colonel didn't *know it*, know it, but he understood sex was part of my toolkit by then. That and my mother's disappearance were the reason he started bringing in his men."

"Still gross."

Just keep listening. "So, the Colonel said I couldn't shoot any of his guys. They didn't have any rules, though, other than accomplishing their objective. I convinced Scott it was in his best interest to keep my pimp happy, so he drove to the parking lot of his church and I pulled it out."

"The bodies in New Orleans."

"My father said a man's never more vulnerable than when his dick is out. One of the truest things he ever said. And let me tell you, for a guy who wasn't on board at first, Scott sure got comfortable. Said if anyone asked, he was bringing me in so I could receive guidance and penance for my sins."

"I honestly thought he was a good guy."

"He was being manipulated. And he sure as hell didn't deserve what came next." Lori forces down the puke pooling in her throat. "While Scott's eyes were closed and he was telling me about how grateful my country would be, I pulled his gun out of his center console. I couldn't shoot him, so I settled for beating him with it. The Colonel had been watching and listening—"

"Christ almighty."

"Yeah. So, the Colonel pulled me out of the truck while I was still working on Scott, who was still breathing. My father said he would drive him to a hospital in his truck, so I took my father's keys and went home."

Lori lets Boudreaux sit in silence for what feels like a full minute, likely recalling his part of the story. She'll be happy to never hear it.

"He lied to me at first, too," Boudreaux finally says. "Told me Scott had been an invited dinner guest and stayed for Scotch and cigars. Said he found Scott having his way with you and beat him. I think he told the truth about trying to get Scott to the hospital. Your dad called me from Scott's pickup, and it's hard to fake that kind of panic."

"I think you're right, which made it even crazier when he wanted to continue. There was one guy who survived after Scott. I stopped when he went unconscious. On my own. That's why there was a third."

She wants storytime to end there, but Boudreaux clears his throat. "Well, go on. I've wanted to know how and why you punched Dennis's ticket for a long time now."

"Fine. Same setup as before, only this time Dennis takes me for a long drive—so long the Colonel had to back way off. He had a tracker on me but lost visual. Dennis left the main roads at Knox Street and took his old Bronco into a clearing off to the east and followed some abandoned train tracks into the woods. We were less than a mile from a residential neighborhood to the east and the railhead to the west, but the trees were thick enough to make us feel secluded. Might's well've been ten miles out in the country."

"That location makes no tactical sense."

Dammit. Lori wanted to spare both their ears from this detail. "So"—she takes a breath to steady herself—"when I said the setup was the same, I lied. I didn't find out until later, but this time the Colonel wasn't testing one of his men. He suspected Dennis shouldn't've passed his psych evals and knew he'd been caught soliciting in the past."

"It was a sting?"

"Yes, though that was a secondary objective at best. He mainly wanted to test me in a less-controlled situation. I suppose the Colonel might've doled out some internal punishment if Dennis had lived, but I think he'd've recommended a promotion. Birds of a feather and all that."

Boudreaux's breathing intensifies. "Okay, so you're out by the railroad tracks where nobody can see you."

"I was suspicious on the drive that he never mentioned anything other than having a good time, but I figured his interrogation technique could just be different than I'd expected. After a few minutes down there I stopped and broke character, asked why he wasn't interrogating me yet."

"And that's when he realized you were Colonel Young's daughter."

"I don't think he got that far. He knew I wasn't a hooker, maybe even that I was an undercover detective. Either way, he knew he was in deep trouble. Dennis's first reaction was to slap me, so I bent him the wrong way and got out of the truck. I didn't make it to the clearing, though."

"How'd you get the better of him?"

"He was preoccupied with getting in trouble, I guess. And I was still good enough to beat a lot of men in a fight. After rolling around for a few seconds, I kicked him off and made it to the tracks. He tackled me again, but my hand found the spike. I hit him in the temple, but that just dazed him. Dennis was on his knees trying to get up when I stabbed him with it."

"Good girl."

"Maybe if I'd stopped there. But the spike wasn't in deep enough. I'd knocked him to the ground, but he started pulling it out."

Lori pauses, hopes Boudreaux will tell her to stop.

He doesn't.

"I straddled him and knocked away his hands," she says, queasy. "Then I used my palms to push in the spike as far as my hundred pounds could manage. When he stopped fighting, I pulled it out and started beating his face with it. That's when the Colonel pulled me off and jabbed *his* thumb in."

Lori stops, listening to the replay. But this time she's also feeling the steel slide into his flesh.

Disgusting.

Satisfying.

"The Colonel told me his keys were in the truck," she says. "He didn't say it, but I knew Dennis was dead before I put it in gear."

They both know the rest of the story. Boudreaux and her father buried Dennis that night. Three days later, the Fayetteville and Charlottesville papers posted an article about two Fort Bragg soldiers missing within two months. Local TV picked up the story the following morning. By the evening news, all the media had a statement from the Army. They were working with local law enforcement to find the missing men.

Internally, the Colonel's story that he had the first operator on a solo deployment was falling apart. So, rather than lie again, her father came clean.

Except he didn't know how to tell a straight story, so he said Gloria Young really had been hooking. As far as the Army is concerned, she and her imaginary pimp had killed the men, and Col. Wyatt Young's sin was covering up for his daughter.

What officer wouldn't do the same?

Bragg Media Relations could manage local managing editors. But a leak could produce a sensational headline and stories describing sex and illegal activity by an officer's underage daughter. That would attract major international media, who would dig into the nature of their service. *The Washington Post* had already run a brief, and that was without knowing the missing soldiers were less than six degrees from POTUS.

The Army couldn't risk the media exposing the Unit and its command, so they planted leaks. All reporting revolved around a love triangle between two soldiers who worked in the same non-combat unit on base and a woman who's wanted by CID. Nobody's identity was revealed, and the news cycle moved on.

When the Colonel was discharged, they moved into a house her father inherited from his folks. When a homicide detective from North Carolina called to say Misty Young had been found dead of an overdose in a homeless camp, the Colonel inherited some money from her parents that had been tied up with her status as a missing person.

The money didn't last long, not even with a second mortgage on the house, and he had to list an OTH discharge on employment applications. The Colonel wouldn't take a service industry job, and he refused to quit the expensive booze and Cubans.

With no path forward, he finally fired the bullet with his name on it.

Lori's body starts shaking and Boudreaux wraps his arms around her. But she's not cold. She's sick and anxious, so he releases her. He stays beside her, though, making sure their legs remain in contact through denim and polycotton.

She clenches her teeth to regain control of her nerves. "Neither of them deserved it. Not even Dennis. He was human garbage, but what he did doesn't even meet the Old Testament, eye-for-an-eye threshold for the death penalty."

"I don't know about that." Boudreaux sounds confident, as though he's given this topic some thought. "If that's your criteria, neither do the guys who swing outside of Republic prisons for kiddie porn. The way I see it, anyone who disagrees with that ought to be put on a list."

Lori doesn't know if Boudreaux's right. And as someone who deserves the noose herself, she's as far from the Judgment Seat as a person can get. "Let's hope I never draw you for jury duty."

She laughs, but it's not reciprocated. Lori's used to chasing her dark secrets around, but Boudreaux must not be the type to ever let his peek out of their compartment.

"I did so much for him." His voice is a lonesome, mournful mix of syllables. "I knew he had a bad side, but I thought the good we did in our official capacity far outweighed my off-the-books work. But if I'd known all this, I'd've left and never looked back."

"He was a master manipulator. It's understandable for you to help him bury the bodies. Disappearing people is SOP for Delta operators, right? And choosing you must've made sense when you figured out I'd killed them."

Boudreaux's leg trembles as he scoots away. "Maybe if that's all I'd done."

What other terrible things had Boudreaux done for her father? Lori doubts he's talking about something that happened on a deployment. Is he guilty about ops that went bad, or ones that bordered on assassination? Probably. But he'd have no reason to bring any of those up now.

It's about her.

Lori wants to know, but she can't ask the question. Her brand of self-harm is numbing pain, not causing it.

"What do you remember about your mother's disappearance?"

"For starters, it wasn't a disappearance." Lori doesn't know where this is going, but she doesn't like it. "She stopped taking her medicine and left. The doctors said it's common."

"The doctors talked to you about your mom?"

No. They talked to the Colonel, who relayed the info to Lori. The picture's coming into focus. "Are you telling me my father kicked my mentally ill mother out of our house?"

"Not exactly. Your dad told me she stopped taking her antipsychotics and wanted to move back home to be with her parents. Problem was—"

"They'd already passed. The doctors ... my father ... told me that's why Mom stopped taking her meds."

"I got the same story. He told your mom he'd give her time and money to go get the house fixed up so they could have a vacation home, but only if she went back on her medicine. She either did or was lucid enough to fool him for a bit, then took off."

That's one of the most human stories Lori's ever heard about the Colonel. But why is Boudreaux the one telling it?

"This is the part you're not going to like," he says. "After three days of radio silence, he tasked me with tracking her down. I found her shot up with heroin in Oklahoma. She was pretty incoherent, but I gathered she was trying to reconnect with her ancestors."

Boudreaux even knows her heritage. A man Lori met less than a day ago knows more about her than the man in the next room who shared her life for years, and she's having trouble reckoning with the cognitive dissonance.

Then it hits her.

Her mother only left once.

"If you found her, why didn't she ever come home again?"

"I extracted her and delivered her to Colonel Young. He said your mother couldn't move back in until she agreed to get straight."

There's the prick I knew. "And you helped him."

"He told me to keep an eye on her and—"

Boudreaux keeps talking, but Lori uses her newfound ability to focus and thinks instead about the last time she saw her mother.

It had been a good day. The sun was bright after days of rain, and gone were Mom's ramblings about her past life, of the voices telling her to drive to her homeland. That morning, a Sunday, she made breakfast. Fluffy pancakes with her special blend of vanilla and nutmeg. Thick bacon, homemade hash browns, eggs cooked to order. Lori could only stomach scrambled, but her mother always asked, as though one day her daughter might wake up a different person.

While Lori and her father went to church, her mother stayed behind and made the house. The Colonel and the rest of the community were okay with her not attending. She'd had a few outbursts during services. During the last one, she started speaking in tongues, though Lori later heard some of the words during a museum exhibit on the early Native American tribes of the great Plains. Her mother had been speaking Comanche.

When they returned home, the Colonel helped Lori's mother pack the car. She was only supposed to be gone for a week, and there was no shortage of underlings to serve as Lori and her father's chauffeur.

Her mother hugged Lori last. I'm going to be fine, she said. You'll see. Then, after the Colonel was nearly to the house, her mother said one last thing.

Sometimes you have to listen, baby girl. When the time comes, listen.

***

LORI'S HAD ENOUGH. She's dry and jonesing and just found out a man she'd been trusting with her life is the biggest liar of them all. As she bolts upright, Lori's legs threaten to give out. But she holds it together long enough to mule-kick the door.

"Get me out." She's screaming, mimicking the volume and tone from that night beside the railroad tracks. It's the only time she's been loud enough to be heard over the banging of her feet on the door. "I'm getting sick in here. Somebody open this door now."

Boudreaux's still talking. She's back to recording his pathetic excuses, and maybe she'll listen later. But right now, there's nothing he can say that'll make up for what he did. If he would've helped Lori's mom get right, the Colonel would never have taken his sick games as far as he did. Lori wouldn't be a murderer. She wouldn't know the joy that comes with taking a life that deserves to be taken, or the guilt that comes with prematurely snuffing one out.

Boudreaux's not trying to stop her. He's still jabbering on about trying to be a good guy and wishing he'd realized how dangerous her father was. As he raises his voice, Lori switches to kicking with her left leg and her screams bleed into belligerent nonsense. Her legs are about to give when she hears a key in the lock. Lori squeezes her eyes shut to protect herself from the unforgiving halogen waiting outside.

"What'n the hell's going on in here?" the guard asks. He's the youngest one who entered earlier to get the bucket.

She turns toward the light and opens her mouth, expecting words to come out.

Instead, she vomits, and by the sound of the guard's cursing, he was caught in the crossfire.

"Goddammit lady, you could've warned me."

"Please help me," she says, eyes still closed. "I need medicine."

"What kind of medicine does she need?" the guard asks Boudreaux, as though she's incapable of knowing what drugs will get her right.

She opens her eyes. The guard is looking over his shoulder at Taggart.

"Based on what I've read, she needs pain pills. Two Oxy ought to do it."

"For my leg," she says, the lie popping out reflexively. "I was shot earlier today in New Orleans."

Her eyes are adjusting, and she can see that the kid isn't really a kid. He's about her age, though the sandy beard's never going to grow in like the SF guys he's trying to emulate.

"All right, Dust Devil," Taggart says, leaning in. "Y'all smell terrible. Get cleaned up and give her a fix." He probes her with his brown eyes. "You're lucky I need you alive and cooperative."

Dusty leads her past the nurse's station and toward the patient rooms. "I'll take you to one of the empty rooms so you can wash yourself off. Then we'll get the pills."

The door to Room 5 is open, and she sees Ramirez lying in the bed. He looks peaceful enough and the heart monitor sounds steady.

"He going to be okay?" she asks.

"Don't know. I heard the doc say something about a coma and needing blood. Not that it matters."

She gets to live and a hero like Ramirez has been slated for death. "Doesn't seem fair."

"Hey, stuff's rough all over. Not up to me who lives and who dies."

Just following orders. Dusty strikes her as a good soldier, one who got in to do good and looks up to those who've been in longer than him.

"What branch were you with?" she asks.

"Army Rangers."

"Seventy-fifth?"

He lowers his head and comes to a stop beside a door. "Well, I was Ranger qualified. When Oklahoma seceded, I decided I'd rather come back and serve in the Guard." He opens the door. "Ladies first."

The room's clean and appears to have a large bathroom. Lori immediately starts devising plans that involve sex. But is that necessary? They need her alive, and Taggart has already decided to let her get clean and high.

She wants to try a different approach this time.

"Sounds like you really wanted to serve in a Ranger battalion," she says before disappearing into the bathroom, which does have a full shower with a detachable head. "You want to be Special Forces, too?"

"Oh, yes ma'am. Since I's a kid."

She walks back out into the room. "You can wash off your boots and pantlegs in here. I'll need a set of scrubs. I'll be back in—"

"Can't do it." He's not being mean about it, just matter-of-fact.

"Got to respect me for trying, though."

Dusty cracks a smile.

Rapport.

"You ever hang out with a guy in Delta?"

"Would I know if I had?"

He's quick. If he weren't holding a lot of innocent people hostage as part of a plot to blow up modern society, she might like the guy.

"The guy I was in the closet with was in the Unit." She steps closer. "And my father ran it. Back in the day, of course."

Dusty's reaction confirms it. He's a military starfucker. And if she's lucky, so are the rest of them.

50
ERIC

Even Boudreaux is broken now. It only takes one of them to escort the grizzly from one cage to another. The only difficulty lies in which seat he'll take. He takes one beside Eric, which puts them both opposite Hansen and MacLaughlin, who's back at the table but soaked and coughing.

Eric and Boudreaux are catty-corner from Moore and Reynolds. Lori's still somewhere in the bowels of the hospital, but based on her outburst, she's not handling the situation any better than the rest of them.

"Y'all're the saddest sacks I've ever seen," Taggart says. "Makes sense, though. All but one of you"—he tilts his head toward Eric—"used to be badasses. But now here you are, fixing to get taken out by a couple of regular Joes."

Eric wishes Taggart were wrong. But everyone at the table knows what it's like to set up and take out high-level targets—say, the people who are about to blow up an entire town and an eighth of the continent's oil reserves. But they can't seem to defeat this joker and his band of morons, who are acting at the behest of someone who named himself after Colonel Klinger.

But with only two guards in the room, now would be the perfect time. Boudreaux may look like he's been hit with a tranquilizer, But Moore doesn't seem worse for wear. Add in Jeremiah, who was DEVGRU, and Hansen's Special Forces skills, and even with their hands zip-tied behind their backs, those three could lead a successful charge against Taggart and the guard he keeps calling Prickly Pear.

And surely there's something sharp enough in the unguarded closet across the hall to cut through the flex-cuffs.

Eric may not have what it takes to neutralize the guards. But getting others to do what he wants is Eric's specialty.

"What do you mean when you say *regular Joes*, sergeant?" he asks.

"I mean us grunts, you goddamn spook."

Eric snorts. Nobody's ever called Eric a spook. Not in real life, anyway. They do it in movies and books, but that's always made him laugh. "You've never worked with intelligence officers, have you?"

"Hell no. Spies and all them covert military operations are the reason the country's in such bad shape right now." He scans the table. "I understand giving Title 50 authority to spies in the cold war, and I appreciate those men who helped us kick all that commie ass."

That's not how it worked, but Taggart must be referring to the fact that CIA and other officers in the former United States intelligence community were authorized to conduct covert operations. Which means Taggart's about to move on to the military, which are Title 10 operations.

"But when the military's involved, Congress and the American people were supposed to hold cowboys like you accountable."

That's basically correct, but nobody involved would ever put it in such black-and-white terms.

Before Eric can correct him, Moore scoffs. "That's such a simplistic view. But what should I expect from such a simple mind?"

"Says the guy who sold out and started doing the company's dirty work."

Here we go. Eric doesn't have much time to start a brawl. When the other guard comes back with Lori, it'll be that much harder to get control of the room.

"The way you talk, I'd say you never even served," Eric says. "Only a civilian would talk the way you do. See, we're the guys proud to have taken out the leaders of Al-Qaeda and ISIS. I guess y'all are the other guys."

Taggart rushes to Eric and jerks him to his feet. "I'm Sgt. Jack Taggart of the United States Army. That's who I am. You're the one in the room who never served, asshole."

Taggart draws his pistol and whips it across Eric's face. As he falls to the table, Eric kicks Boudreaux's leg, hoping he'll react and rush Taggart while he's preoccupied.

Boudreaux nods and stands. As he does, movement in the background catches Eric's attention. Through eyes spotty from the impact, he sees the door to the conference room open.

Lori steps through first, wearing the same shirt but scrubs for bottoms. Her escort's wearing the same clothes, but they're wet, like he washed them and didn't bother to dry them.

He may be wet, but the man they call Dust Devil moves just as quickly as ever as he races past Lori and shoves the butt of his rifle upside Boudreaux's temple.

51
JEREMIAH

Jeremiah stands, determined not to let Lori face the same hell he just watched Mac go through. He makes it two steps when a gunshot brings the room to a standstill.

His ears are ringing, but Jeremiah sees Taggart pointing his M18 in the air, debris from the cheap ceiling panels falling in front of his face.

"If y'all want to get this party started early, I can do it." Taggart's words are muffled, but everyone understands or gets the gist.

Jeremiah sits beside Lori, and the rest of the hostages follow suit like a kindergarten class after the teacher finally loses his shit. Said teacher and his assistants, Prickly Pear and Dust Devil, have a confab in the corner, though Jeremiah can't hear what they're discussing.

Lori leans in, keeping her eyes on the guards. "I told Dusty I heard commotion out in the lobby, with the doctor and nurses. He said he'd send Taggart out there since apparently the doc has to be handled with kid gloves."

As they watch Taggart holster his pistol and leave the room, Jeremiah wishes things had turned out differently for Lori. She is so capable. He's told her before, but Jeremiah has dreamed of an alternate reality where they met while he was still in DEVGRU. She would've been the best female asset his team—or any of the teams in Black Squadron—would've ever worked with.

Even now, after years of treating herself like garbage and a day that would make most people give up, Lori had the presence of mind to get out of that closet and convince the enemy to divide their forces and leave the dumbest in charge of securing a group of elite operators.

He hates that they met when both their lives were so jacked up, him a drunk, her an addict—though hers wasn't always chemical. When she was addicted to being murder police, Lori was a major asset to her community. Had she the chance to channel that obsession into AFO and OPE work with Jeremiah, maybe she could've stopped wars, been an anti-Helen, acting as her own Trojan Horse.

"Follow my lead," Lori whispers before turning toward the two remaining guards, who are now standing sentry at either side of the door, rifles leveled. "You two okay? I didn't mean to get anyone in trouble."

Are *they* okay? Jeremiah's not sure what game Lori's playing. What the hell lead is he supposed to be following if she's sucking up to the enemy?

"Yes ma'am, we're okay," Dust Devil says. "And thanks for the help. I guess you and the doctor are our primary objective."

And the rest of us are to be neutralized. Did Lori want the rest of us to know we're on the chopping block? Could be motivating. It definitely pisses off Jeremiah.

"Well here," Lori says, "before Sergeant Taggart comes back, why don't I get started introducing you to everyone like I said I would."

Prickly Pear looks at his buddy, confused. "What's she talking about?"

"You know the guy you brought out of the closet after I left?" Dust Devil leans over like he's telling a dirty joke. "He was in Delta."

"Bullshit. If he was, you'd never know."

Dust Devil looks at Lori, appealing to his new friend.

"Let's start at the bottom and work our way up," Lori says, nodding to Fowler. "First we have a former intelligence officer with the CIA. You were the deputy director, right?"

"Not quite," Fowler says. "That was my boss, Randall Gates. He's the one—"

"Yeah, he was working for K," Prickly Pear says. "Sergeant Taggart told us. Said you're too big a pussy to go through with the mission."

"Boys, there's no reason to call names," Lori says. "Especially when you know he won't be with us for much longer."

Jesus, Lori.

"Like I said, I was starting at the bottom." She tilts her head toward Moore. "This man's name is Robert Moore. He also used to work for the Agency, but he was a Marine before that."

"We heard sarge earlier," Dust Devil says.

"Well, what he didn't tell you is that Moore was one of the CIA's top assassins."

Moore flashes anger. "That's not very accurate."

Lori forces a smile. "Oh, don't be modest. You used to be an American James Bond. But I bet you drank Kentucky Bourbon, not fruity martinis."

Is this where I start taking her lead? If not, Jeremiah can't fathom what Lori's doing.

"I know you can't talk about it, but c'mon, we all know what you military boys do for the CIA." She turns to the guards. "I'm sure you two have heard the rumors."

They nod.

"You missed it earlier, but Sergeant Taggart said guys like him ruined America's defense by operating without proper authority," Prickly Pear says. "He told us not that long ago that an assassination started the first World War, and we were one assassination from a third. That's why our mission with K is so important."

Dom hocks a loogie and spits. "American armed forces never assassinated anyone. We eliminated the leaders of enemy states as part of our national security. Your sergeant wouldn't know a damn thing about what it really takes to defend this country."

"You mean the Republic of Oklahoma?" Dust Devil says, grinning like he'd just caught his teacher writing the wrong answer on the board. "I'd say we know more about protecting that than you do, old man."

The kid giggles. Jeremiah grins.

Dom growls.

"Calm down, Dom," Jeremiah says. "It's okay. I'll explain it to him."

Jeremiah understands where Lori's going with this. Her new buddies are obviously interested in special operations forces. They probably wanted to be in units like DEVGRU and Delta before the secessions, so they're immersed in an interesting situation.

In other words, these two are distracted.

And while Lori was never a military wife, she always understood one thing when Jeremiah went off on a transport.

A distracted soldier's a dead soldier.

52
LORI

Lori taps her boot against Jeremiah's, letting him know he's right. She doesn't know how much time they'll have with just these two guarding them. Since she was lying about the commotion in the lobby, Lori's surprised Taggart hasn't come busting through the door yet.

But she needs another minute or two before Dusty will be impressed enough to leave his post. If she can trip him and slip her handcuffed hands under her ass, there's hope of getting control of a gun.

Lori also needs time for the drugs to kick in. She took one and a half Oxy and Dusty took the leftover. She's getting right, and he'll be feeling real good soon.

"In fact," Jeremiah says, "Dom here wasn't just Special Forces. Tell'em where you ended your time in."

"Can't. Classified."

Dusty takes a step their way. "C'mon man," he says, a drunk trying to convince his sober buddy to take a shot. "Who're we telling?"

Hansen shakes his head, but Jeremiah leans toward Dusty. "He was Intelligence Support Activity."

Now Prickly moves away from the door. "No freaking way. Gray Fox?"

"Only in Afghanistan," Jeremiah says. "We call them Orange, and they keep secrets even I don't know. Hell, I've known the guy since we called him Undertaker in JSOC, and even I can't tell you what rank he retired at. He was a master sergeant in SF, but everything after that's classified."

Hansen looks satisfied. Jeremiah always said he was racist, misogynistic, and an all-around prick—likely a result of his weird-ass upbringing—but Dominic Hansen was the second smartest SOB he met while working with Joint Special Operations Command.

Right below MacLaughlin.

"Hey Mac," Lori says. "What was your nickname?"

"You just said it." She turns away for a few wet coughs. "Mac."

Jeremiah translates. "I think she meant when you were in 24 STS."

Prickly takes a few more steps in their direction. "24th Special Tactics? I didn't know they had women."

Almost there. Just keep them talking.

"Just one," MacLaughlin says. "Four of us completed special warfare training, but I'm the only one who got into special operations. Made chief master sergeant as a combat controller."

"Hold on a minute," Prickly says, stepping so close Lori thinks about jumping him now. "You're telling me that we have 24 STS, ISA, DEVGRU and Delta all here at this table."

Dusty's pupils are nearly pinpoints as he speaks. "So, y'all're all"—he puts up slow air quotes—"Tier One operators here. Commanded by Jay-Scotch and shit."

Prickly puts a hand on Dusty's shoulder. "You okay, soldier?"

Lori can't afford for Dusty to blow up the plan yet. "He's fine. He just wants to hear Mac's nickname when she was working with the rest of these guys."

MacLaughlin coughs again, but with a grin. "Special Sauce."

Jeremiah alleviates everyone's confusion, including Lori's. "Because advance field ops always went better when she was in the mix. Plus, everyone thought Big Mac was too on-the-nose."

Even Prickly laughs at that.

Jeremiah and Boudreaux are both a little farther down the table than she is, which is why she saved them. Lori needs one of the guards to feel the need to be close to the most well-known of the elite operators. That's when she can strike, with Jeremiah as her backup. And Boudreaux—if he's done pissing and moaning.

"And then there were two," she says.

"Yeah, yeah," Prickly says. "Master Chief Jeremiah Reynolds was DEVGRU."

"Were you there when they shot UBL?" Dusty says, a bit more coherent.

"Christ, how old do I look?" He pauses for another round of laughter. "No, though I was with the tribe before going to Black Squadron."

Prickly gets closer. "But you started in Red, so you probably knew some of the guys who were part of Neptune Spear in Abbottabad, right?"

Lori could do it now, and Taggart's been gone so long she's beyond antsy. She taps Jeremiah's shoe again. Even if he wasn't, Jeremiah needs to lie so the kid's in enough awe for them to take him down.

"Affirmative. I knew at least—"

Dusty stumbles forward, nearly into the table, as he rounds the corner. "Wait a damn minute." He's nearly to Boudreaux. "I came back in here to meet this guy. He was in goddamn Delta, man. I want to hear one of *his* stories."

Now both guards are in the ambush zone. Jeremiah already knows what to do, so Lori looks at Boudreaux. He's been reading her mind all goddamn day. He needs to do it one more time.

But when they make eye contact, he looks sad. "Not really. I was mostly G Squadron. AFO and battlespace preparation, that stuff."

Lori widens her eyes and clenches her jaw. She didn't want to be so overt, but it's now or never. She tilts her head to Boudreaux's right, where Dusty is leaning against the table.

He seems to get it, and Lori kicks Jeremiah one more time.

But he doesn't jump up. Instead, Jeremiah starts talking. "You were in G? I was Stingray. How do we not know each other? I did more than a few joint ops with your squadron back in the day, and we're just about the same age."

Hansen points his chin at Boudreaux. "Same here."

MacLaughlin also looks curious. "I knew all those guys, too. I never knew anyone called Boudreaux, real name or otherwise."

This is not the time to solve a locked-room mystery, but Lori has lost everyone, so might's well get it over with. "Fine," she says. "What do you say, Boudreaux? You been lying to everyone?"

Or just me?

Boudreaux glances at Fowler and Moore, but they look too amused to do his dirty work.

"I worked with all of you, at one point or another. Back then, Reynolds and MacLaughlin knew me as Big Easy."

The recognition is almost instant, with simultaneous exclamations of *no way*.

"But Hansen over there," Boudreaux says, "he knew my rank and real name."

"Command Sgt. Maj. Michael Hawke." Hansen looks like the biggest sixth-grader on the planet. "But we used to call you Mike behind your back."

Dusty's the only one impaired enough to say the name quickly and out loud. And since they're in a hospital, he found it amusing to phrase it as a nurse paging a patient.

"And that's why I needed an alias when I went private. That joke's too easy to remember. Hard for Michael Hawke to stay hidden. Easy for a guy named Boudreaux in Louisiana."

"Why Boudreaux?" Lori asks.

"I liked Louisiana and knew I wanted to live there. Plus one of my favorite bad guys from TV once used Mike Boudreaux as an alias."

Mac hacks up another piece of her soaked lung. "But you weren't as"—she curls her neck muscles, revealing her own nice peaks—"and your chin had a human beard, not that thing. And your voice is all wrong, too."

"The Unit prioritized running over lifting. The beard and voice—"

Prickly shoves one of the empty chairs across the room. "All right, enough with the family reunion."

Lori nods at Boudreaux. "Couldn't agree more."

She bolts upright. Jeremiah follows a second later, and together they sweep Prickly's legs out from under him. She doesn't see Boudreaux take out Dusty, but his grunt and the sound of his rifle hitting the floor tell her the plan's working so far.

Prickly still has his rifle, but not for long. Lori bends in half and works her hands down past her ass. The skin around her wrists is burning, but nothing dislocates. She sits and finishes the move, her legs slipping through her arms like a hula-hoop.

They're still cuffed, but her hands are in front now.

Jeremiah's kneeling on Prickly, but he hasn't lost control of the gun. Lori kicks him in the side twice, then reaches down to relive the solider of his weapon. By the time she does, Boudreaux is beside her, untied hands holding Dusty's rifle.

"How the—"

"I'll show you the trick sometime," he says. "Let's go to the closet and get something to cut off everyone else's."

They rush across the hall, which is still empty and not yet filling with more Oklahoma Guardsmen. Boudreaux opens the door and flips the light switch and rushes inside. Lori's not sure what he's doing until Boudreaux returns with a pair of red-handled pliers. She puts down the rifle and holds out her hands. When he's done cutting the flex-cuffs, Boudreaux hands her the tool and points to the conference room.

"Cut one of them free, then come help."

Lori pockets the pliers and picks up the gun.

"Oh yeah," Boudreaux says. "And shoot the guards."

Boudreaux follows her out of the closet but turns left, muzzle out, eyes down the barrel.

When she reaches the conference room, Lori lets the rifle hang by the shoulder sling and motions for Jeremiah to turn around.

"Cut everyone loose." She snips free one hand. "I'm going to help."

"No," he says as Lori rips away the rest of the plastic. "Let me."

They don't have time for a protracted staring contest, but Lori doesn't want to budge.

"I'm the better shot," he says. "Or, actually, Dom is." He motions for Lori to give him the pliers so he can cut Hansen free.

"Fine." She walks over to Hansen, rifle still dangling by her side. "But I'm following him. You cut everyone else loose."

When she's done freeing Hansen, Lori tosses the pliers to Jeremiah.

Then she puts two each into Dust Devil and Prickly Pear before handing the rifle to Hansen, who bolts for the door.

Lori's in the hall but still catching up when they hear a burst of gunfire. He stops and holds up a fist.

"At least two rifles," he says. "Maybe more."

They listen. More gunfire. Hansen flicks his fingers forward and Lori follows him down to the nurse's station, then right. Another shot, then one more before a gravelly voice shouts.

They're are still walking down the hall when the double doors burst open and two new men appear, both in black tactical gear and pointing short-barreled rifles.

"Hold your fire," says a voice from behind them. She's still searching for a match when the face appears.

Hansen curses, then lowers his weapon.

"Novak."

53
ERIC

Eric's the last one Reynolds snips free. He tries not to read much into it, especially since they've been hearing gunfire for the last minute or so.

But with full use of their hands, everyone—including the one suffering from pulmonary edema—seems ready to head into the fray without weapons or body armor.

Moore walks over to Eric while the soldiers talk strategy in their corner. "Assuming Boudreaux and Hansen were able to get the better of Taggart and his men, you need to figure out how to stop the nuclear detonation in Cushing. They smashed my cell, but last I checked my contact in China said they weren't going to launch anything until someone attacks them." He turns to the wall with a round analog clock. "We've got less than twenty minutes before the Allied Nations think Iran has joined China. There's no holding off after that. It wouldn't surprise me if President Ramirez has already put the USA into snapcount, though I don't know how many missiles would launch."

The only way to make sure China doesn't either nuke more cities or detonate one at high-altitude is to stop Novak. Then they can worry about contacting Alex Ramirez in Philadelphia.

"Is your cell backed up online?"

"Yeah, but I've never tried to access the cloud account outside of The South. You think it'll work here?"

"Most hospitals have access to the open internet since they have to transport patients internationally. It's worth a shot to see if you can access your contacts and call Anderson, let him know what's happening."

Moore walks to the conference room door, joining Reynolds and MacLaughlin.

"I'm going to head back to the offices and see if I can call out to someone for help," Moore tells them.

Reynolds looks over his shoulder at Eric. "Your girlfriend joining you?"

Screw you. But instead of saying it, Eric walks toward the group. "I'll help him. We'll come and get you when we know more."

Reynolds nods and opens the door. He and MacLaughlin take off with military precision to the right, while Moore and Eric break the other way. They're nearly to the office doors when an explosion draws their attention toward the hall.

Thick smoke drifts their way, as does shouting.

"Flashbang," Moore yells before opening the door and pulling Eric inside.

Moore slams the door and together they race behind the messy desk of Dr. Rahul Patel.

"Sounds like Boudreaux and Hansen didn't overtake the guards," Eric says. "I thought there were only two and Taggart. How the hell did they get the better of—"

The door flies open, and a canister ricochets off the wall and the desk.

* * *

AFTER HIS SIGHT and hearing return, Eric sees the conference room. He's in another chair and handcuffed again. The rest of the group is present at the table, all hurting from the flashbangs.

As he blinks away more of the smoke, Eric realizes there are two new faces.

The doctor, who's sitting beside Reynolds.

And Novak.

He turns to one of the new guards, who seem much more capable than the yokels Taggart had been using. "Everyone accounted for?"

The guard nods. He's not intimately familiar with them, but Eric assumes these guys are Republican Guardsmen. When he was on the phone with Robb, Novak was in the background saying they were running late. Eric hadn't known what he meant, but he never imagined Novak and Robb would be catching a jet.

Eric finishes scanning the room. The bodies of Dust Devil and Prickly Pear have been shoved into the back corner of the crowded room. Novak has seven of his Guardsmen and Taggart.

Only one person's missing.

"Where's Robb?" Eric asks.

"Well, now I know it was you who called earlier," Novak says. "Robb was a blubbering idiot. He broke on the way to the airport. Didn't give up your name, though. Something to remember him by"—he checks the inside of his wrist—"for a little while longer."

Why the hell is Novak here? If he's supposed to be handling the nuclear situation for President Cole, what good is he in Oklahoma, let alone this tiny hospital in this tiny town. And why risk being so close to the blast? It was dangerous enough just flying into and driving through the snowstorm.

Eric's default is to think a situation through. Analyze it to death until the answer presents itself. But he doesn't have days to do that. Or hours. He barely has minutes, so there's only one course of action left.

"What the hell are you doing here?"

Novak leans toward one of the guards and says something. Eric's ears are still ringing, so he might's well be whispering. But whatever Novak says, the guards spring into action and begin rifling through the pockets of their hostages.

"First," Novak says, "you should know it was always going to end this way. Right here in this hospital."

The henchmen are Republican Guard, based on the sleeve digging into his pants pockets. He pulls out a keyring and wallet, his cell having been confiscated and presumably destroyed in the field just south of the Kansas Territory border. His items are slid into the middle of the table with the rest. Among them are a cellphone somebody must've kept hidden from the previous guards and a piece of crumpled up paper with sloppy handwriting.

Novak walks to the table and picks up the phone. "Why, Doctor Hosseini, you're a sneaky one. That wasn't necessary for this to work, but hopefully you're even shadier in real life than we planned on making you look."

"Sir, please, you're making a mistake. My name is Doctor Rahul Patel. I'm from India originally—"

"Cut the horse shit," Novak says. "I know all about you, Doctor Sasan Hosseini. Hell, you're the key to all of this. I mean, Cushing was always one of our targets, but we could easily have sent the cruise missile here after saying Iran bombed any place in the country. But with an Iranian-born doctor practicing in the very same province, our story is that much more believable."

Novak has a patsy. But how would a doctor in Farefax, Oklahoma, sneak an unknown nuclear bomb onto the continent? More importantly, how would Novak's story hold once the material was tested? Scientists can tell which area of a nuclear facility a sample comes from. No, lying about the origin of the bomb or the delivery logistics wouldn't work.

Unless Hosseini's alleged involvement in ends with the planning and payoff. Those elements can be faked by anyone with the right computer skills. Then the source and movement of the bomb don't have to be faked.

Novak doesn't have a patsy.

He has a group of them.

54
JEREMIAH

Novak's going to blow up a town and blame it on this poor soul. The documents he forged were really Dr. Hosseini's ticket to hell on this Earth.

Novak's too sick to just shoot him. He'll turn Hosseini over to the Joint Republican Council, which oversees the elite counterterrorism force for Texas and Oklahoma. Novak will say he discovered Hosseini's plan and couldn't quite foil it in time to stop the detonation in Cushing, but another attack is imminent and only Hosseini knows when and where. The Councilmen will take it from there.

Unless Jeremiah can sort through this cluster.

"You've made your point," he says. "China's already on the brink of war after you bombed Southern California, and you have, what, a dozen more long-range missiles on that bomber? That's enough threat to get the Allied Nations to fold. You don't need to kill thousands more and ruin this man's life."

"You had your chance to die with dignity back at the plant, but you chose your ex-wife over the greater good. Fortunately, my priorities didn't change so drastically after I left the military."

"You were kicked out for being a nutjob," Jeremiah says. "You don't even live on the same planet we do."

"Which planet is that?" Novak starts pacing the room, a college lecturer finding his element. "The one whose storms are getting exponentially worse? The one that produced the epic blizzard outside? That forced New Orleans to build that monstrosity of a wall to protect its people against super hurricanes? The one that made Los Angeles a wasteland long before today's nuclear strike?"

"And nuking the continent off the face of this apparently awful planet's going to help?"

Novak stops. "I'm only detonating one more. And, yes, it'll bring a nearly instant end to our dependence on oil."

Fowler croaks, as though he tried to stop mid-giggle. "You think shutting down oil trading's going to suddenly turn the world onto green energy?"

"Not suddenly. Because without forty more years of progress—and people at the top committed to that—the science'll never be advanced enough to plug the oil wells. But if they don't act quickly, if they don't realize what's best for the world is best for the individual, they'll let the planet turn into a Stephen King novel."

"It's unreal how crazy you are," Jeremiah says.

Novak glances at the clock. "I have enough time to explain it so even you can understand. After all, Dr. Hosseini should know a few details if he hopes to deliver a reasonable confession to save his family from the same torture he'll undoubtedly receive from the Councilmen."

Dr. Hosseini, who had been quietly sitting beside Mac, begins sobbing uncontrollably. She can't properly console him, but she leans over and talks softly.

"So right now the truck Reynolds and his team snuck out of Amarillo—"

Jeremiah spits in Novak's direction, but he doesn't have enough saliva to make it dramatic. Dom tries hocking one, but the adrenaline dried him out, too.

"As I was saying, your semi is parked outside the Columbus Petroleum Terminal just south of Cushing. It's one of the few places West Texas Intermediate crude is physically delivered. Columbus also helps set the sulfur content and specific gravity for WTI."

"And they'll find somewhere else to get their specs and be trading within the week," Fowler says.

"That's a possibility. But that's just future money. Might's well've come from old Pennybags himself. Blow up the pipelines near

Cushing, and more than a dozen major companies lose out on the three million barrels of crude that flow through them every day. At close of business last year, the price of oil was hovering around seventy-five dollars a barrel. So, in addition to the markets losing their billions in futures, the companies will lose a cumulative total of about two hundred twenty-five million dollars a day."

Jeremiah's never been one for math or budget sheets, but he's beginning to grasp the magnitude.

"And that place'll be radioactive for years," Novak says, "meaning that money only gets recouped after they invest in new pipelines and related equipment to skirt the area." He turns to Fowler. "You more than anyone knows how much that'll cost."

Fowler doesn't speak, but his bulging jaw muscles say enough.

"And what about Cushing's famous storage tanks? Those eyesores can hold up to ninety-one million barrels, but let's call it an average of seventy-five. And let's say the price of oil drops by twenty-five points almost instantly. Even at fifty dollars a barrel, you're looking at nearly four billion dollars evaporated into thin air."

Novak starts pacing again, and everyone—even Jeremiah, God help him—tracks his movements. "But the panic will be much worse than four billion in instant losses. Oil's becoming as valuable as diamonds. There's maybe forty years of the stuff left inside this dying planet, so anybody in that game was banking on the price going up. Most of the major firms probably thought that four billion was really more like seven billion, which is why they're all overleveraged and have invested those trillions in borrowed capital. And the money that trickled down to the contractors has been going into cities and towns all across the Rural Bloc, and they've all set out budget projections using those numbers. Hell, think about what happens to the fifth-wheel camper industry when the pipeliners and other contractors can't get work?"

"The industry flatlines," Fowler says.

"Oh yeah. And think about the drillers. Why would a company keep pumping ancient swamps out of the ground when they have nowhere to store them? Refineries only have so much capacity, and that was before the pipelines that get the finished products out were blown up. But let's say they can offload that. How will they get more crude to refine? Can't take sour and heavy crude unless they're set up for it, and those modifications take millions of dollars per refinery."

Novak takes up a post behind Fowler and puts his hands on his shoulders. "Nearly every single pipeline that runs to nearly every major refinery on the continent goes through that little town south of here. Doesn't it?"

Fowler nods.

"So," Novak says, "it won't be long before the continent is no longer producing gasoline. And diesel? Well, that's a byproduct of refining the gas, so you can't have one without the other. Looks like the electric car guys out on the West Coast will be happy. Until the asphalt shortage creates a lack of drivable roads. And so on."

Novak sounds so confident, it's hard to remember that he's a stark-raving lunatic. Though for all the crap he's talked on K and his morons, they do have the world in a vice right now.

"I know you think I'm crazy," Novak says. "But why do you think all the dystopian movies have gas as the most valuable commodity left on the planet. So, faced with that possible outcome, why wouldn't an alliance of governments come back together to both stop a nuclear war and to ensure that the continent's citizens have access to the fuels that still make society possible."

Fowler jerks so violently Novak steps back. "You're exactly right, and that threat can still work. There's no reason to do the deed. You still have time to call it off and give the Allied Nations a chance to do the right thing."

Novak tells his men to lower their weapons. "See, that works in a perfect world. But it doesn't account for the ignorance, greed, or tendency for people to feel invincible. That's how we got into this mess to begin with. Without consequences that hurt the elite in their own bank accounts and food supplies, nothing changes."

Jeremiah shakes his head. "Jesus H. You think you're the good guy."

"My ends are justifiable. Just as yours were when you chose to drive out of the plant with the nuclear weapon that will fix the current plagues on our society."

The crazy man releases Fowler and walks to Dr. Hosseini. "Now, doctor, you're smart enough to have understood what I just laid out. I suggest you memorize it as best you can. The more forthcoming you are with the Councilmen, the better it'll be for you and your family." Novak looks across the table at Lori. "Now, you won't be expected to know all of this. Hell, I need you to deny till … well, you know the rest."

PART IV: EMERGENCY DISABLEMENT

55
LORI

She knows the rest of that phrase, but not the rest of Novak's plan, which is what she needs. Because she's going to stop him.

Or go down trying.

If Lori can go out being righteous again, even for a moment, she can handle death. But to get her chance at redemption, Lori needs more information.

"If the doc's your fall guy, why keep me alive?"

"We need someone to satisfy the world's bloodlust." For the first time since he arrived, Novak's eyes stop conforming to his smug, cool act and reveal the crazed lunatic underneath.

"See, the good doctor here can't act like a terrorist," Novak says. "But if he's smart, he'll tell them he was approached by someone from the Iranian government while working in Los Angeles who convinced him to move, scout the area, and help plan the Cushing strike in exchange for the millions of dollars now in his account. Then they keep paying him as he recruits the rest of you for his piece of the mission."

Dr. Hosseini begins rocking in his chair and repeating words that Lori assumes are a prayer.

"But the doctor here's only a useful idiot. You, on the other hand, have a long history of violence that'll be fed to the media, including the incidents that led to your father's discharge. And you'll resist interrogation, which means the Councilmen will be granted permission to torture you. And let me assure you, Retired Detective Gloria Young, you will reach that breaking point and reveal your role in this plot just to stop the pain. After that, the country will rally around your public execution and demand the world's governments take action to restore peace."

He wants to keep her breathing just long enough to endure more pain than humanly possible.

Fuck that.

"Well then," Lori says, "sounds like you better do me the same courtesy as Dr. Hosseini here and give me the talking points."

"Oh, it's pretty simple, really. Your ex, trying to keep you sneaking into his bed every so often, got hooked up with the doctor via his piece-of-shit father." Novak turns to Jeremiah. "That paperwork's already been forged. So you would call in Vicodin prescriptions for pickup at the in-store pharmacy where you've stopped nearly every trip through Oklahoma City since before the secessions began."

If he really has forged prescriptions, nobody can argue Lori takes pain meds regularly. "So?"

"So, after a while the doctor threatens to expose the illegal prescriptions unless Reynolds goes along with the plan to hijack the bomb. The plan involves you pretending to be kidnapped with the help of the good ol' boy network of Fowler, Moore and Boudreaux, allowing everyone else at the plant to claim Reynolds went rogue with his team."

Novak backs up and addresses his patsies as a whole again. "Y'all executed your plan, and I tracked you here, taking out everyone but the doctor and Miss Young. But I was just a bit too late to stop the detonation. However, with the two living suspects in custody, I am given authority by the Council to oversee the information extraction, which will lead to the realization that the Chinese and Iranians wanted the war and decimated oil industry—with the hope that Russia will join the war effort—which will bring everyone to the table to stop them with a re-unified United States military." He begins pacing again. "See, all your efforts today barely inconvenienced me. We had to put Gates and Clarke in the truck so they get vaporized along with Levine. Gates was supposed to live, but with Fowler taking the fall for planning the New Year's Eve shootings on behalf of Dr. Hosseini, he's just a rich retiree who got lost in the woods on a hunting retreat in

Wyoming or Idaho. And Clarke, well she was going to be just another Cushing victim either way."

Lori refuses to believe this would've worked. Novak can't be an evil mastermind who outplayed everyone in this room. It's been a while since she felt pride, but dammit, Lori can't let this fucking guy get the better of them.

"So, what now, you just gun everyone down here in the hospital, wait for the bomb to go off, then haul me and the doctor back to The Republic for interrogation?"

Novak's eyes sparkle again. "Pretty much."

Dr. Hosseini stops praying. "Sir, may I ask one indulgence before you commence with the rest of your plan?"

"Why would I do that?"

"If you permit this one act of kindness, I will offer no resistance and admit to everything you've outlined."

Novak nods for the doctor to continue. "Just before your friend arrived"—he looks at Taggart—"we were going to call Mr. Ramirez's family to let him know what had happened. Given the circumstances, I'd like to give him morphine and let him drift off, then tell his family he died in no pain. The numbers are on that piece of paper"—he nods to the middle of the table—"Mr. Ramirez was my last patient, and I'd like to finish my job."

Novak works his jaw for a moment, then shakes his head. "I admire what you're trying to do, but I can't let that happen. He needs to look like he died fighting me and my men, not in a hospital bed." His hand brushes past Dr. Hosseini's cellphone as he secures the slip of paper. "I probably should know who the media can contact when it comes time to have family members cry over the deaths of men led astray by their compromised commander and his ex-wife."

He unfolds the note and clears his throat as though preparing to deliver the Gettysburg Address. He reads Sarah Grace's name and number. "Panhandle Province area code. Must be the wife."

Novak continues with the next entry. The name is Lexi Ramirez. The country code is unfamiliar at first, but Lori matches it to the USA. The area code is Washington. She's surprised to find a match to the next three digits. They're for a cellphone carrier she once called, the number for a member of the DEA task force in Amarillo.

Novak's voice tapers off and turns breathy as he reaches the last four digits. Lori catches them, which is good news. As spooked as Novak is, they're bound to be important.

But why? One of Jesús Ramirez's relatives has a working cellphone issued by the United States government. If the number still functions, Lexi Ramirez must still work for what remains of the federal government, now in Philadelphia.

Lori. Gloria.

Lexi. Alexia.

President Alexia Ramirez.

Holy shit.

If she hadn't done the same with her name, Lori might not have put it together so fast. Then again, Lori's smart.

Less-than-ten-seconds smart.

Lori has no proof she's right, other than Novak's strong reaction. But if his goal is to get the relevant Allied Nations leadership together quickly enough to keep China from striking, it would have to be on a conference call. Which means he has direct lines, including the one he just read.

Everyone's underestimated Novak because of the untethered drivel he and his UNIC followers spout, but he's no moron. He's smart enough to have been a step ahead of everyone.

Until now.

Novak eyes the clock, then pockets the piece of paper.

"Taggart, tell one of your men to get Ramirez out of bed and into his gear. Have someone else go check the security cameras and make sure there's no activity outside. We're eight mikes away. That's just enough time to do this, long as nobody calls it in to the locals early."

With only eight minutes left, Lori knows it's time to get free and call President Ramirez. Anything. The lack of a plan can't be an excuse for inaction. She scans the room, and everyone else seems to know it, too.

All eyes shift to the conference room door when a guard throws it open. "We have a situation." He rushes to Novak, who listens, then puckers his lips.

"Goddamn superstorms. Everyone but Taggart, go do a physical perimeter check."

Ice on the security camera lenses, her father says.

Her father? "What the …"

Novak quits sucking on his sour candy. "Something to share with the class, Miss Young?"

Lori shakes her head, at both Novak's question and her own. Because it wasn't her father. At least, not the Colonel whose voice takes up years of space in her head. This voice was an idealized version of her father. It had a softer tone. A loving tone.

A dad's tone.

Not only is the voice wrong, but the process is wrong. She searches the archives and replays the voice. The recordings have never played on their own. Then there's the fact that the voice was responding to current events, which means it wasn't a recording.

She's not listening to voices. She's hearing them.

Just like her mother.

When the time comes, listen. That's what she'd said.

Lori's mother wasn't schizophrenic. She had the same fucked up thing as Lori. And she at least suspected Lori had it, too.

Her almost-father interjects. *You don't have time for this. There are only three of them in the room, and one is directly behind you. Now's the time to act. Stand and kick your chair into Taggart, then charge Novak. He'll underestimate you, so you can side-step and knee him in the stomach or balls, whichever presents itself. Then put him in a headlock and drop his head onto the floor. Do it now, Gloria.*

"My name's Lori."

Lori didn't mean to say it. Somehow her inner monologue is gone, replaced by whatever psychotic break has taken over.

But it works to her advantage.

"Secure Miss Young," Novak tells his remaining guard. "We need her out of here, anyway."

As the guard approaches from behind, she decides to listen.

Lori's chair is just enough of a distraction to charge Novak, who looks more curious than worried—just like the delusional narcissist he is. When she's a few feet away, he cocks his right fist.

As she ducks under his haymaker, Lori sends her left knee into Novak's stomach. When he doubles over, she raises her cuffed hands up her back, slips his head between her left elbow and side, plants her right leg, and executes a move worthy of any pro wrestling ring.

By the time Lori gets to her feet, everyone else has done their part. MacLaughlin is cutting Fowler loose with the guard's combat knife while the rest of the former servicemembers are either checking a weapon, restraining Novak and Taggart, or barricading the door.

"Hey MacLaughlin," Lori says, "cut me loose."

With her hands free, Lori rushes to get the doctor's cell. "Fowler, do you know any local cops or sheriffs in Cushing?"

"Yeah," he says. "What terminal was it?"

"Columbus," she says.

Jeremiah follows up with the new license plate numbers. They now have the means to locate the bomb before it detonates, but it won't matter if Lori can't get the code to cancel the detonation.

Nobody picks up on the first ring, so she texts.

Friend of your bro, x-wife of cmndr Reynolds. Nuke missing from the plant in AMA. Will det in 4 min. Need universal cancel code now.

She dials again. No answer.

Redial. No answer.

Then an incoming call.

"Put Zeus on."

The connection is bad, but she races through her spiel. "I can't. He's hurt. It's a long story, but I'm Jeremiah's ex-wife, and you're going to have to trust me. I need that code now so we can get it to law enforcement here in Oklahoma. Otherwise—"

"You're breaking up. You said you're Lori Reynolds?"

"Yes. Well, I—"

The call drops.

President Ramirez knew to ask for her brother, which means she got the text. So rather than waste time calling again, she sends another message. As she does, Lori prays for the first time since her mother left.

Yes, Lori R. Nuke to det in 3 mins. Need code.

Three dots appear a second later, followed by sixteen alphanumeric digits, which she says out loud.

"Fowler, are they at the truck yet?"

"Yeah, and we talked them through hooking the keypad up."

Lori reads out the digits as bullets splinter the door to the conference room. Boudreaux and Jeremiah return fire. The rest drop to the floor. Fowler yells the last few numbers and letters into the phone as the rest cover their ears.

Lori's done everything she can.

Now she can die.

56
ERIC

The guy in Cushing's doesn't get it. Yes, it's loud. And sixteen digits and letters is a long code. But with two minutes and change until detonation, you'd think a guy standing over a nuclear bomb would step up his game.

Instead, the guy's asking for the code again to confirm what he's already written down, which he decided to do rather than just punching it in.

"Slide me the phone," he yells to Lori. "Guy's asking for the code again."

She says something to herself—Eric can't hear, but he's sure it's mostly incoherent cussing—and sends it his way.

It gets hung up on debris just in front of the porous door and table that's barricading it. He hesitates for two seconds, then crawls to the cell.

Eric's calf takes a round. He screams in pain but keeps moving, securing the cell before crawling across the floor to the side nearest Lori.

"Okay, I'm giving this to you one more time," Eric yells into the satphone, "then you're going to have to put it in and pray it's right."

Before he starts, Lori puts herself between Eric and the mayhem, hunching over his head and the phone. She yells at MacLaughlin, who does the same, giving him something that resembles a sound buffer. Eric repeats the numbers and wishes Godspeed to the sheriff's deputy, who says he'll stay on the line to report the outcome. The wait will be less than ninety seconds either way.

But before he gets confirmation of the bomb's neutralization, Boudreaux yells that the room's been breached.

MacLaughlin and Lori abandon their positions, leaving Eric exposed. MacLaughlin moves toward the door, staying low and close to the wall, holding her knife by her side. Lori crawls the opposite direction and gets to Taggart just before he completes a barrel roll away from the room's center. After socking him in the face couple of times, Taggart's body goes limp again. She searches him and pulls an ankle pistol one of the others missed or never searched for.

Hansen has started firing another tactically acquired pistol. He's not firing many shots, but every time he does, one of the bodies drops through the door. At this point, they're crawling over each other to get in.

Moore has another knife and has taken up a position similar to MacLaughlin, ready to clean up any garbage the firearms don't take out.

Eric and the doctor are the only ones without weapons. Dr. Hosseini is in the fetal position in the corner farthest from the shooting. He's not moving, but Eric doesn't see any blood. He's about to crawl over to check the doctor's status when Reynolds yells.

"I'm out."

Boudreaux says the same ten seconds later. Hansen's been diligent, but he only hangs on another five seconds. By this time, the bomb's either exploded or someone's on the line screaming with joy, but that's secondary.

Eric sees three more Guardsmen through the doorway. They're firing as they charge but nobody's in their line of sight but Novak and Taggart. As the first steps through, MacLaughlin shanks him in the hamstring, then the neck. The second finds a similar fate at Moore's hands, though he uses the thigh and throat.

The third doesn't attempt to cross the doorway, choosing instead to wildly empty his mag into room. Boudreaux cries out and so does Taggart. Eric hears the Guardsman drop his rifle, then start with his pistol. After a few dry clicks, everything goes silent.

Then Eric sees another flashbang bouncing directly to him.

Before he can think himself out of it, Eric grabs the cylinder and shovel-passes it back in the direction it came. Then he curls up and hopes his aim was true.

Eric isn't sure it worked until he sees MacLaughlin and Moore rush out into the smoke. He can't hear much, but somehow an electronic voice cuts through the noise. Eric picks up the satphone.

"Repeat, we had no detonation. No detonation. Is anybody there?"

57
JEREMIAH

Fowler's voice is the first noise that rises above the ringing. Jeremiah can't make out all the words, but it's clear the bomb didn't detonate. Next comes Mac yelling *all clear* from the doorway.

With that knowledge, the next objective is tending to their wounded.

"Everyone alive?" he yells, keeping his eyes and muzzle facing the door in case they missed one.

Boudreaux—or Big Easy, or whoever he is—answers in the affirmative, adding that he's been hit in the leg.

"I took one in the calf," Fowler says. "But I have Payne County calling Osage to send medical units."

Mac's hacking turns into a laugh. "Guys, we're in a hospital." She walks to Dr. Hosseini. "Are you hurt?"

"I do not believe so," he says.

"I know you're shaken up," she says. "But can you help them?"

"Yes, of course."

Mac helps the doctor to his feet and Dom joins her. Before they lead Dr. Hosseini and the wounded to the trauma rooms, she calls out for Moore. "All clear out there?"

"All clear."

Jeremiah peeks outside to satisfy his paranoia, then helps them navigate the bodies. As Dom rounds the corner, Moore comes back in.

"Everyone else good?"

Taggart groans. "Not me. I'm hit."

Jeremiah walks over. Taggart's bleeding from his side and likely won't make it without prompt medical attention.

Oh well. "You can wait until more help gets here."

Next on Jeremiah's list is Novak, who's alert but not talking.

"Where's that plane going?"

Novak's eyes dart his way but return to the ceiling a moment later. "What plane?"

Jeremiah punches him in the nose. "That big ugly fat fucker you used to blow up LA. Is it still in Amarillo?"

Novak turns his head away from Jeremiah and spits out blood. "You won't get shit out of me. I'll die before talking."

Jeremiah grabs his face and turns it to him. "That's pretty tough talk. But I know guys who really would die before giving up intel. They're loyal to a cause. You're only loyal to yourself."

He lets go of Novak's face and kicks him in the ribs. "Hey Moore, give me that knife."

After palming the Ka-Bar, Jeremiah drops a knee to Novak's chest. "Last chance."

"My name is Corporal Alan Novak of the—"

Jeremiah shoves the blade into Novak's piehole and slices into his cheek. The scream is from a bad horror movie. The cut isn't long, but it's enough to fill Novak's mouth with blood. After a few seconds, Moore taps him on the shoulder and Lori yells for him to stop from her post in the corner.

Jeremiah isn't out of control, but he wants Novak to think otherwise.

It works.

"It's grounded until Robb or I give them new orders," Novak says after Jeremiah removes the blade.

With Robb dead, the plane will be secure until presidents Cole, Anderson, and Ramirez get the situation under control. That needs to happen fast—right after Jeremiah lets Zeus talk to his sister.

"Where's the paper with those phone numbers?" Jeremiah asks Novak.

Novak shakes his head. "Dropped it. Need the doctor to sew up my mouth."

He's still bleeding, and Jeremiah knows he's right. If Taggart dies, that's a casualty he can live with. But they need to keep Novak alive. Not only will many governments want their pound of flesh, but—as he put it earlier—they'll need someone to satisfy the world's bloodlust.

Jeremiah hands the knife back to Moore. "Cut him loose and stop the bleeding. Sew him up if you can. The quicker, the better."

He turns to Lori, who's muttering something in the corner. "Help me find that number."

"Don't need to. I have it memorized."

"I'm sure you do, but I'd feel a lot better if—"

"Will you quit being a dick for once?" She's never interrupted him with that tone before. "I have it. I'll explain how later, but first let's go see if the doc's cellphone gets any better signal in his room."

Voices fill the hall as Jeremiah and Lori walk past the nurse's station. A few of them are laughing, including Mac and Dr. Hosseini, which brings a smile to his face.

Then it registers. There's no heartbeat coming from Room 5.

He sprints down the hall, hoping the monitor is malfunctioning but everything else is working. The door's half open, but not enough to see Zeus, so he kicks it open so hard it bounces back and gets him on the shoulder.

He doesn't feel it.

Doesn't feel anything.

Zeus's eyes are open and glassy, a pair of 9mm holes in his forehead. Those motherfuckers double-tapped him in the head when the shooting started. Why? In case he revealed his superhuman healing powers and joined the fight?

Jeremiah slides to the floor and rests his shoulders against the side of the bed. Lori enters a second later. She covers her mouth at first, then approaches, slowly, like she's trying to coax a wolf into eating from her hand.

"Do you still want to call his sister? If not, we can call her first. But one of her first questions will be ..."

Jeremiah can't talk to Lori. But talking to Lexi Ramirez is his job—his duty—so he holds out his hand for the phone, hoping Lori understands and doesn't make him say it.

She doesn't. Lori enters the number, then puts a hand on his shoulder as she kneels to hand him the phone.

"I'll see if Moore can contact his asset in Beijing, or maybe President Anderson." She wipes a tear from her cheek, and his eyes threaten to release theirs. "Come get us when you're done and we'll all fill her in on the rest."

Jeremiah feels the burn on his cheeks before realizing he's crying.

58
LORI

She turns quickly. Lori wants to give Jeremiah deniability, but she also needs to stay on task.

Moore's still working on Novak a few doors down, but she needs him to hurry so they can figure out whether stopping the detonation even mattered.

"You almost done?"

Moore looks up but keeps his hands working. "Just tying him off now." He jerks on the thread and Novak grunts, his hands still cuffed and feet now secured with white medical tape.

"Good," she says. "You have a way to call your spy in China?"

"I think so. If the Internet and phone in the doctor's office are as good as he says." Moore slaps Novak on the fresh stitches, which are jagged and are bound to leave a scar nastier than the one on her thigh. "We're going to drop you off in the room with the guys so you don't get any ideas."

As they escort the prisoner across the hall, Moore glances back to Room 5. When his eyes find Lori's a moment later, she shakes her head.

Moore sets his jaw and tosses Novak into the room. He lands face-first, a satisfying thud followed by a more satisfying scream.

"Remember, he can't die," Moore says. "But a few kicks never killed anyone."

Lori starts toward the nurse's station while Moore stays behind. She assumes he's relaying the tragic news but doesn't want to be around when he does. Instead, she hustles to the office and rounds the desk to wake up the computer.

She barely has time to open a browser when Moore steps in.

"All yours," Lori says.

Moore takes her place at the computer. Lori shuffles around and clears a spot on an old couch that hasn't been used for sitting in a long time.

Lori's thankful Moore gets through to his contact on the first try. She can only hear one side of the conversation, but she gathers that President Ramirez has already called and told them that something is wrong on this side of the globe and not to react yet.

When he hangs up, Moore tells her as much and immediately dials his boss, who gets a summary of the news.

"And you'll call President Cole and tell him to cease all nuclear activity? ... Excellent. And for heaven's sake, please tell him to keep that B-52 on the ground. ... Thank you, Mr. President. I'll call back after locals get this area secure and I can find a flight home, though with this weather that may not be until tomorrow."

As he hangs up the receiver, Lori's attention is drawn by a knock on the open door. It's Jeremiah, followed by MacLaughlin, Hansen, Boudreaux, and Fowler.

"He just finished up," Lori says. "China's got their finger off the trigger, so we're good for now. Do you want him to dial President Ramirez?"

Jeremiah points to the cell. "She's on mute." He touches the screen twice then lays the phone down on the desk. "Okay Madam President, you've got everyone now."

"And who is everyone else?" President Ramirez asks, her voice a thicker version of the South Texas accent than she uses on TV. "I assume your wife's in the room, too?"

Lori looks at Boudreaux. Or should she start calling him Mike? "Ex-wife, actually. It's Lori Young now, Madam President."

"Oh, my apologies, Miss Young. Who else?"

The group looks around, so Jeremiah takes the lead again. "We have two other members of my team, ma'am. Shaye MacLaughlin and Dominic Hansen."

"Oh, right. Zeus mentioned both of you. I know you served, too, but I forget the details."

Mac coughs into her fist, but her expression returns with a Scout-on-a-field-trip smile. "Hello, Madam President. Chief Master Sgt. Shaye MacLaughlin here, retired Air Force Combat Controller, 24th Special Tactics Squadron."

Hansen is far less enthusiastic. "I was Army Special Forces, then Intelligence Support Activity, Madam President."

Lori's not sure what to make of Jeremiah's giant of a subordinate. The more she's around him, the more she wants to know. But Lori has a feeling she and Hansen will be spending a lot of time together.

The group pauses to wait for the presidential response. "That everyone?"

Boudreaux attempts to loosen a few rocks from his throat. "No, Madam President. Command Sgt. Maj. Mike Boudreaux, retired Army 1st Special Forces Operational Detachment–Delta, G Squadron."

Lori has her answer. He's Boudreaux now. Whoever Michael Hawke was, the guy standing across from her killed him.

"Quite impressive," President Ramirez says. "If I'm not mistaken, you were all JSOC, with the exception of Miss Young."

Fowler hobbles toward the phone. "Actually, Madam President, I was, well, involved."

"And you are?"

"It's me, ma'am. Eric Fowler."

"Oh really. Involved? For which side?"

He bites his lip, so Lori steps in. "He was instrumental in our success, as was—"

Everyone coughs at once, and Moore looks terrified. He, apparently, was only here covertly.

"What was that?" President Ramirez asks.

"Oh, nothing, ma'am," Lori says, though she does a terrible job hiding the fact she's lying. "I was just going to say that we also made good use of his company's facilities, too."

"Well, if that's everyone, I want to thank you all for your service, today. Mr. Reynolds filled me in on most of what happened already. Acting on your own to stop a terrorist plot of this magnitude is nothing short of heroic. I don't know how the rest of the nations feel, but the United States of America owes you all a debt of gratitude."

Jeremiah picks up the phone, sensing the conversation's imminent end. "Just doing our job, ma'am."

"Aren't we a couple of talking clichés," the president says, her smile nearly visible through the speaker. "I'm not going to let it go at that, though. A president like me could use a group like you."

Boudreaux takes a step toward the phone. "With respect, ma'am, you have a military."

"And today proves it's not worth a damn."

Lori loves hearing powerful people curse. Reminds her that nobody's as good as they pretend.

"However," President Ramirez continues. "My checks still cash. And if you let me take credit for what happened today publicly, I'll have no problem paying everyone with some discretionary funding."

Politics on the day she learns her brother was killed. You must have to be an iceberg to survive the heat of her office.

"So we're what?" Boudreaux asks. "The A-Team?"

"I was thinking Task Force Zulu."

"Because we're the last people you want to call in an emergency?"

"Actually," President Ramirez says, not messing around, "I was thinking it would be a way to honor Zeus."

Lori smiles. That shut him up quick.

Jeremiah sucks in a breath. "I think we can do that, ma'am."

"Excellent. And I have your first operation in mind already."

"What's that?" Jeremiah asks.

"We need an emergency disablement of that nuclear weapon that you kept from detonating. I think we all agree it can't go back to The Republic, and I have nowhere to store it here."

"Tell you what, Madam President," Jeremiah says. "I don't think we can destroy the bomb for you, but I have a secure place to store it."

"Where?"

Boudreaux takes the phone from Jeremiah's hand. "Ma'am, respectfully, if we do this, you can't know where. We'll stash the bomb in one location, keep the keypad with us, and let you retain sole access to the codes."

"That can work," she says. "For now. It sounds like you're taking charge of this outfit, Mr. Boudreaux?"

He and Jeremiah share a look. They both make sense as leaders of whatever the hell this is, though she doubts either will ever take orders from the other.

"For now," Boudreaux says.

Jeremiah nods.

"Good. How can I reach you? This number?"

"Not our phone," Boudreaux says. "But we'll call your cell when the weapon's secure. By then we'll have a better comms solution."

President Ramirez's pause makes it clear how unhappy she is with that answer, but there's not much she can do.

After they agree to the terms, Lori stares at Boudreaux. It'll take a long time to forgive him, if ever.

But after watching him take charge and politely tell an Allied president to go screw herself, Lori's prepared to swear off drinking and getting high in exchange for ten minutes of personal time in the next room.

I always knew you two would be good for each other, her delusion of a father says. *Even if he is a little old for you.*

"Shut up," she mutters.

"What's that?" Boudreaux asks.

Every set of eyes are on her.

"Nothing," she says, searching again for something reasonable to say. "Just talking to myself."

Everyone seems to dismiss it as the idiom most people use when thinking out loud. Lori wonders how long that'll work, and how long it worked for her mom.

Boudreaux shifts his attention from Lori to Jeremiah.

"So, where is this secure location?"

59
LORI

Secure facility, San Juan Mountains, La Plata County
Free State of Southwestern Colorado

Lori's not made for this kind of cold. Even sitting shotgun in their new Telluride—an on-the-nose gift from Sheriff Edwin Hansen—she sits on her gloved hands to keep them warm as they wait for the massive overhead door to open.

"You sure the heat's on full blast?" she asks Boudreaux, who drove them up the tunnels.

"It'll get warmer when we're not in the mountain," he says. "But yes, it's up all the way."

"That thing needs to hurry the hell up," Jeremiah says, his voice barely audible over the heater and rolling metal.

As Boudreaux drives out, Lori reluctantly removes her hands and pulls a satphone from the center console.

President Ramirez answers on the second ring. "Is this line secure?"

"And untraceable." Lori doesn't try to hide her annoyance.

"According to whom?"

"The best combat communications specialist either of us have ever met."

Lori trusts Boudreaux and Jeremiah when it comes to Mac, who's resting in her Amarillo apartment with the bomb's permissive action link. Fowler's doing the same back in Cushing. Moore said he was headed back to Birmingham and left an encrypted email as a contact.

"Very good. And the payload?"

"Parked in my backyard."

One of the guys snorts trying to suppress his laugh. The woman on the other end of the line sighs. "Fine. Hard as you fought to keep it from detonating, I trust you to keep it safe."

Dom is a few hundred yards behind them in the blue tractor. Sure, the bomb could be moved by another hauler or transferred to a two-ton pickup. If exploded without being armed—which can't happen without an armed assault and a genius-level hacker—the B83 would become a dirty bomb. A devastating blast with radioactive fallout, yes, but a millionth the size of a nuclear detonation.

And that's a huge upgrade from the rest of the Free State of Southwestern Colorado's munitions, which so far have only been used defensively. Once again, Lori has no proof it will stay that way.

But Dom trusts his uncle, and Jeremiah trusts Dom.

Like most things in Lori's life, that's good enough for now.

"Safe as can be," Lori says. "So, you ready for our account number?"

Lori gives her the digits, which correspond to the TFZ Corp., a new private security firm in The Republic, which is known for its hands-off approach to paramilitary contractors. The fee Boudreaux negotiated for the New Year's Eve save was generous, which means they'll use TFZ to buy a nice piece of High Plains ranchland and enough building material to construct a proper base camp.

There's no reception as they navigate the switchbacks, but Lori's confident the money will be there when they can check.

"That should do it," Lori says.

"For now," President Ramirez says, a bit of relief in her voice. "But here's hoping I don't need Task Force Zulu for a good, long while."

And with a jinx like that, what could possibly go wrong?

ACKNOWLEDGMENTS

First, I'll address the elephant in the room: This novel was not written as a reaction to the current state of American politics, no matter how hard that may be to believe.

The idea for the first scene—including the post-secession setting and coordinated attacks across several nations—hit me in late 2018 while I was watching the ball drop in New Orleans on New Year's Eve. It came so vividly and completely that I wrote it shortly after watching the Sugar Bowl. The rest of the first chapter and a synopsis were also written more than two years ago.

With that out of the way, I have some folks to thank profusely.

I will be eternally grateful for the team at Black Rose Writing, including Publisher Reagan Rothe, who believed in me and was patient as I rewrote and edited this novel as events unfolded in 2020 and early 2021.

I must also thank the former intelligence officer who has let me pick his brain and run ideas past him for the last few years. You know who you are.

The same goes for the many veterans who provided insight, both specifically for this novel and throughout my life.

Any mistakes are mine and mine alone.

Amber Guffey is my forever editor, and as such I will forever be in her debt for the many hours she put in helping me with this story.

I wrote this novel in an office built by my father, Rick Treon (I'm the fourth of my name). He, along with my mother, Julie, and sister, Nikki, are the people who allow me to continue writing novels.
You would not be reading this without their love and support.

ABOUT THE AUTHOR

Rick Treon writes about life and death in the Lone Star State. His debut thriller won the PenCraft Award for Literary Excellence in Suspense, and his essays have been syndicated across Gannett Media. Before making up stories, he worked as a reporter and top editor for several newspapers. For more information, visit ricktreon.com.

NOTE FROM THE AUTHOR

Word-of-mouth is crucial for any author to succeed. If you enjoyed *Divided States,* please leave a review online—anywhere you are able. Even if it's just a sentence or two. It would make all the difference and would be very much appreciated.

Thanks!
Rick Treon

CPSIA information can be obtained
at www.ICGtesting.com
Printed in the USA
BVHW071320010621
608546BV00001B/50

9 781684 337699